WHOSE SLEEVES?

Jonathan Abel

For Simon and Julia.

色よりも香こそあはれとおもほゆれ誰が袖

ふれし宿の梅ぞも

Iro yorimo ka koso aware to omohoyure tagasode fureshi yado no
ume zono
KOKIN WAKASHU (905)
Deeper than the flowers' shade
Their fragrance haunts my sense –
Whose sleeves so scented brushed against
Plum blossom by my door?
(Trans. JA.)

Chapter One.

Charlie had been only twelve years old at the time, but a few details of the ceremony were scratched on the window of his memory: the whole experience of evacuation was hidden behind a coffin and some stained glass which could not be shifted aside.

That stained glass echoed in the colours of the Kimono hung on frames around white walls or pulled gently from drawers in lacquered cabinets, which slid out with the merest rustle of tissue paper in a large music room not much used for music. The frames were shaped like the shrine gates of Japan and artfully folded silk gowns spilled down to show the bold and clashing colours of an other aesthetic, while gold splashed from the Obi sashes folded below them on the matting floor.

Each of the Kimono represented a time of year, the design reflecting what was yet to occur in nature. For the plum blossom season, the design on the Obi would show cherry blossom or at the time of the finest autumn leaves there might be a spray of early winter narcissi. All this had been gently and elegantly explained, illustrated with patiently unwrapped swathes of silk by the man in the coffin whose widow sat beside Charlie wearing a black Kimono that he himself had tried on a few short nights before. She looked serenely comfortable and perfectly out of place in the small gothic church with its sombre congregation and the stained glass looked kindly on her.

Now Charlie was sitting beside his own son and daughter in law in a different pew. The two grandchildren had not been allowed to attend. Charlie thought they should be there but he supposed that they would have been bored rather than particularly upset. So best not. They were gathered to say goodbye to his wife though Charlie felt that he had said his goodbyes a while ago, when she was still around to hear them, knowing that she would soon be off, as she put it, keen for him to know that she would miss him. White rooms and someone else's flowers. Bridie wouldn't let him bring her flowers, didn't really think you should cut them while they were still so pretty. Even in the pub she had insisted on growing plants instead, never discouraged by accidental or malicious damage. Her prerogative, the decoration. Did a lovely job. She even fought off a lucrative Brewery offer because she knew that they would turn the pokey old bars into one big Gin Palace with bogus antiques and shelves of books well out of reach and thus doomed never to be read again. She had been outraged when they visited a chairman of the Licensed Victuallers, no less, and saw an old set of Jane Austen treated in this way; obscure or foreign books might just pass, but not the classics. Charlie doubted his wife had ever read a classic. God knows he never had, but Bridie knew what was right and appropriate. She was such a lovely woman.

What are you supposed to think about at your wife's funeral? Pious thoughts did not come naturally. Loss? Well, he had dealt with that while he was slowly losing her. He certainly couldn't sob into his hanky, though one or two others were giving it their best shot. He missed the children. Then his thoughts turned to the pub.

***

And when he got back, and Bridie had been burned in her box and the men from the LVA who had stood pallbearers had shaken his hand or put their arms around his unsagging shoulders with an unwelcome solidarity, he was glad to get back. The big room at the front was busy with lunchtime drinkers some regular, some not (good, he loved passing trade) and in the small back bar there were none but the deeply familiar. A couple of the old girls kissed his cheek, smiling, and good old John Cusson said, "You have a little one with me". But they had also said their goodbyes to Bridie elsewhere and in a different way and were ready for a drink.

Julie and Annette were busy with lunches in the kitchen, he knew, but they rustled up bits of chicken (on the bone because he preferred it) and some roast potatoes to feed the little gathering. The girls shyly brought in a grapefruit stuck with cocktail sticks holding pineapple chunks and mousetrap; they had always laughed at Bridie for taking so much trouble with free Sunday lunchtime nibbles when you could just microwave some chicken nuggets and open a few bags of cheesy wotsits. Bridie liked to do it for the back bar, and she didn't encourage strangers to partake either.

He had them all out of the door for two thirty as usual. They hadn't the money to drink out of the old hours, these people who had been coming to his pub as long as Charlie had been waking up here; longer, some of them. Not many now and getting fewer every year: but he didn't go to their funerals and they wouldn't be going to his. The bloody LVA would be there in force.

The big room up front stayed open all day now, there was such pressure from the breweries that almost all the other pubs in town did the same. With two staff on he just about broke even. He said hello to the two lads on the afternoon shift. They'd been with him a year now, which was rare and welcome, lads moving on as they did. His evening girls in the back bar had been with him twenty years. Even then he had inherited them barely old enough to serve. Behind the bar anyway.

He wandered through to the kitchen to see Julie and Annette and got another little kiss, then back to the bar to get them a nice drink, He didn't stay to see them drink it. He went upstairs and closed the stout door behind him; the staff rarely got past this point, however much he liked them. It was just his flat now. Bridie and her greedy little cancer hadn't been here for a year. First the hospital, then the nursing home. Now gone.

The parcel still sat on the table in the hall where it had been for the last eight months. He knew the contents, could guess the patterns. He also knew the grammatical oddities of the note that would accompany it. But he wasn't ready for it just yet.

From the glass-fronted cabinet to the left of the empty fireplace he took a shapely brown bottle painted with red plum blossom (after all it was cold enough for March even in May) and a shallow cup in a matching pattern with a short stem. In the kitchen he had to stretch up to the top cupboard for the bottle of Sake given to him by a passing Japanese student. He encouraged them in the pub, and they usually came back. He filled the flask and warmed it in the microwave for a while, imagining the old man and his kimonoed widow glaring over his shoulder at this anachronism. Or maybe not. She would have liked microwaves. And this was a Toshiba.

Chapter Two.

Charlie's memory had space for only two images of his mother. The first was a photograph taken before the war when he was about five years old: she stood behind their busy bar, all mirrors and bottles; in the background you could just make out those old town pub oddities which his father called 'Gentry Screens'. These were vertical oblong wooden frames holding engraved and frosted glass, mounted at head height and pivoted so that a customer in the Saloon could communicate with the barmaid but still be shielded from the (slightly) lower orders in the Public Bar.

She looked tired, she probably was, still smiling gaily and pushing up her hair on her head at the back with one hand like a film star. The other hand held a small glass of something dark, probably port according to Charlie's ever sketchier memories. He could remember her smell and her voice exactly.

The second image was one of those memories. The face he fitted to it was the one in the photograph, but as this was almost three years later, the insecurities and loneliness of her war would in reality have taken their toll. In this last look at his mother he was waving from a train full of children as she was being efficiently manhandled behind a barrier by the WRVS at their sternest and most sympathetic. "Come on, dearie, they're all in the same boat" with a gesture at all the other mothers in varying states of distress. He had never seen her again.

Shortly after the evacuation his father came home on leave and Charlie's parents died in an air raid along with most of their regulars. It took a while for the news to get through to Norfolk, so there was no funeral then for Charlie. He still kept her picture on his sideboard.

At least his parents had seen each other again, unlike so many couples eternally separated by combat. This nice thought was not original to the boy, but gently planted by the woman who tried all too briefly to fill the motherly gap, and whose photograph was on the mantlepiece, not the sideboard.

***

Charlie recalled the slow and wretched journey to the country; a fabled place highly and condescendingly recommended by a rich aunt (on his mother's side) who had not only been there but also to the seaside. As publicans the Moultons were not badly off, but there was no such thing as a family holiday. Too many other people spent their money in the pub on holidays.

As it trundled deeper into Norfolk the train gradually emptied of children, most of whom seemed smaller and unhappier than himself. Indeed, he began to feel quite cheerful once they had cleared fenland (which he could not have identified as such, but which looked bloody miserable from the train), and the land began to roll again. A shunt and a change, most enjoyable, and eventually they stopped at a place called Great Walsingham, a name which town-boy Charlie thought a bit extravagant.

Two others, a brother and sister team who had fought noisily throughout the journey to the point (sin of sins) of tearing each other's labels, also got shoved off here. The three were told to wait. Charlie stood apart. Planes droned in the chilly air. A Vicar in a trap with a scabby-jointed pony gathered up the snivelling siblings, who had only been snivelling at the prospect of being separated and now were ready to resume a cheerful mutual hostility. The Vicar shouted over his departing shoulder that someone would deal with Charlie presently. Whatever that meant. It meant an hour later; Charlie sat on the fence, feet barely touching the top of his trim little cardboard suitcase. His gas mask, which seemed silly in all this fresh air, poked the small of his back. He dared not move. An hour's a long time. Curious elderly people who appeared to be held together with string and facial hair ambled past and looked inclined to prod him like a side of meat. But they didn't. They just grunted something that sounded like "Aarnin" or spat and passed by.

Just as tears were about to burst through his stoic loneliness, he saw a tiny person leading a donkey towards him and waving. Or at least he assumed that was what she was doing, but as she kept her rapidly wagging palm out at waist level, he thought it risky to wave back just yet. Her feet moved remarkably quickly for one making so little progress, which was just as well since the donkey looked elderly (though donkeys do) and disinclined to move at more than a gentle stumble. It also tended to meander slightly, but the woman with her active hand waggling palm out at the midriff simply skittered from side to side with it.

Charlie had forgotten tearfulness by the time this vision came close enough to say

'What your name, little brother?'

And although nonplussed by the grammar and the declared relationship he stood very upright and looked down at her from his fence and said

'Charlie Moulton, Missus.'

'That's right'

she said, although Charlie thought he should know without confirmation what his own name was. She had a way of speaking that he had never encountered. Not the accent, because he'd come across all sorts in the pub, even the odd foreigner. The words were kind but not authoritative like his father's or tersely loving like his mother's. And he thought that in his opinion she was the most lovely person he had ever seen. Personally.

She was shorter than the ears of the donkey she was theoretically leading (although to be fair it looked quite a big donkey) and kind of fluttery. Her gestures and her manner of speaking; quick gushes of soft words with muted consonants corresponded to the kindness of her strangely flattened eyes. But it was the hair that he instantly fell in love with. Like coal in the rain or his Granny's jet beads; blue and purple in the black of it and incredibly shiny and straight. At the back it reached almost to her knees, centre parted in front and gathered in a simple bunch tied low down so that it covered her ears and the sides of her neck. It sat heavily (or so it must seem for such a tiny person) on her shoulders. Her face recalled the Chinese Princess in the library book which he now remembered was still by his bed, and he felt a pang of worry.

Since she did not correct him, he continued to respond to her sparse questions with "Missus" tagged on the end. She tried, quite firmly to persuade him to mount the donkey.

'That is why he with us.'

Charlie was reluctant to plunge so precipitately into the rustic life, so they walked on either side of the erratic beast's head, but after about half an hour he allowed himself an only mildly plaintive

'How far now, Missus?'

She simply smiled and pointed to the donkey's back.

With some difficulty (she really was determined) they got him onto the oblivious creature's dipping spine. He balanced his dear cardboard luggage between his thighs, anchored it with his elbows and held tightly to the scraggy mane, having been reassured that

'He not hurt'.

Charlie was uncertain whether it was the donkey or himself that would escape discomfort.

The hedges grew higher and the banks on either side of the stony little road grew steeper until they could see nothing before or behind them except the next and last bend. Suddenly and to Charlie's alarm a huge tanned woman wearing a bright headscarf tied up on her head like the cleaner at home leaned over the top of the hedge high above them and called out

"Hello, Missus Wife!"

with a pleasant laugh. The little woman leading him (he had thought about Palm Sunday and felt vaguely guilty) put one hand over her mouth and laughed in a different but equally pleasing way, her hand waving away from the waist as it had when she had first approached Charlie. The gesture was confirmed as a greeting.

At last they turned into a drive with straggly yew hedges on each side, which Charlie thought looked important, and he was deftly pulled off the imperturbable donkey with only a minor dent to his precious hand luggage. His new companion poked his gas mask sharply

'You not need that.'

'You bloody have it, then.'

Charlie thought but did not say.

An enormous, lean brown-and-white dog appeared, almost as big as the donkey which it licked affectionately on the nose. The donkey seemed not to mind and fluttered its eyelashes as donkeys will. The lady was tripping off carrying his suitcase. His mother would not have allowed this, but the lady had disappeared through a green arch in the yew before he could protest or retrieve it.

Its brick seemed both torn apart and held together by the ivy and the roof didn't look at all secure about the deep eaves. Charlie was as immediately taken with the house as with the extraordinary woman who had brought him to it. He almost wished it was a pub. There weren't many people about.

Chapter Three.

He had kept the parcel waiting so long that the dry tape was beginning to flake from the cardboard. Charlie's knowledge of Japanese was small; he could only speak a few phrases, nothing like the stringing together of a sentence, but he recognised the characters for England on the address labels and was pleased. He had laboriously practised writing them under the patient tuition of his friend, using a pen that produced results he could have bettered with a frayed twig. The sender's name was also written in Japanese characters, but across the top were the rather shaky capital Roman letters MATSUI TOMIICHI, the man Charlie called Mr. Matsui and Bridie had called Tommy-san. Charlie did not approve of this latter, thinking it disrespectful to invent pet names for people you hardly know, but he would never have said so.

He felt ashamed at not having shared this gift with Bridie in her last months at the nursing home, but some perverse logic convinced him it would be an unfair reminder of the life that went on without her. Small white rooms. Someone else's flowers. What place there for the dazzling article that he knew to be in the parcel? She didn't really like Japanese things anyway. Had an uncle in Burma. He took his first sip of the hot sake and wished suddenly that he had taken the box for her to open. He had better get used to these little bursts of regret.

Inside the official, standard Japanese Post Office box were two parcels of stiff paper like outsized office files, fastened with lengths of coarse ribbon wound around bamboo toggles. He lifted the smaller one from the top and set it aside, then poured a little more sake, determined not to rush. He unhooked the ribbon and lifted out a long narrow piece of heavily embroidered cream silk; it was covered in peacocks and cranes and bridges over streams running together at random in uncountable colours. He laid it lengthways across both arms of the three-seater sofa, but it still touched the floor at both ends. Then he folded it into a manageable length and hung it on the small lacquered stand to the right of the fireplace. He had acquired a pair of these from a stall in the covered market. The second file was bigger and quite heavy: he looked again at the red and white sticker with the cost of the postage on it, but he had no idea of the exchange rate, so the four figures could have amounted to anything. He remembered his son bringing rupees back from India, valueless in their abundance. The yen was probably a bit like that.

He carefully peeled back the tissue paper and pulled out the kimono, which he held up with the back towards him. It was of lilac silk with deep purple and white wisteria blossom and leaves of variegated greens all spun through with gold thread. He laid it across an armchair and poured some sake, then draped it over the second lacquered stand. He went into the kitchen and from the sink retrieved three football sized Chrysanthemums that he had also bought in the covered market. Plonking them fairly unceremoniously in the tall vase in the cold fireplace, he sat back with the last of the warmish sake and admired the effect.

***

Charlie always went downstairs for the first couple of hours on weekdays to see to the back bar until the girls came in at seven. This was the time that he would have used the pub himself had he not been a landlord. Daft thought. What else would he ever have been, or have wanted to be? The front bar was staffed by a couple of nice lads (from a pool of six) but didn't really get off the ground apart from the food side until about eight, so he wasn't needed there. Just popped his head in now and again, determined not to interfere more than a landlord should.

So this evening, his new objects cluttering up Bridie's orderly sitting room - no his now, he really must get used to that - he went down at five o'clock for his habitual patrol. First into the big, spotless kitchen, where Larry the peculiar but reliable evening cook (he liked to be called 'Chef" which the lads mockingly did: Charlie knew enough about the man's CV to know that it wasn't deserved) would be pootling about creating among other things the cheapest Lasagne in the city. The food was no great shakes, but it was plentiful and reasonably healthy, so they did a good turnover with the students and other youngsters up front. His back bar regulars didn't come here to eat.

A long corridor led from the kitchen to the front, passing the back bar on the right. Old tobacco-darkened frosted windows high up on the left stole what light they could from the enclosed garden outside. Pews from a redundant Methodist chapel (best sort, miserable lot) ran under the windows. They had occasionally thought of furnishing this poky garden for customers, but half of it was a useful bottle store and for the other half, honestly he couldn't be bothered. The Brewery would have paid for it if Bridie hadn't blocked anything they suggested: get their foot in the door and you'll be up to your eyes in flock wallpaper before you can say knife.

He went into the back bar and shuffled the newspapers, though the lunchtime staff always left them tidy. He provided them all for his customers except the Sun, which he thought was disgusting. Actually he thought the Telegraph was close to sordid as well, but at least it was serious. It was also the most popular with the old boys, and he sometimes had to pop out for an extra copy to avoid unpleasantness.

On the biggest wall hung (or rather was nailed, since it was amazing what could disappear) a big copy of the Annigoni portrait of the Queen. Next to her was a facsimile (the original had been there once, but Bridie had got nervous) of a deed signed by illegible granting the freehold of the Crown (as it then was) to a Giles Montague, which probably sounded posh in 1709, but now had the ring of some advertising nitwit in a loud bow tie. These days the place was called the Two Brewers, which was equally unimaginative, but made for a better sign above the entrance. The pair of vaguely antique workmen on his sign were clearly pissed.

Around the wall from our own dear Queen above the bulging plaster where once had been a fireplace were a group of black and white photographs of the regulars taken a couple of years back by a passing (weren't they all) Australian barman. Some of them were really good and the old boys (and a couple of girls) were as pleased as punch to see themselves up there, although they complained like hell for appearance sake. Neville, a retired Estate Agent had had plastic surgery a few years back to remove the complicated alcoholic bloom from his nose. He had been less than tickled to return with bandaged face and see a Band-Aid stuck across the appropriate part of his portrait. Those lads again, probably.

A doorless doorway led to the tiny room, more a porch, between the back bar and the street, which contained a couple of tables with benches built in on either side. Use of this space by strangers was particularly frowned upon, and when one of the old men had mischievously pinned a note to the outside saying 'Please Use Other Entrance' Charlie had quietly replaced it with a permanent wooden plaque to the same effect and the regulars' arch satisfaction. Now the little band of clingers to the wreckage had their own entrance. Officially.

Sometimes Bridie had moaned about him pandering to the exclusivity of the back bar crowd, but Charlie saw little harm in it. The rooms were really too small to accommodate the large groups that gathered up front, and the tables weren't big enough to eat anything but sandwiches from. Which they didn't sell. And anyway, she knew that he loved these old fools: added to occasionally after suspicious silent vetting, sometimes suddenly subtracted from. Just as Bridie had now been deducted from the sum of nice things. She had loved them too, grudgingly.

Charlie lifted the hatch and got behind the bar. Sacred area, this. Strictly staff only and then only after a thorough interview. Bloody spotless. Of course, by ten the front would be awash with beer and old cardboard boxes were laid down to soak it up and avoid accident, by eleven it would be filthy. But it started and finished the evening spotless. His staff complained that they had to do such a thorough clean up after closing (what, they muttered, does the cleaner do?) but Bridie made the rules and when she first made them the daytime cleaner had been her cousin. Saw no reason to change after the silly girl got pregnant and went to live on an army base in Germany.

He checked all the optics and the free bottles of Sherry and so on, but nothing needed replacing. Archie the cellarman saw to all that, as often as not by drinking any half measures ('dodgy tots' he called them) before replacing the bottle. Charlie wasn't supposed to notice, so he didn't. Perk of the job and good cellarmen were hard to come by. It was hard to believe that half measures of spirits were worth drinking before ten thirty in the morning, which was when Archie left off, but then.

At twenty past five the lads arrived, polite and smart in jeans, white shirt and ties. Charlie provided two shirts and left a selection of ties in the staff room so they didn't have to buy their own, but these two had some sort of competition going on and scoured the local charity shops for the loudest. Doesn't matter if they take the rise, as long as they wear one. The lads wandered off towards the kitchen to see Larry and order something to eat for their break. Charlie was surprised, when he visited the other licensees, to hear that they either didn't feed their staff of gave them something cheap. Larry fed this lot off the menu, but then that in itself was hardly extravagant.

He switched on the machines in the front, their various beeps and whistles turned to the lowest level. There was a fruit machine of dazzling complexity and a quiz game which was more popular with the townies than the students. And the bar staff liked it. No juke box or piped music; Bridie's rule and happy to follow it. The place was noisy enough anyway. I'll provide the walls she said. Bring your own atmosphere.

Then he unlocked the doors at the front, saw the lads smiling from the bar and went to let Duncan in at the back door. He was usually waiting with his long-redundant briefcase full of crumpled paper, ready to be shooed in like a cat. If Duncan wasn't there Bridie used to walk the two streets to his house to make sure he was alright. Sometimes he met her half way and grumbled at the interference.

Chapter Four.

Dear Charlie-san,

I hope you like this small gift for your enjoy. I had great time Two Brewers always. Thank you so much. Maybe I come back next year same month.
Your friend, Matsui Tomiichi.

It was eight o'clock, and now that Coronation Street was over there was not much on the television for the rest of the evening. Charlie preferred a good book to read, as a rule: James A. Michener's 'Texas' had been a recent favourite, and he was about to embark upon a Richard Adams about a bear, to judge by the cover, which he unashamedly did. He bought his new books from W.H. Smith, which provided him with an approximation of quality without the burden of great choice. There was a flashy Dillons in the town, but it was a bit poncey for his tastes. The nice manager whose name was Catherine often came in for lunch with her chum. She had offered to get Charlie a discount on her personal account, but he was a bit shy to take it. Nice of her though. Drank halves of bitter in a mug. Like Bridie.

The hours between his finishing in the back bar of an evening, handing over to one of the girls and closing time (which he liked to supervise) stretched a bit now. He and Bridie used to take it in turns to cook dinner and drink a glass or two of wine. Maybe play whist or rummy; she never did get the hang of cribbage. Diddicoy's game, she called it. They used to read sometimes, or just discuss what was going on downstairs, laughing or tutting as appropriate, talking shop.

Thursday was their regular night out. Both girls worked the back bar that night; between them they would know how to handle anything that needed handling. Two or three courtesy calls around town and a spot of dinner somewhere. She loved her Chinese, and there was a good place over Miss Selfridge in the High Street for Duck with Plum Sauce and Special Fried Rice. He didn't envisage going again for a long time.

During the year he had reluctantly done his stint as chairman of the bloody LVA she had taken over, as he would expect and prefer with such things. They had visited each of the thirty-odd pubs in their area at least once a quarter. Very impressive to the committee, but less so to Charlie who would have preferred not to visit a goodly number of these establishments at all, never mind four times in a year. He liked a clean and orderly house. Kept one, too, against considerable odds.

He put on a jacket and proper shoes (he never went downstairs during opening hours in slippers or shirt sleeves) and popped into the back bar for a nice bottle of Guinness. At one time he had drunk bitter, like Bridie and that nice girl from the bookshop, but these days it didn't agree with him. Shame, really, because they got some interesting guest beers in now: Greene King Abbott was his favourite, and though it was a bit strong, when it arrived he usually let Archie the cellarman persuade him into a half. Archie liked to show off his talents and Charlie appreciated his staff. But it was always a mistake and he would be up and down all day.

The front was filling up nicely by this time, with the food side winding down to make room for the serious boozers. The back bar was ticking over, as was its wont. He chatted idly to Sylvia, whose shift it was on a Wednesday, and whose hair seemed to be a particularly vibrant shade of copper this evening. Her young man Ivan was sitting at the corner of the bar on a high stool doing last Sunday's 'News of the World' crossword, occasionally soliciting the dubious assistance of other drinkers. It would be no use asking Sylvia, bless her. Charlie drank his Guinness behind the bar, trading nonsense with the old boys (and three old girls tonight, made a change) because he didn't really want to go back upstairs yet. But he knew he was cramping Sylvia's style, so he took another bottle upstairs with him.

Dear Mr. Matsui:

Thank you very much for the beautiful gift of Kimono and Obi which is much appreciated. As you know I have wanted to own a real Japanese one for many years. You might say that you have made my dream come true. I am sorry to tell you that Mrs Moulton (Bridie) died last week, of cancer, and that is why his letter is late. Sorry about that.

If you come back to England you are welcome here at any time and for as long as you wish. I enclose some bar towels for your collection, including Abbot Ale which, I know you enjoyed. Do you still use them in the bath?

Yours sincerely,

Charlie Moulton.

The next morning, being Thursday, was supposed to be the start of his day off once he had finished the banking. He spun the chore out a bit, then he wrapped Mr. Matsui's parcel of bar towels with brown paper and masking tape to drop off at the Post Office. It was a warm morning and the plane trees in the High

Street looked clean and bright: even the winos sitting beneath them seemed less aggressive than usual, although that could have been because Tennant's Super was on special offer at the Off License.

It was after eleven o'clock by the time he was done in the bank, and they still wanted half an hour to sort out his change order, so he decided to mark time in the Talbot on Pitt Lane with a Guinness and a chat with Jimmy behind the bar. Jimmy was the biggest and blackest black man that Charlie had ever encountered (which admittedly wasn't that many). He had a strangely high-pitched voice and a tendency to knock things over, but the Talbot was the most peaceful pub in town. On their popular Disco nights order reigned. Even on football Saturdays when the fainter hearts closed altogether, there was no trouble and most of all Charlie loved an orderly house. On match days The Two Brewers locked the front doors and let regulars only in at the back, policed by Charlie and two of his Australian boys on extra time.

Jimmy's declared main purpose in life was to 'shoot the breeze' which Charlie thought a splendid, if meaningless expression, and they talked companionably about nothing for a while. Charlie watched in awe as Jimmy's huge hands tried to get inside a pint mug with a drying cloth but was jolted to listen when he heard the man tell him he should take a holiday. In the spirit of their banter Charlie supposed aloud that he probably should but wouldn't know where to go or what to do. A half-serious offer of introductions in Cameroon was half-seriously declined. Charlie went back to the bank for his change.

Carrying several hundred pounds worth of coins in a beaten-up old haversack with "Kajagoogoo Are Lush" painted on it in once-

Dayglo pink which matched not at all his tweed jacket and cravat, Charlie thought about it. But sadly he dismissed the idea of a holiday. He wouldn't know where to go or what to do all by himself. Have to get used to that. Alone.

Back upstairs he sorted the change into the safe and thought about what to do on his day off, never mind a bloody holiday. His first Thursday without her. While she was in the hospital or the nursing home, he had spent most of the day there, waiting for her to be able to look at him, not wanting to beg help with the pain, because they both knew what that meant and Charlie wasn't strong enough and she was too bloody lovely to let him know that she knew. He didn't want to go wandering off now among their old friends' pubs like some sad, lonely old man. Well, at least he wasn't poor. Bridie had done all the arranging when they went out together. Stop it!

He took the car keys from their hook in the flat's off-white kitchen and went down through the back bar. He thought for a moment that he might ask someone to come with him, but he shook it off. From behind the Gordon's Gin optic he picked up the tape of Dolly Parton which the cleaner listened to on a leaky walkman as she made her desultory passes across the carpet with the hoover. "You can't clean properly without a nice bit of Country". He walked out of the side entrance (Please Use Other Door)
and down the street to the mews where he rented a garage.

They had bought this car in 1972. A lovely old-fashioned Rover with its bumpy bonnet and comforting radiator grille. The paintwork was cream, and the leather seats a cracked ox-blood. They had never seen any reason to change it. Archie the cellarman's eldest boy Ian looked after it inside and out. Even the engine shone as if oil would be an insult to the engineering. Dolly clunked comfortably into the cassette deck and he eased the big car through the mews arch and into the street. He glanced at the pub in the rear-view mirror as the lights changed and saw Sylvia in a regal headscarf and Jackie O sunglasses sashaying in for her wages. Bless her. After the number of times he had said that she must be well set up for the afterlife. Then he turned into the High Street and headed out of town towards the low hills in the west.

Chapter Five.

Charlie followed his new companion across a broad lawn spattered with daisies, avoided the occasional molehill and passed a dark ilex tree under which lay a circular carpet of brown cast-off leaves, a perfect noontime shadow which had killed off the lawn. The yew hedge enclosed the whole grass area in a garden with no flower beds, disappointing Charlie who had expected lots of flowers in the country. The house on the right almost blocked out the sky, and was so covered in shaggy ivy that it might have been another hedge were it not for the deep-set windows; these included an impressive set of French windows with a small paved area in front containing three rattan garden chairs, one with an extended foot rest, and a small table made of rough-hewn logs. There was also a square brick structure about waist height with a metal grille on top which Charlie could not immediately identify.

Turning the corner of the house they went through another yew arch and entered a cobbled courtyard with outbuildings on two sides. The woodwork bore the flaking and bubbled paint of indeterminate green that Charlie recognised from old pubs, of which, even at his underripe age, he had known a few. More yew hedge filled the third side of the quadrangle and the last was taken up by the wall of the house, this time bare of ivy, but showing signs this had not always been the case.

There was no one about and in contrast to the green and friendly front of the house, the courtyard looked a bit lonely and forbidding. But Missus Wife was waving at him again, this time flapping her fingers towards herself as if she was demonstrating the swan in a game of shadow pictures. He decided to interpret the gesture as beckoning and taking the line of least resistance followed her through the bubbling back door into the house.

The lady, (he was still having trouble with what to call her) was nowhere to be seen, so he stood still and looked around. Although a lot bigger (everything was bigger in the country) it was not unlike his mother's kitchen at home, where she toiled listlessly over stove or sink with a fag hanging out of the corner of her mouth and as often as not a small glass of something dark on the windowsill behind the draining board, next to the dishmop in an old jam jar. Here too there was a five-bar pulley clothes horse hanging from the ceiling with some small white towels dangling down. Three walls supported tall cupboards and the one opposite the door held a huge and complicated range on which stood a steaming kettle.

On either side of this black and hissing monster were piles of rather nasty looking wood. Town boy Charlie suspected this wood of harbouring creepy-crawlies, a fear later confirmed. There was a tiny coal scuttle. Next to the door on its right were two deep stone sinks like the coffins in the museum at home. One of them sprouted a handled pump and held a chipped white enamel bowl with a navy-blue rim. On the windowsill behind the other was a dishmop in a jam jar. No little glass.

He stood still for what seemed like a very long time to see all of this, but it wasn't long at all and soon his rescuer came bustling and smiling into the kitchen and pushed him gently backwards into a Windsor chair at the scrubbed table, which dominated the room from the centre. As she got busy with a kettle as big as her torso, he took in what she was wearing. He had been too busy to look before, hanging on to the donkey and preserving his precious suitcase. Although it was mild outside, she wore a jacket made from what looked like the eiderdown on his parents' bed and which tied inadequately (he thought) in front with a single pair of ribbons. Under that was a simple round-necked shift and her lower body was swallowed up in baggy cotton trousers of blue and white coarse cloth, tied at the ankles. On her feet were green and pink canvas slippers small enough for a doll; the only thing he had noticed earlier was that she had been wearing thick-soled leather sandals without socks. Now he saw the sandals in a row with several other pairs of shoes by the back door. Some were tiny like hers and others were enormous as if in deliberate comic contrast.

She heaved the kettle back onto the hob with a clunk and a hiss of spilled water then came over to him with a small pot. It had a lid and a spout like the one at home which he was accustomed to fill when his father asked him, but the handle which should have curved around opposite the spout stuck out at right angles to it on one side. She then put two small bowls on the table, and without using a strainer poured watery brownish liquid into them; there were little twigs floating about in it. She pushed one forwards and motioned him to drink, then shrieked with laughter when he asked for milk. Well, sugar had long been out of the question, and so he assumed that here in the funny country with a war on milk was out too. So he tried it, a bit unnerved by the absence of a handle to the cup. And he drank it all because he was a polite boy and she was being very nice and at least it was quite weak. It tasted like soil.

Then, to his terrible embarrassment, she knelt in front of him and started to undo his shoelaces. Too much.

'I can do that, thanks.'

He jumped from the chair and tugged nervously at the tight double knots his mother had made him tie in another world, ages ago. She watched him tolerantly until he had pulled his boots off and she nodded with approval

'That's right'

when he put them at the end of the line by the back door next to a pair of brown and cream co-respondent shoes almost twice as big. Then she handed him a pair of canvas slippers the size of the co-respondents, but he was getting into the swing of things and just shrugged, smiled his most grown-up smile and slipped his feet into them. She said 'That's right' again and used her beckoning gesture, then disappeared through a door to the left of the range. Charlie followed her into a dark panelled hall, and it was just as well that the enormous slippers made him shuffle or he would have trodden in one of a row of shallow bowls and saucers running along the side of the staircase. As it was, he just knocked one slightly and spilt what looked like milk, but because in the gloom he couldn't be sure he decided not to be cross about not getting any in his tea.

Beyond the bottom of the stairs he could just make out a few paintings on the panelled walls and at the end of the corridor was a large front door with a fanlight above. In its light, pale late spring sunshine filtered green by the ivy, he could make out two mysterious figures perched on boxes. But there was no chance to study who or what they night be, because a large but slightly hesitant voice called from an open door to the left

"Are you there Mr. Moulton?'

His little protector skipped out of the same door and deftly shoved him through it with one hand while closing it behind him with the other, forcing him to move quickly to one side in order to avoid getting shut in it.

He was dazzled after the dark passage, but as his eyes adjusted, he saw a room unlike any other he had seen. The walls were painted a simple creamy colour as was all the woodwork and even the fireplace. In the grate was a tall green vase stuffed with peacock feathers, like the one he had filched from the arboretum near home, but there were loads of them, shoved together like flowers in a bunch. The room was lit by a single bay window, but with glass from floor to ceiling and at the top of each of the dozen lights was a lozenge-shaped panel of green and gold stained glass. In the bay stood a simple empty desk of white oak with a chair similar to the ones in the kitchen, only squarer. All around the walls at the height of his own head (rather than high up like his grandmothers brooding pictures) there were massive unframed panels of pure shiny gold with pictures of tigers and trees and monkeys and birds, all picked out in bold colours.

It was the most beautiful place Charlie had ever experienced. He looked at the floor, which was of plain polished hardwood, then to his left, opposite the window, where there was a small raised area with a low, square table at its centre. At this table, with a bowl of what looked like mud tea a la Missus Wife in front of him, was a large, smiling white-haired old man who seemed rather pleased that Charlie was gawping around like a goldfish. His father would have been cross, and Charlie remembered his manners, stopped staring at everything, pulled himself together and said

  'I'm Charlie Moulton, sir'.

  'That's right'

  said the big man, which was beginning to get on Charlie's nerves.

Chapter Six.

It took only a few minutes to reach the edge of town where the road began to rise into the gentle hills beyond. At this time of year they were a thousand damp shades of green in the sunshine, and Charlie soon decided to turn off into the smaller country lanes where the wide verges spelt out the better estates in the area. May blossom clouded the hedgerows and the tall stems of cow parsley (Bridie called it Queen Anne's Lace) which had yet to be cut down by the vicious blades attached to the back of tractors waved slightly, more from gravity than the vestigial breeze. He had never seen an Arnold Schwarzenegger film, but he imagined that those blades would make an excellent prop in the right imagination. Perhaps he could write and suggest it.

Having so decisively escaped the town Charlie's thoughts began to wander over what to do next. He decided he was hungry, turned back to the main road and headed for the village of Barton. It was undistinguished, when he got there, in the manner of most local villages (although there were a few noble exceptions). It began and ended with grey prefabricated council houses, some with replacement windows, Georgian doors and patios, showing off their ex-tenants' recent purchase. Others displayed the traditional cabbage patch, denuded car carcasses and pigeon lofts. This Charlie preferred. He had been increasingly upset by the disintegration of the welfare state into which he had been ungrudgingly been paying all his life, but which was now begrudging any return on his investment. Not that he had anything to worry about financially, but his back bar was full of those who had, so he worried for them instead. They could talk about it all lunchtime and pick up from where they left off the next day. There was a newspaper photo of the Government Minister responsible taped to the otherwise pretty much redundant swear- box on the bar. Unfair perhaps, but as a big a bloody liar as any of that mendacious lot.

The point of this detour (although he was unsure that you could have a detour without a plan) was of course the pub: not one favoured by Bridie, but the quiet object of Charlie's affection. It was called the King's Shilling and had a rather good sign; a traditional proud Great War recruit on one side and an eighteenth-century press gang on the other. It was run by a lovely (Bridie said odd) couple called Bella and Clive; she was American and ample, he was a wiry, bearded ex-lecturer in something at the University of somewhere else. In an unusual reverse set-up for this traditional trade (well, it used to be, still was in favoured pockets of resistance to the bloody breweries) she ran the wet side (bars and cellars, tough work) and left him free to rustle up some of the best country food Charlie had ever tasted.

The building itself was an unprepossessing Victorian brick job painted slightly too dark a shade of blue. The woodwork was rust coloured. Probably the brewery's idea, but with these two you couldn't be sure. Charlie parked the car in the small front courtyard (there was a carpark at the rear, but few used it) and entered by the front door, which announced a Lounge Bar. There was a wood-burning stove in the middle of one wall and a door to the right for the loos; bench seats upholstered in shiny blue vinyl took up the rest of the wall space and tables of assorted age and type were scattered around, all with faux-walnut formica tops and metal rims. The ash trays were battered tin. A threadbare carpet had once been red-grounded paisley and a bit nasty: it was still nasty but quieter. Behind the plastic pine bar was a wrought iron monstrosity from which hung the optics, and visible behind this (because lit by a pinkish neon tube) was a photo-mural of a tropical beach. It was at least spotlessly clean, and the worst decorative highlights were blotted out by the stately bulk of Bella. She was wearing a homemade cable-knit sweater in a wide variety of coloured wools, which must have been created from balls of wool joined at random from a knitting bag as the garment progressed.

For some unknown reason this woman from Seattle was in the habit of greeting all comers in an exaggerated West Country accent. Charlie politely 'Hello-ed' back to her feisty 'Orroit My Luvver!' There was only one other person, a young woman, in the Lounge, but the clack of dominoes and rattle of poker dice from the Public Bar reassured him that Clive and Bella were doing some trade at lunchtimes. With his bustling town business, it was easy to forget what a struggle it could be out in the sticks.

Given the decor and greeting it always seemed strange to look up at the joys on offer from the chalked-up menu, so much of it wasted on salesman and bank managers from town. But today, being quiet, must not be an expense account day. There was home-caught eel pie with cheesy cream potatoes, salmon fish cakes, and a warm squid salad. But Charlie wasn't in a fish mood. There were venison burgers with either burgundy or blue cheese sauce (or both for an extra quid) and pigeon breasts with petit pois. But Charlie was looking for a particular favourite and he was in luck. Clive got a bit irritated that he always chose the same thing if he could, but it amused Bella (although frankly what didn't) so she poured him a Guinness ('Have it with us, my love') and wrote down his order for breadcrumbed joints of rabbit with mustard sauce.

Bella had been at the funeral, but as Charlie didn't mention it neither did she. They talked about trade and Clive's latest brush with Gilbert the gamekeeper. Giblet she called him. It's a thin line between 'Oops!' and poaching and Clive trod it well. When his lunch arrived, Charlie took it with him to sit in the sunny window and watch the world pass by, although not a lot of it passed through Barton. The Rover sat there in all its glory, and he was gratified when a couple from the Public Bar stopped and looked at it. He was surprised when the young woman, who he had quite forgotten, sitting reading by herself, stood in his sunlight and asked him if the rabbit was nice. It was and he said so. She thanked him and ordered the same from Bella ('Right you are my lover') and sat down two tables away in the light of a different window with a glass of red wine and went back to her book. Her hair was slightly longer than shoulder-length, black with a mild-mannered curl. Shy but laughing eyes and a pale skin that looked as if it would blush nicely. She smiled at Charlie, not shyly, so Charlie smiled back and got on with his rabbit.

Quite suddenly, in a tone that suggested that something had been bothering her, she asked 'Aren't you the landlord of the Two Brewers?', and since he was Charlie said so. She said that she really liked the look of the back bar but didn't dare use it so Charlie issued an open invitation to meet the scarier inhabitants under his protection. She laughed and went back to her book as he tucked into the last of his rabbit. Charlie was used to these empty rituals of recognition and thought nothing of it. But her name was Hilary something. He could see it on the address of the postcard she had been using as a bookmark, which now lay address side up on the table. Charlie fancied his detective skills.

Clive appeared behind the bar in his kitchen whites, although he eschewed what he called 'The turkey-leg frill jobbo' in favour of a little square hat as worn by the carpenter in a childhood copy of Alice. Charlie was finished with lunch, so they popped another Guinness. Charlie had to insist on paying; he hated the tacit post-mortem sympathy. Clive had a pint of lager and (O, dear) lime, and Bella had a ('Who am I kidding, my lover?') slimline bitter lemon.

Clive, great cook or no, often annoyed Charlie by prefacing his pronouncements with 'What you want to do is...' as if he had some second sight. However he might have been right about Charlie's itchy feet.

'Take that lovely tank of yours and do the Lakes. Or Cornwall'.

A wistful Bella, who hadn't had a holiday in five years contributed 'Oo, yes' and 'Sounds great', her Bristolian burr drifting briefly back across the Atlantic. Stay in pubs, they said, go as you please. Charlie was quite sold on the idea after a couple of Guinnesses and said he would consult the travel agent in town. Bella kissed him wetly as he left, and Clive came to wave him off from the doorstep. The girl called Hilary something said 'Could I beg a lift back to town? I walked here.' and was ushered into the front seat. She laughed at Dolly Parton and sang along with 'Here You Come Again' on the way.

Chapter Seven.

'I'm not so much a Sir as a Professor, really'. The large old man was still beaming at Charlie from his odd little perch, now revealed as a square cushion on which he was sitting cross-legged like a very distinguished frog. He beckoned in a more expansive and immediately recognisable manner than the lady for Charlie to come closer, talking the while.

'It's a complex business, you know, the naming of people. I wrote a small thing about it some years ago when I was in America. Not a very nice place, that. About how different cultures use names to identify status and define relationships. Quite well received over here. Nomenclature, you know how it is. You, for instance, are not, I assume, accustomed to being addressed as Mr. Moulton?'

He raised an impressive white eyebrow. Charlie took it that he should shake his head, so he did.

'Hmm. Quite so. Then is it acceptable for me to call you Charlie, is that the variant of Charles you prefer?'

Charlie was following the eyebrow, which seemed to indicate a nod was appropriate.

'Very well. This raises the question of what you should call me. My given, or as you might say Christian name. is Benedict. Not a name I favour, but for various reasons either linguistic or silly and emotional I have a particular aversion to the shortened version Ben. So you may call me Benedict, if you wish, but I suspect that you would be less than comfortable with that, given my apparent age and presumed status, eh?'

Charlie, who was beginning to tire of all this, grinned stupidly and said

'Yes'.

'My wife'

(Aha! thought Charlie, let's talk about her)

'who you have already met and who is, incidentally, quite taken with you, thinks you're a nice polite chap, which our current encounter would seem to bear out, would in your position call me 'Grandfather', or at a push 'Uncle'. If either of these appeal to you? No, I can see not, since I am neither to you, although she is likely to call you 'little brother' on occasion, whether you like it or not. Do stop me if I am being over disquisitive'.

Perhaps if he had known what the hell it meant he would have agreed. As it was Charlie merely smiled feebly.

'I think that we should settle, for the nonce, on Professor. As we become better acquainted you may feel moved to shorten it to 'Prof', which in turn would free me to call you Chas. Which was the name of a dear friend at school about three thousand years ago. Which is by way of being a joke. eh?'

Charlie said

'Yes, Professor'

and was twinklingly called a good study, whatever that meant.

'Is there anything you would like to ask me?'

Since they were already on the subject, he ventured;

'What should I call Missus Wife?'

Professor Benedict whatever laughed gently.

'I think perhaps you have encountered Mrs Boldero? A large lady, working on the land?'

Charlie nodded a 'probably'.

'I do indeed call my wife Missus Wife, although in her own language, that being a literal translation which I once foolishly vouchsafed to the said Boldero woman, a good one incidentally, and worth cultivating for her eggs alone. She, my wife that is, and not Mrs Boldero, calls me 'Papa' much of the time, which I am clearly not, although I admit to being old enough to have fulfilled that function. You see the many difficulties we encounter in naming people?'

Charlie made suitable acknowledgement but was beginning to understand 'disquisitive' to mean baffling and daft.

'I think that in her own tongue you would call my wife the equivalent of 'Aunt' as perhaps you do with close family friends of your mother's generation.'

Not many of those, thought Charlie.

'Her given, though definitely not Christian name is Yukiko, which means snow girl. Auntie Yukiko has a pleasant lilt to it that will please her. Try it'.

Charlie nodded again, but this time his head nearly wouldn't come back up again, and tiredness hit him like a wave. The old man seemed to realise that he had been going on rather longer than necessary and got up.

'I think perhaps you might like a bath.'

His head almost touched the ceiling above the platform. Stepping down into the beautiful room where Charlie stood, he caused great surprise by taking the boy's hand and leading him gently to the door.

'You are welcome in our house, Charlie Moulton. I'm a boring old man, I know, but I look forward to a little of your company. When you can find the time.'

He squeezed Charlie's hand as he turned to the little lady who had appeared in the doorway and addressed her in a short burst of very foreign. This ended with the words 'Auntie Yukiko', and she bowed to Charlie with a big grin, so he smiled back.

'Come on Charlie',

she said, but for years after he would remember the strange inflection 'Chiarry'.

***

Charlie was now so exhausted that he registered very little of the surroundings. He concentrated on putting one foot in front of the other. He managed to convey to his new Auntie that he preferred to undress alone and unaided, so she giggled companionably and went away while he changed, ignoring the thin cotton dressing gown laid on the enormous bed. He pulled off his smelly blazer, jumper and shirt (he hadn't noticed that they smelled until he took them off) and then peeled off his socks, which were always a bit on the pongy side. His grey flannel trousers came off last and he put on the dressing gown over his vest and long underpants, but it was too long so he took it off again. Then because the bed was so soft and big, he lay down and began to drift away.

'I thought perhaps I should explain the bath'.

The Professor was standing over him like a tree. Charlie sat bolt upright, but sank back into the bed involuntarily, ruining the effect.

'It's probably a bit different from your accustomed bathing practice, you see, although it can be a lot of fun'.

He gave Charlie an inadequate looking towel like the ones hanging from the ceiling in the kitchen.

'You wash with the bath water before you get in, you see'.

In his befuddled exhaustion and long drawers Charlie didn't see at all. He allowed himself to be led downstairs and out through the kitchen across the courtyard with the green bubbly-painted doors and into an outbuilding, which revealed itself to be full of steam. The Professor lifted the lid from what must once have been a laundry tub and handed Charlie a wooden bowl that looked like the cut off end of a small barrel. He put his great mitt into the steaming water and Charlie nearly fainted, as if the man had plunged his hand into a kitchen stewpot.

'Hmm. Not too hot.'

It looked bloody boiling to Charlie.

'Hang 'em up there, then'.

He appeared to mean Charlie's dressing gown and underwear, and Charlie was not ready for this at all. He shook his head firmly. The Professor looked a bit nonplussed and called for his wife. Charlie grabbed his forearm and shook his head even more firmly, his lips pressed white together to stop them from trembling, but the tears of confusion, tiredness and embarrassment came like rain.

Missus Wife came scuttling across the courtyard and batted the Professor away with one hand while tilting Charlie's chin upwards with the other, apparently in order to stare up his violently running nose. He just couldn't help himself and began to sob like Judy Garland. He was immediately swept up into the air, apparently by the Professor because it was a long way up, but he couldn't see or hear because of his own distress and weeping. He felt the move back into the fresh air followed by the hiss of the range in the kitchen then they lurched up the stairs the Professor carrying him with difficulty. He was lowered into the crisp white-smelling bed and fell asleep to the sound of water being poured into the wash basin on the night stand.

Chapter Eight.

Charlie was surprised, but on reflection pleasantly so, that his new acquaintance from the King's Shilling should actually turn up in the back bar one Saturday evening just as he was opening up. She parked herself delicately on a high stool (they were all of different sizes, but the higher ones brought you more or less level with the bar) and had a glass of red wine while he flitted around serving the regulars as they all arrived in a rush. As usual Duncan was first in with his briefcase full of rubbish. He was served a pint of whatever was cheapest, which on this occasion was Morland's, then went to settle grumpily into the porch room, where he rummaged around in his papers and muttered to himself. He could actually be quite charming, especially with Sylvia, and once in a blue moon would take a shine to one or other of the lads up front and change venues for a while, leaning limply on the front bar. He always came back in a huff when the boys became too busy to pay him attention or were inadequately responsive to his shrill, direct questions about their ancestry. He was especially fond of Australians who made up a considerable core of the itinerant front staff. As a once well- respected criminal lawyer, he still fancied that he retained a Rumpole-like rapport with the criminal classes even, as he put it tactlessly, at the distance of a few generations. Charlie did not rule out the fact that they were young, fit and often handsome as a contributing factor in Duncan's interest.

By the time he had satisfied the various (although seldom varying) requirements and returned to Hilary he had remembered her name, which he usually did, given thinking time unlike Bridie. Her solution was to call everyone 'Dear' altering the tone to suit the occasion. Hillary's glass was empty, so he bought more wine: he never stood the first in his own pub, business was business. She was by now sitting next to a man called Ernie who was looking mildly put out because she was in his usual seat, so Charlie introduced them; if he wanted the seat, he would just have to ask for it.

Ernie worked in the porters' lodge of the Art College in town, which provided him with plenty of fuel during the regular back bar sessions complaining about the 'Younger Generation'. Which with this lot would include at least ninety percent of the population. Mind you, Charlie had to concede that the Art students could be a scruffy and belligerent lot, some of them. The Poly students were a more sober (moot point) lot; though not so much as to significantly affect his takings. Anyway, it wasn't the Poly any more, it was called 'Figgis Barnes University' which didn't seem a title likely to conjure up more respect, more likely to make people giggle than attract them to its higher purpose. Charlie's son was a teacher there, of history. They were so proud of him when he went to University, but when he became a Doctor of Philosophy Bridie was fit to burst, and Charlie took delight in addressing postcards to Dr. Charles Moulton. The proud father also thought that there was a more secure future in pub management than University lecturing but bit his tongue on that one. More security and a decent pension. Shut up, Charlie.

Ernie had his Castella cigar on the go, and a pint of lager with a scotch on the side. He didn't touch the chaser all evening until the bell went, then he downed it and had a last one before 'Time' was called. It sounded extravagant, but Ernie only came in on Saturdays, and as far a Charlie knew didn't use any other establishments. As usual he was worrying at last Sunday's Express crossword, a step above Sylvia's Ivan, but most of the other old men cut through the Times before noon and were distinctly snooty about general knowledge puzzles. And about help from anyone else. Ernie was enlisting Hilary's protesting aid now, and she seemed to be quite good at it. Despite what he might say when the old boys wound him up Ernie enjoyed young company. In his first years out of the navy he had run a successful boxing club in town, which had kept many a potential hooligan on the straight and narrow, even if after a few rounds with Ernie they couldn't always see straight. He must be getting on a bit now. Older than Charlie anyway.

At seven o'clock Lizzie came on for her evening stint. She was of an age with Sylvia, but you wouldn't know it when they were together. Lizzie wore her years more heavily, and certainly would not have resorted to the bottled carrot top or have sported the tighter outfits that her colleague favoured. She smiled at Charlie and asked him, as she had done every working night since he could remember what he was having for his tea. On this occasion Charlie realised that he really hadn't thought about it, which as Lizzie was swift to point out, was not like him. Suitably chastened he went upstairs to poke about in the fridge and cupboards because the alternative would be Larry's lumpen lasagne, and he couldn't face that just now. Hilary, now head to head with Ernie over the last few clues, smiled and waved as he went from behind the bar. He didn't mind leaving her.

Upstairs he changed into his carpet slippers and an old cardy with leather buttons and elbows. There wasn't much in the kitchen, but he cracked some eggs, grated some cheese and picked a few random herbs from the back window box, where he had quite a little selection going. The front and side window boxes over the street were already blooming with petunias, geraniums and lobelia; it was nice to put on a bit of a show for the few tourists that made it here, and although it wasn't cheap it brightened up the otherwise plain regency facade of the pub. Quite inviting, really.

Expertly Charlie cooked up a fluffy, runny Omelette. He switched on the television. There was sometimes quite a good detective thing on a Saturday, which he would watch with his feet up until about ten, when he went back down for the last hour or so. He didn't feel like a drink just now. Maybe later.

The doorbell of the flat rang shrill and for too long. He could hear footsteps running up the wooden stairs from the back bar, then a banging on the flat door and Lizzie shouting 'Charlie, Charlie'. She sounded as if she was crying. He fled down to the door, wrenched it open (bloody thing still stuck at the bottom) and caught sight of Lizzie already retreating to the bar calling 'It's Ernie!' over her shoulder. Charlie ran down after her.

All the back bar customers were sitting on the pews in the kitchen corridor or standing dazed as evacuees from a burning building. A big leather-covered chair had been placed in the doorway to the bar. Charlie noticed that the upholstery was ripped at the back. Have to get it seen to. He could hear a young woman's voice saying 'Fuck, O, Fuck', which he automatically disapproved, not liking language from ladies. He squeezed past the chair and there was Ernie lying on his back being given artificial respiration through a rather grubby hanky that might have belonged to Hilary, who was standing there muttering 'Fuck, O, Fuck' and swaying from the hips in a gentle aerobics exercise with her hands tucked under opposing armpits. She wasn't crying. First aid was being administered by the nice young Indian (or possibly Pakistani) doctor who used the front bar quite regularly, but now he stopped and said

'I'm sorry. He's gone. Massive coronary.'

Without thinking Charlie said

'Thank you doctor'

and felt foolish. An ambulance crew bundled in with a machine they must have known was now redundant, but applied to Ernie anyway, probably to be comforting or show willing or something. The body jerked about like an expiring fish. An ambulanceman stood up, said 'Sorry' a bit unconvincingly and went to get a wheelchair from the van.

Charlie saw that Ernie's trousers had been undone in the fray and that his penis was poking out. He knelt down, tucked it in and zipped him up like a little boy. They wrapped dead Ernie in a blanket and wheeled him bumpily (as if it mattered) away. Charlie squared his shoulders decisively and moved the chair out of the doorway. He waved his dazed and murmuring customers back to their places, as if in a rehearsal of a drawing room farce. Lizzie sat down on a pew in the corridor with Hilary and Charlie fetched a bottle of cheap brandy from the store cupboard.

'Fuck, O, Fuck'

said Hilary.

'All right, love. That's enough'.

said Lizzie.

Charlie passed out brandy fairly liberally and returned to his station behind the counter. He'd seen off a few of this lot, but never in the bloody bar before. Lizzie, trouper that he knew her to be took over from him straight away. He asked Hilary if he could give her a lift home or anything, but she said not and asked to use the phone.

He went back upstairs, suddenly aware and ashamed of his carpet slippers and cardy. Just a little more fed up than he had been while cooking his now inedible omelette. Wondering how he could get in touch with Ernie's sister in Nottingham before the authorities did. Bridie would have known.

Chapter Nine.

Charlie woke in the soft white bed that had claimed him the day before, the day of the bath that hadn't happened. There was sunlight, tinged with ivy-green shining bright across the room. He woke up confused, but quickly came round enough to shudder with embarrassed guilt at his behaviour. He felt rude and selfish at his reaction, and childish, which was not the impression he wished to give to the nice man, although he thought it would be less of a problem with Missus Wife. In spite of, or perhaps because of the Professor's ramblings on the subject he was still unsure what else to call her: he couldn't remember the foreign name the old man had given her and somehow Missus Wife worked for him, seemed appropriate.

It was quiet. Charlie knew that he was beginning to feel lonely and potentially tearful, the unfamiliarity too raw to be exciting. A sudden thump caused him to sit upright in spite of his nascent misery, but it was only some old cat rubbing up against the window, where it must have just jumped. Charlie was not fond of cats: they made his mother sneeze.

It really was very quiet. He began to sense that he was alone as well as lonely. He looked down to the foot of the bed and saw to his horror that his long underwear was folded neatly over the board. He was naked. One of them had taken his clothes off. Maybe both of them. He could feel his cheeks colour as he drew the slightly fusty garments under the bedclothes (which smelt spicy) and pulled them on. He had not noticed this fustiness in his stuff before and it was beginning to irk him, especially as he had slept under this wonderfully clean white fluffy thing. He didn't even let his mother see him without his clothes these days.

Had he not been so keen to hide his shame he would have saved himself a prick in the chest, as he now discovered a note pinned to his vest:

"Good morning, or possibly good afternoon, Charlie. My wife and I have gone to Walsingham in search of provisions, but will be back before you miss us, I don't doubt. Please give in to curiosity and explore as you please, but I would prefer you to begin outside, as I wish to show you the house myself."

It was initialled B.G. so he assumed it came from Professor Benedict whatchamacallit beginning with G. A new step forward in the naming game.

He spotted his trousers and jumper folded across a chair, though the shirt was missing. He grabbed them over his smalls and went to the window. He looked down onto the drive at the front of the house and the yew hedge that led away towards the road (or what passed for one in this country). In the middle of the gravelled area in front of the main entrance lay the enormous dog, befriender of ancient donkeys, in an apparent stupor. Two cats were curled into its stomach, a puzzle to Charlie who had been brought up on the mythological antagonism of the two species from comics and common knowledge. He had no idea what time it might be, so in search of bearings both physical and temporal he decided to brave the world outside his new room.

He opened the bedroom door, which was not as heavy as it looked. Two more cats, which had clearly been waiting for the opportunity sped past him without a nod and jumped onto his crumpled bed where they began washing themselves with noisy intimacy. Charlie went to the bedside and made shooing noises and gestures at them. One of the cats looked up with obvious irritation, lifted its hind leg higher and began vigorously to lick its inner thigh. The other ignored him completely. Physical ousting seemed risky to Charlie, who was intimidated by anything larger and less caged than his grandmother's tatty budgerigar. In the face of potential violence, he admitted defeat and abandoned the cats to their reverie. He left the room with the door ajar in the hope that they might leave of their own accord, but he secretly admitted their higher proprietorial claim.

The dark landing outside his door seemed if anything more silent than his bedroom. The staircase swept up the middle and divided in two switchback stages, with an elaborate wooden bannister around the top. There were five closed doors identical to the bedroom he had left. It was clearly a big house, but Charlie was used to living in pubs, which tended to be pretty big even if the living quarters were cramped. Above his head were three domed lights let into the roof, but they were glazed in red and blue and gave little light. To his right was a tall sash window, so overgrown with ivy on the outside that any attempt to look out would have been futile.

Aware of his instructions (or rather the Professor's wishes; instructions did not seem to come into it here), Charlie resisted the temptation to open doors and began to walk gingerly down the wooden stairs. Half way down a sudden rattle of crockery stopped him. Heart athump, he peered through the bannisters to his left, whence the sound had come and remembered the row of bowls and saucers near the kitchen door. Disappearing white fur. Yet another cat. He was wondering a bit anxiously how many of these unfamiliar and unpredictable creatures lived here when there was a loud clanging of a doorbell. His first inclination was to ignore it and go back to bed but remembering the cats and his duty to the people who lived here he crept downstairs and peered through the wobbly glass of the front door. The bell rang again, and the letter box popped open to reveal a pair of hostile puffy eyes.

'Open the door!'

The voice was female, commanding in a WRVS bully sort of way. He rattled the doorknob half-heartedly and shouted

'It's locked,'

Hoping that this was true.

'Then unlock it.'

He saw a bolt high above his head but no prospect of shooting it. He rattled the knob again for want of anything better to do, then the letter box shot open again and the strident voice commanded 'Kitchen!'

He was so startled by this tone that he didn't have time not to remember where the kitchen was, although his hurrying bare feet only managed to avoid the line of saucers under the stairs by sheer luck. In the kitchen the back door was now being rattled with unnecessary force, so whoever was outside must have sprinted around pretty sharpish. Once again, he was at a loss. He could see no bolt but couldn't believe that he was locked in, because the Professor's note had specifically invited him to explore outside. Then he saw a key on a string by the letterbox. Why would they need a letter box in the back door? Later, Charlie. He tried the key in the lock and with a little difficulty sprang it. Before he could open the door himself, it was blasted open by the stranger outdoors. This was not his house, so he stood firmly in place on the doormat by the row of shoes even though this meant head-butting the considerable midriff of the woman who was so intent on entry. This was instinctive: tradespeople and others were always trying to get into the pub when they shouldn't, and his father had taught him to keep them out.

When it became clear, after a five second stand-off that Charlie was not about to budge, the copious bosom which was all he could see to go with the puffy eyes made a small retreat to the doorstep. the same commanding voice that had shouted through the letter box said

'Professor Gunton!'

Perhaps because it was a statement rather than a request or question, and perhaps because as yet Charlie didn't know anyone called Gunton, or more particularly because he was cross and had just woken up in a strange empty house full of bloody cats he said

'No!'

quite loudly and began to close the door.

There was a brief and undignified scuffle, but Charlie was outclassed. The woman burst past him and settled herself immediately into one of the Windsor chairs. She looked about with snooty curiosity, although she seemed remarkably at home. Charlie was so cross he almost told her to take her muddy shoes off, but recognizing her social and generational advantage, simply said with bad grace;

'They're out.'

'I'll wait.'

'But it's not our house.'

Charlie managed to sound plaintively outraged, but she was not moved.

"What d'you think of the Jap, then?'

Chapter Ten.

It really was the last bloody straw. Charlie wouldn't have had to go to the funeral at all if Ernie had croaked anywhere but the back bar. He would have sent flowers. As it was, he found himself sitting at the back of the church minding his own business and failing to follow the Catholic mummery, staying well out of all this, when the Undertakers' mate, or whatever they called them, tapped him on the sleeve of his camel-hair coat and asked him to help carry the box. Well refusal seemed churlish, so he took off the coat and handed it to Lizzie, who was sitting in front of him. His black suit seemed more appropriate for the duty.

He had to walk down the centre aisle in front of everyone (which basically amounted to most of his regulars) his arm around the shoulder of some obscure relative, carrying what remained of Ernie out the back door to the waiting hearse. Charlie surprised himself by being quite upset. Ernie was not a friend; perhaps it was carrying a coffin so soon after following one. As the congregation (not the audience, as Duncan insisted on calling them) stood around waiting for the hearse and the single family car to disappear he was startled by the voice of Hilary saying 'Do you fancy a quick drink?' He should not have been surprised to see her, of course, since her acquaintance with Ernie, however brief, had been pretty intense. And he really did fancy a drink.

They walked along the leafy High Street from Saint Aloysius, passing several suitable hostelries along the way, but the afternoon was pleasant, and they agreed to stroll down to the

Talbot. It was only when Jimmy raised an arch eyebrow that it occurred to Charlie that he was out for a drink with a twenty-five-year-old girl, and a pretty one at that. She seemed not to mind, so nor did he. She laughed when he said, "Your usual?' which raised JImmy's other eyebrow, but she nodded at the same time, so he ordered for them both and they went to sit by the window. Jimmy was probably put out that they didn't sit at the bar, because the place was empty and he liked to talk, but Charlie was not in the mood for trade gossip. Anyway, he had company.

They watched in companionable silence as people trotted up and down the street, unaware of the voyeurs in the pub. A childhood spent in pubs trying to be invisible had given him a taste for observing people that had never palled. But eventually the silence did, and Charlie found himself talking. He told her he was contemplating a holiday, surprised himself again by confiding that he was weary of the pub, weighed down by a life without Bridie. She had shouldered so much of the business and supported him just by being there. Hilary had not known that Bridie was recently dead, was brief and succinct in her commiserations, moved swiftly on. He talked about how his wife had handled the staff, farmed out the accounts, fought off the pushy Breweries. The Two Brewers was the only private Freehouse left in town, but Charlie's thoughts were turning to a sellout. His son wasn't interested in the place, and it was probably too much for a single private buyer. He could make a tidy sum and retire. But what on earth would he do then? He couldn't imagine. The brewery would put in a flashy young manager and convert the back bar into a tarts parlour or worse, a games room, and push out all his old regulars. And what would old Duncan do then, poor thing, So perhaps not.

Hilary listened patiently as he talked himself out of retirement then went to the bar for another bottle of Guinness and a glass of red wine. Charlie appreciated that she didn't refer to it as "A Red Wine' as so many did these days. Bridie always said "Certainly, sir (or madam). Would you care to specify?' Which never got much more than a quizzical look, but well done for trying. By the time Hilary was back with the drinks he had decided to take the car to East Anglia, just for a week. Sylvia and her Ivan were always ready to stay in the flat and there were plenty of staff. Sod it, he was going on holiday. The impulse nearly extended to asking Hilary to join him, but he stopped himself. She would laughingly refuse. And he didn't really want company; Charlie on his own now. Might as well get used to it. Bridie would not have relished East Anglia: she would have talked him into Tenerife. Again.

At half past twelve Hilary said she had to get back to work: there would already be a pile of notes on her desk. She said her boss was incapable of dealing with clients on the telephone, a handicap for a solicitor. Was she a secretary then? He had never thought to ask her. No, she was a solicitor, too. Oops, sorry. She smiled and went.

Sylvia was on the back bar, so all would be in order there, and Annette was in the kitchen to make some bits and pieces for the regulars to nibble as they gave their harsh critique of the funeral service. He could imagine Duncan's shrill pronouncements. He harboured an anti-Catholicism born of a Jesuit education whose physical unpleasantness he doubtless exaggerated. Charlie would join them all in an hour or so, when they had had a chance to mellow a little.

Having settled his mind on an Odyssey to the east, Charlie decided to arm himself with some suitable literature, and for once W.H.Smith seemed unlikely to be able to cater to his special needs. He determined on Dillons, poncey or not, because it had a big travel section. The trouble turned out to be precisely that it was so big, and he couldn't locate anything that wasn't a Rough Guide to somewhere far more exotic than the back streets of Norwich. Fortunately, he had been spotted. The nice Catherine who drank halves of bitter in a mug strode towards him with smiling purpose to offer him assistance. She immediately produced a Bed & Breakfast guide and the Shell guide to East Anglia, which were ideal. For once he accepted the offered discount. He would buy her the next half.

Walking back towards the pub he felt an unfamiliar reluctance to go home. It was not that he had fallen out with it, of course; it was still his life. The morning's dissatisfaction was hardly surprising under the circumstances, he now told himself. Sternly. But having made the leap of faith required to get himself away on holiday, he now wanted to go somewhere quiet and read his books, plot a route, imagine the rooms where he might stay.

Duty called slightly more strongly, and he entered the pub through the front door with a smile, checking the crowd and that his license to print money was still in order.

The back bar seemed little different from usual, since most of its habitués wore dark clothing all the time. The occasion was marked with small plates of sausage rolls and roast potatoes in front of the drinkers. There was always an atmosphere of sombre merriment among this lot, which reminded visitors of nothing so much as a wake. Today they were actually holding one. Duncan was stuffing a newspaper parcel of finger sandwiches into his decrepit briefcase with such an air of furtive guilt that Charlie was tempted by easy outrage but smiled to himself instead.

Before Charlie could decide who to greet first, Ernie's sister from Nottingham breezed in amply through the private door, which set off the usual chorus of tutting and harrumphing until the locals realised who she was. She was fresh from the Crematorium where none of the drinkers had wanted to be. Charlie bought her a sympathetic Gin and Bitter Lemon. It lasted about thirty seconds. She could buy the next, he had already bent the rules. She was kissing him on the cheek in a small cloud of powder when the nice Indian doctor who had tried to resuscitate Ernie arrived. Charlie introduced him to the sister who enveloped the hapless medic in black nylon velvet, nudging his glasses onto his forehead.

As Charlie took over the bar his earlier reluctance to engage faded. He sent Sylvia to offer her condolences and get a sausage roll before Duncan nicked them all. Jim Dixon, who was rumoured to be a de-frocked (if that was the right expression) monk, but who had probably started the rumour himself came to the bar and asked for a pint on tick as usual. As always, he was refused, and he cheerfully paid up with a twenty pound note.

This ship of fools was Charlie's metier: there were only about a dozen of them, but fascinating, story-laden and grumpy, not a real spender among them, they made Charlie's the best pub in town. They certainly didn't encourage new members to their group, but there were those came to observe and soak up some of the bizarre humour of it all. He wasn't going to sell anything

Chapter Eleven.

Charlie was good at silent glaring, but he couldn't keep it up for ever. This hateful woman kept plying him with questions that were personal, even rude; some of them about himself, but most about the nice people who seemed to have agreed to look after him. He knew he was a well brought up little boy because the barmaids at home often told him so, and his innate good manners forced him to respond, however monosyllabically. But he couldn't deal with was the way she said 'Jap' all the time: it was a dangerous word for a little boy in wartime. Of course he knew who she meant, but to Charlie a Jap was a little yellow faced man with thick specs, squinty eyes and buck teeth who bayonetted the innocent and bombed Pearl Harbour. Nothing to do with this lovely giggly new friend with her odd gestures, her unladylike shuffle. Charlie had noticed this particularly because his father was always muttering to people to pick their bloody feet up.

He was longing to ask the smug and wrinkly face across the table what she meant, exactly, by 'Jap', but he desperately didn't want to have to dislike Missus Wife before he even got to know her. The interrogation was interrupted by a knock on the kitchen door. A loud voice of a different stripe, jolly and a bit smoky calling out

'Missus wife! Yer eggs!'

Being, as the Professor had pointed out, a quick study Charlie recognised the Mrs Boldero who had greeted him and the Professor's wife on their journey from the station. Was it only yesterday?

He jumped down from his confrontational seat and opened the back door with as bright a 'Hello!' as he could muster, and the corduroy and cleaning scarf-wearing woman on the doorstep handed him a small gardening tray containing about a dozen fresh eggs. Charlie was awestruck at such riches and took them with exaggerated care. Mrs Boldero's face darkened as she greeted the woman at the kitchen table with barely a flared nostril.

'Professor not here, then?'

Mrs Boldero was looking at the woman, but Charlie got the impression she was really addressing him. He shook his head firmly.

'Better wait, then. Mrs Desborough.'

Mrs Boldero nodded very slightly at the other woman, who smiled unconvincingly. Charlie go the impression that he was being protected, a bit like when at home he came down in his pajamas to say 'Goodnight' and the public bar went quiet.

'I'd say put the kettle on, but they don't have proper tea in this house, do they?'

She appeared to be making a joke. So Charlie shook his head shyly.

'Your name Charlie?'

He nodded again, although the temptation to reel off another half-dozen possibilities courtesy of the Professor was strong.

'Well I'm Edna Boldero. This here's Gilly Desborough.'

Charlie, who had not yet retaken his seat, said

'How do you do?'

Mrs Desborough said;

'That's Gillian, actually.'

She said it with a hard 'G'. Which seemed appropriate. Mrs

Boldero obviously assumed that the older woman would not have introduced herself.

'You'll be alright here, love. They're eversuch kind people. Fell on your feet, I'd say.'

She looked at Gillian Desborough with a raised eyebrow, but the only retort was a crossed ankle and a brief snort.

Charlie felt terribly awkward with these two formidable women in someone else's kitchen, but as the nearest thing to a host he couldn't leave them. On the other hand, the obvious mutual hostility was quite scary for such a little man.

'Would anyone like a walk outside?'

As soon as he had said it, he felt a fool. But the two women just looked at each other more fiercely.

'No.'

Said Mrs Desborough.

'I'm alright for now, love.'

Said Mrs Boldero.

Charlie sat.

Silence.

The dog heard it first and began to woof deeply, but soon they all caught the sound of splutter and cough from a rather dodgy motor. Charlie's first impulse was to run out to meet it, but the atmosphere required calm:

'Perhaps that's them.'

Staying put.

Mrs Boldero smiled at him and said she expected so, while the other one recrossed her ankles and looked grimmer than ever.

An old dirty Austin with no apparent roof chugged into view through the kitchen window. A be-goggled Professor held the wheel and his wife sat in the back seat surrounded by bags and boxes. She jumped down almost as soon as the car stopped and fiddled with bits and pieces in the back seat, while the Professor swatted at her wrists as she had done to him in the bath house. He lifted out the biggest box and was hidden by it as Charlie opened the door and said

'Hello, Professor.'

He greeted Charlie genially, but his eyes were behind the boy's head, and from the door he could only see Mrs Desborough, so Charlie quickly said

'Mrs Boldero brought your eggs.'

The Professor looked relieved as the egg-provider came up behind Charlie and briefly put a hand on his head.

'Hello, Mrs Wife.' she said, brightly, glancing at the Professor.

'Harro, harro!'

The little woman tripped across the courtyard but stopped dead when she saw Mrs Desborough before recovering her composure and brushing past them all. She kicked off her sandals and slipped into the canvas slippers by the door all in a single motion. Mrs Boldero moved to let her pass and touched her lightly on the sleeve. Mrs Desborough remained firmly seated and didn't smile at anyone.

'I've come about the boy.'

'Yes. I see. Shall we go into my study.'

'Have you got any seats in there yet?'

As they went through the hall past the saucers of milk Charlie could hear her ask why the boy was not at school and the Professor reply that he needed rest and recuperation after his long trek. Charlie hoped she would step in the milk. He didn't hear any more.

Mrs Boldero was laughing about the choice of beverage here as Missus wife poured three tiny cups of tea from her strange little pot, but she took a sip all the same. The big countrywoman ventured another sip and grimaced while Missus Wife giggled at her.

'Tastes like dishwater, doesn't it?'

she said to Charlie, and although he knew she was just being funny he shouted;

'Well I like it, it's everso nice!'

and bolted through the kitchen door without his shoes.

A few minutes later Mrs Boldero came to him where he sat against the ilex tree, back to the house, staring into the great expanse of hedge.

'Don't worry, love. I'm on their side, you know. They'll look after you.'

She patted him on the head again and walked off through an arch in the yew.

Five minutes later he heard the front door slam and someone, he assumed Mrs Desborough with the hard G, trudging across the gravel. The yew hedge was too thick for him to see through, but he was fairly sure that the Professor and Missus Wife didn't usually use the front door. There were no shoes by it.

After he had sat for half and hour, a pair of his own shoes plopped down by his side and he looked up to see Missus Wife a few feet away making her beckoning gesture.

'Come on.'

He followed her back into the house (without putting on his shoes, but slipping on the big slippers at the back door to approving nods) and upstairs. She gestured to him to open the door,

'Your room, Chiarry.'

She closed the door behind him.

In front of the fireplace, where a tiny fire had been lit, was an ancient enamel hip-bath full of steaming water. A fluffy towel hung over the back rest. Charlie saw the bed had been remade, but the cats were still there: well, they didn't seem to make him sneeze, anyway. He was tempted to lock his door, but he knew that he had been understood and that it was not necessary. He took off his clothes and lowered himself into the water. Which was very hot.

Chapter Eleven.

Carefully Charlie folded his Kimono back into the tissue paper. He strove to return it to the form in which it had arrived, but this proved a frustrating task, and after the third attempt he contented himself with getting it into the cardboard folders at all. He threw out the three huge Chrysanthemums. The preposterous blooms would not begin to shed for a good week yet, but he didn't want to leave behind anything that Sylvia might find irksome. She and her Ivan were staying in the flat while he was away.

Sylvia and Lizzie had advised him to get away, but now perhaps they thought his plan, only briefly explained, rather frivolous. Nevertheless, their blessings were at least three-quarter-hearted.

He had never really relished the thought of someone else, however familiar, in their home while they were away. Bridie had always neurotically scrubbed the place from side to side (in a flat there was hardly a top to bottom) though the mess she claimed to be eliminating was hardly visible even to Charlie, who had a keen idea of tidy himself. This time he didn't really mind. Sylvia was a good girl, and her Ivan wasn't a bad lad, if a little shiftless. Brute strength and ignorance had their attractions equal to copper-coloured hair.

Charlie sat at the bureau with chipped walnut veneer and wrote a list of where things were and what to switch off when and how. Sylvia had done it all before, of course. The hot water was constant, being connected to the pub supply, and the kitchen was so small as to present little problem. They would probably use

Larry anyway. Still, best to be thorough.

His middle-sized leather suitcase with its peeling labels, stood by the front door battered from years of biennial treats. Majorca: before the plebs had taken it over, they had sailed into Palma on the Edinburgh Castle. Tenerife; well Bridie had liked it but Charlie secretly regarded it as a bit of a dump. Malaga; they had both enjoyed Malaga. No label for this trip, though. Just a change of trousers, pants and socks; a couple of shirts and a bag with toothbrush and shaving stuff. He planned to buy anything else he needed en route.

That sounded good, on the road like Bing and Bob. Not like Kerouac, whose book Charlie's son had recommended to his uncomprehending Pop. Charlie liked being called Pop; his grandchildren called him that, too. Or sometimes Grandpop when their father was about. The naming of parents and grandparents was important: nothing too formal but a bit different. Bridie hated 'Nanny.' She said if they wanted a nanny they should buy a farm or ring an agency. The kids called her Granma, which she didn't object to openly.

That morning he had framed the photograph which now sat on the mantlepiece in the bedroom. It had been taken a couple of months before the diagnosis, when she was still up to weight: perhaps even a little plump. Her hair was newly done, with that familiar lacquered blonde halo; she was stood behind the bar with her hand on a pump. Funny, she was still hopeless after all these years; never learned to pull a good pint. After all those years, he should say. The picture had been taken by a photographer for the LVA newsletter after some marathon fund-raising effort. Which charity it had been he couldn't remember, they had sponsored so many, but her last favourite had been the LVA retirement homes, God forbid he ever ended up there. He had been going to put the portrait next to that of Missus Wife in the living room. Stiff-backed she stood, white moon faced and unsmiling in a dark Kimono holding a furled paper umbrella in her left hand and a single paper flower in her right. Must have been paper; looked unreal even in the shades of brown and cream that may once have been black and white. It was a professional job done in Yokohama with 'Yoshizaki, photographer' printed in flamboyant Art Deco script on the lower border. He had pinched it from the Professor's library after finding it in an old book. Then he thought of putting Bridie next to his mother on the davenport. They had never met, so perhaps not. Bedroom then. His three women in their different continents of his shrinking world. All gone. Almost equally missed. He checked the electrics once more and arranged the note prominently on the davenport, where Sylvia couldn't miss it. He clicked the door shut and toted his light suitcase down the steep stairs to the bar. He put his spare keys into an envelope with Sylvia's name on it and popped it into the back bar till as arranged. He could hear Archie the cellarman in the front, sloshing around pipe-cleaning fluid or some other arcane attribute of his liquid trade (he ought to have webbed feet to go with his blossoming nose) but didn't feel the need to say goodbye. Charlie slid out of the back door and almost fell over Duncan who was sauntering past with his head down. He looked at the battered suitcase and laughed girlishly.

'I'll write you a label. Then you'll look like a real evacuee.'

Charlie smiled vaguely and said

'See you when you're older'

which was his standard au revoir and set off down the street for the mews and his waiting chariot. Archie's eldest Ian had given it the loving once-over last night, so he knew that it would purr; he recalled that he should have given Archie a twenty to pass on, but it was too late now, he was ready to get going.

He pulled out of the mews entry and into the street just as the sun came out from behind a light grey cloud and would have felt good omens if he had any time for all that rubbish. The old girls in the back bar read out everyone's stars from the papers each day. The inconsistencies between astrologers allowed them to pick the most likely to fit each person. Charlie said he would believe in Horoscopes the day everyone born under the sign of Scorpio was run over by an egg lorry.

As he drove through the traffic lights by the pub, he saw Sylvia sauntering across the road in a Brigitte-Bardot-incognito belted mac, headscarf and sunglasses, a large tote bag over her shoulder. Ready to move in. She would be getting the back bar sorted out for opening at ten thirty. The front bar, like all the other places in town, opened at eleven, but if his clientele wanted an early pint, he was not about to stop them. Outside the Talbot Jimmy was using a long rigid hosepipe to water his hanging baskets and upstairs window boxes. Charlie gave him a friendly toot and he turned round in true Carry On fashion, spraying a passing wino who seemed about to complain until he saw who was blotting out the sun.

The road east out of town passed through all the council estates and ratty terraces that once housed the working population. Not many of them could really be called that anymore. Not what a 'working man' had meant to Charlie's generation. Poor young buggers. Where once had been a whole industry there was now a single small pottery and a big craft museum: good old market forces. There were a couple of clothing sweatshops which employed mainly women, most of them Asian and a furniture distribution warehouse for one of the trendy chains that had spilled across the country in the last decade, and which now advertised a permanent sale. Boom and bust, the legacy of a bunch of greedy, spineless politicians in thrall to philistine business. Charlie loved making money, voted Tory and had little enough time for whingers and new age travellers, but he recognised a spiteful political ideology when he saw one. The bloody national lottery, which Bridie called the tax on the stupid, was just a symptom of our decline into the third world. They'd be using it to shore up the NHS next. Oh, well. So much for a buoyant mood of adventure. He shook the clouds of urban decay from his thoughts and concentrated on the road ahead as he took it south towards Peterborough. Another bloody awful place, but it had a decent bypass. No need to dwell on the shame of that beautiful Gothic spaceship serving mostly empty light industrial units. Speed on. Big road driving didn't suit Charlie, but he intended to be on the Suffolk/Essex Border for lunchtime, then turn back up into the sticks to begin his holiday at the right pace.

By half past twelve he was ready to eat. It had to be a pub and it had to specify food on sturdy professional sign. Gems like the King's Shilling were a rarity, and a fluorescent cardboard sign by the road in barman's handwriting (not usually joined up) as often as not meant sausage and chips in a basket and only a pool table to eat it off.

***

Responding to a discreet, well-lettered advert, Charlie found the

72

Churchwarden's Pipe in an attractive double-barrelled village four miles west off the dual carriageway. It stood on a small green with brick red-tiled houses, not particularly distinguished and all similarly painted, suggesting that they were either estate owned or in the grip of an unusually powerful parish council. The pub was also of brick, but with a slate roof. It stood squarely opposite the pretty church, which was dwarfed by a disproportionately tall and elegant limestone tower. Barnack stone, probably signalling a brief spurt of prosperity in the early fifteenth century. He would have looked it up but was not yet in his guide book's area. Still he took out his books when he was safely parked under the bright beech trees spreading over on the green. The Shell guide, a bed and breakfast listings book and a guide to the pubs of East Anglia given to him the night before he left by Hilary. Lent, rather, as it had her name rather boldly written on the fly leaf: Hilary Ghent *Chelmsford* 1984. What buried prejudice against the place caused him to wrinkle his nose at that? He took them with him and walked to the front entrance.

The Lounge Bar, as it advertised itself, was empty and dim, lit by low windows with leaded lozenge lights, bottle-bottom panes thrown in at random for authenticity. These were partially obscured by curtains displaying hunting scenes in dingy brown and green with flashes of red on the pursuers' jackets. Bloodthirsty nitwits. This pattern must be produced exclusively for pubs; he had never seen it anywhere else nor had he ever noticed it advertised in trade papers. A mystery.

The walls were plastered in Artex swirls, like Marks and Sparks Christmas cake, the wall lights hacked unkindly from stained wood. The lampshades echoed the colours of the curtains, with windows cut out of pictures of coaching inns. Marks and Sparks Christmas cards this time. Charlie recognised the style of the brewery the place must be tied to. He sympathized with the tenants while thanking God for his decorative freehold.

The counter itself was big enough only for one person. It occupied a corner of the room, which held a dozen small tables. There was a nice-looking young girl standing behind it now, smiling professionally. He smiled back and said 'Hello' but was in no hurry to put his books down at a corner table, check his pocket for cash (which was a nervous tic, as he never left the pub without cash) and hang his light car coat up on a hanger near the door. As he walked towards the girl, she expertly reanimated her smile, so he withdrew the misery pose he had chosen and ordered a bottle of Guinness, impressed when she offered him a choice of one off the cold shelf or from the counter. Although he preferred them cold, he felt he should reward such attention to detail and ordered a warm one.

There was a basic leather-covered menu on the bar offering the usual sandwiches and such ad-speak nonsense as a ploughman's lunch, although to be fair who was he to say what a ploughman might order for his lunch, if indeed such a body still existed. At the bottom of this uninspiring list, however, was a hand-written note advising that a restaurant menu was available, and he decided (with a bit of a cheek and little hope on a quiet weekday lunchtime) to test the claim. 'Just a minute' said the girl as she disappeared, soon to be replaced by a man slightly younger than Charlie, similarly dressed but with a faux-regimental tie in place of the cravat. The man was very apologetic, and Charlie, feeling guilty, offered to settle for a sandwich 'or something', but the landlord knew his client and offered to run him up a nice trout with new potatoes and watercress, or perhaps an omelette there being no fryers on in the kitchen. Charlie was impressed. Any other day he would have introduced himself and they would have talked trade and filed away each other's business profiles. But for all that this was clearly to be a busman's holiday (and none the worse for that; Charlie loved nothing better than a well-run pub,) he also wanted to be private. He settled for the trout and went to sit in his corner with the Shell guide. He opened at the maps and let his eye wander around Suffolk and Norfolk, picking out familiar names some of which, like Aldburgh and Southwold he had visited with Bridie. He had not been to Norfolk since he was a much younger man, but he knew some of the names well enough.

It was only now, sitting at this table in a strange pub waiting for a trout that was causing unnecessary work for the person cooking it when he would as soon have settled for a slab of pate and some microwaved garlic bread that it came to him that he was heading back into untouched memories. Charlie was not the sort to recognise, let alone seek out hidden motivation. So he went back to his book.

Chapter Twelve.

Charlie was up to his ears in hot water, a difficult accomplishment that required him to hang his legs over the sides of the bath. He realised he still had no idea what time it was. He didn't own a watch, but there was always a clock nearby when you lived in a pub, life running to the rhythm of legal opening and closing times. His life heretofore had been partially gauged according to whether or not people over the age of consent were allowed to consume alcohol. Of course, school had a timetable, but he often didn't go to school. His mother didn't know that, but his father was a turner of blind eyes extraordinaire and had in his day been a truant of some note. No-one at school seemed to miss him anyway.

The bathwater was beginning to cool down, the little fire unable to prolong its usefulness. He decided to get out and use the fluffy towel. Now that he was left alone, he felt secure enough to drip profusely onto the red hearth rug. At home he was allowed to be alone as much as he wanted; actually, choice didn't really enter into it. His parents kept unsocial, interminable working hours, and he was an only child, possibly unplanned (grown-ups talk too loudly sometimes, especially when they've had a few). They were always too busy or too tired to listen to him. Not that he said much.

On his own now he wasn't embarrassed about being naked; even the cats didn't bother him as he checked himself for pubic hairs, which he had seen on older boys. He stretched himself in front of the dressing table mirror to make any new muscles stand out. Neither action proved fruitful.

On the footboard of his lovely bed was a thin blue and white patterned dressing gown. He put it on. It was stiff with starch and far too long, but he hitched it up around his middle and tied it with the broad green belt, which looked like military webbing. In the long mirror which he now discovered inside the wardrobe door he thought he looked silly, but he didn't want to put his smelly clothes back on, and anyhow they seemed to have disappeared. So he stuck his tongue out at himself.

The knock on the door was diffident, so he expected to hear a little voice say 'Chiarry', but there was none. The knock came again a little harder, and he realised that he was expected to respond. Being grown up was a bit of a bother but he said

'Er, come in.'

The Professor stooped to miss the lintel and entered wearing a dressing gown just like Charlie's over which he wore a curious padded jacket with box sleeves. He smiled shyly;

'Hello, Charlie. I am sent by my wife to assist you with the post-bathing routine. At least I assume that that is the idea, she is a little unspecific when giving instructions, which as you can imagine I find hard to bear.'

He shuffled his feet and Charlie saw that the Professor was wearing the same slippers he himself had been assigned earlier, but he also saw that the Professor's feet filled them amply.

'I'm afraid that this style of bathing, which I know to be most pleasurable, must be something of a rarity, since the water has to be brought up while still hot and that is no mean feat here where we are without help, and I am too old and feeble to be of much assistance to my wife, who is inclined to refuse help in any case. I do not mean to appeal to your better nature, since your everyday one is quite equal to the task of understanding.'

Charlie was mortified. It had not occurred to him to question how the bath had been possible, being too delighted that it was happening at all. He was sure that it was not the Professor's intention, but he felt guilty and selfish anyway.

'I'm sorry, sir. I didn't ask her for this.'

'No, you didn't. You will discover after continued dealings with my wife that you cannot make her do things. She does them or sometimes not. Anyway, the next part of the proceedings is rather fun.'

The old man reached down outside the bedroom door and produced a small basin and a water jug like the one on Charlie's mother's dressing table. He put them down next to the bath and beckoned to Charlie who came to stand face to chest with him; very swiftly and expertly the professor adjusted and tightened his dressing gown without undoing it or exposing anything embarrassing. He went over to the window and threw up the sash, letting in some fresh country air. It was still light outside.

'What time is it, Professor?'

'Around five, I should say, although I carry no watch for exactitude. Here take this,'

and he handed Charlie the jug.

The old man bent almost in half like some distinguished insect from a library book, and filled the basin with water from the bath, not quite to the top, to avoid spillage. Charlie hoped he wouldn't notice the splashes of water he had made on the rug underneath the bath tub. The old man carried it to the open window and gleefully chucked the water out onto the tiles outside. Charlie giggled, and so did his companion.

'I told you that this part was fun. Come on, fill her up.'

He pointed to the jug. The cat which had presented itself at Charlie's window when he woke up now bounced through the casement and sprang from the windowsill to the bed. It shook its paws fastidiously, disdaining used bath water. Charlie found he no longer minded his bed doubling as a cattery. After a couple of loads each, the water level in the bath was low, so the Professor instructed him to take the handle at one side while he took the other himself. With the Professor bent double and Charlie at full stretch, the old man's free hand (Charlie didn't have one) steadying the tall back of the tub they maneuvered it to the windowsill and tipped it up with the back rest acting as a lip. The remaining water, grimy and soapy, sloshed down the roof into and overflowing the gutter. Charlie heard the slap as water hit gravel, and hoped there were no animals loose around, at least not the big dog or the donkey.

'Well, Charlie Moulton, you must be hungry.'

Charlie thought about it for a second and nodded, smiling.

'Then we had better eat.'

Charlie took the jug and basin while the Professor lugged the bath downstairs not without the odd grunt. They were followed out of the bedroom by the various cats which had appeared apparently at the mention of food. They impressed Charlie by overtaking on the stairs without getting in his way.

Looking over the bannisters he saw that the line of bowls and saucers was now being used by a dozen felines of various colours and sizes.

'My wife is inordinately fond of cats.'

'How do you remember their names.'

The Professor chuckled his amiable chuckle;

'They're all called 'Cat.'

Charlie giggled. The Professor seemed to approve.

'Just as the dog is called 'Dog' and the donkey is called 'Donkey'. Had we a pet octopus I don't doubt that it would be named 'Octopus.'

He laughed a lot at that.

'If I had a pet, I would want to give it a real name. I've never had one.'

The Professor looked sympathetic.

'Well, now you can share all of ours.'

He looked wistful, as if he was about to launch into one of his speeches.

'If you had a pet, what do you think it would call you?'

'Well, Charlie of course.'

'Don't be too sure.'

Charlie didn't have time to ponder the implications of this latest gem, as the Professor pointed to the door directly opposite the beautiful room.

'That is the Dining Room. Please offer to help my wife, whom you will find in the kitchen. She will likely refuse, but I am not willing to make a definite statement on that. You are in her hands now.'

He disappeared into his magical study with a small smile, and Charlie tiptoed through the gauntlet of Cats (who now deserved a capital letter) to the kitchen.

Chapter Thirteen.

It was still only two o'clock when Charlie finished lunch. He thanked the barmaid, paid his bill and set off again. He now found himself crossing the border into Suffolk on a back road to Sudbury. It was time to act the tourist.

He pulled into a tatty layby, where a ruinous caravan appeared to be the abandoned remains of a greasy-spoon truck stop, apparently rendered redundant by the dual carriageway. The deduction was proven wrong when a patched and coughing Bedford van rattled to a halt behind his car. Two men got out, one wearing an outrageous leather hat with fake fur earflaps tied under the chin. They went to the cheesy shutdown plywood service hatch and banged on it loudly. They were rewarded by its being flung forward, narrowly missing the nose of the man without the hat. His thick black hair and idiotic expression reminded Charlie of some old Russian Folk Art he had once seen at the Arts Centre in town. Not that he had any interest in Folk Art, nor even the Arts Centre as such, but they always sent him invitations to things, and a blurred sense of civic duty compelled him to show up and put some coppers in the hat.

The force behind the service hatch was unseen, but the shrill volume of what was issuing from it, suggested it was female. The dialogue that followed produced two Tony Benn sized mugs of tea, and eventually something steaming on a paper plate, which the two men devoured standing up. Charlie decided to concentrate on the task in hand and looked up Sudbury in the

Shell guide index and turned to the page indicated.

The place did not seem to have a great deal to offer, but he had heard of Gainsborough and liked the sound of his house, so he pulled back onto the road, watched with open curiosity by the bizarre pair of al fresco diners.

The centre of the pretty little town was busy with shoppers at all the usual suspects: Boots, God bless it, and a W.H. Smith. He didn't look all that hard as he passed through. He parked his car barely legally off the central market place and walked up a side street to where the museum stood. It was a good, unexceptional Georgian fronted building in red brick and white paintwork, much as one would find in any East Anglian town, no doubt built to accommodate prosperous burghers engaged in whatever made burghers prosperous. Unlike the elegant and ostentatious mansions which dotted the rural landscape, financed largely by the ill-gotten gains of Whig politicians or their ilk. None of this came from the Shell guide. Charlie was recounting to himself the opinions of his son, who had plenty to spare. He spouted them whenever Charlie drove him to or from university. Longest conversations (monologues, really) they had ever had. Charlie recalled them with pleasure and pride. He had asked the boy to help out whenever he was home in the long vacations, but he never would; he preferred to wash up in restaurants or punch out tickets in the tinny little Arts Centre, which now Charlie thought about it had just closed down to be superseded by a wine bar. All those jobs had been negotiated by his ma or pop, who could sadly guess at his terror of being sucked into the family business. Fair enough, Charlie had eventually been persuaded by Bridie. He was just a lad, learning about freedom. Although not freedom from financial dependence on his old man, that was a long way off. Not begrudged, really. Sometimes Charlie was frightened that his thoughts were too similar to the old buggers in the back bar.

The Gainsborough House Museum did not take long to exhaust. There were only a few paintings, though pretty and nicely displayed. He especially liked those landscapes that didn't have some overstuffed landowner or actress on the make posing in front; at least that's what Charlie thought them to be. The furniture was elegant, too, but it was still a Museum, despite the kiln and working studios. Museums weren't Charlie's favourite places: he liked to see pictures displayed on private walls in the big houses his son disdained. Portraits of people who had lived in the houses and had actually bought all their Madonnas and Cupids on the Grand Tour. Trips which represented insurance against their impregnating unsuitable English girls bought by thrusting them among even more unsuitable but far les damaging foreign ones. His son had, Charlie was the first to acknowledge, a most entertaining way of demolishing the English upper classes. Charlie had often asked to attend one of his lectures, but the boy wouldn't hear of it.

It was without a glance in the rear-view mirror that he left Sudbury and drove out towards Long Melford, where he knew even without the Guide's assistance that there was a good church for him to shuffle around. When Bridie arrived on the scene he had more or less given up his hobby of looking around old churches: she didn't really see the attraction of dusty places full of dead delusionists, but Charlie had become quite knowledgeable as a young man. He had even developed a sneaking affection for the Victorian restorers and tinkerers who had so thoroughly buggered up a large number of perfectly good mediaeval interiors. At least they had cared.

The long, broad street that was Long Melford remained much as he recalled, if a little sprucer and brighter, with its magnificent church at the far end. He could only estimate the years since he had been here. It must be at least thirty. He parked the car up at the Sudbury end and walked down, browsing the windows of antique shops and looking at a tempting restaurant menu. Pity it was only four o'clock. In one of the shops he spotted a Japanese screen and went in for a closer look. But he was disappointed; he could tell from the bright paint and the background that it was not very old, and quite probably not Japanese at all. The lady behind the counter who said 'Nice piece, that' looked most put out when he said that it was indeed quite nice, but not particularly antique.

He reached the church with its monumental Victorian tower. Or was it Edwardian? He could never remember when the old broad died. The nave and chancel were independently impressive, with their lovely stained glass and the cleverly knapped flint of the walls. No number of visits to these places could tire him, although he felt not a twinge of religious sentiment as he walked around. Surprisingly, considering his recent brushes with death, it was still the dead hypocrites, or rather their monuments that drew him most. The bigger and more vulgar the better. All Bridie had been allowed was a square foot of yellowish marble with her name and dates in black, no message. The usual sentiments on modern stones sounded like a bloody greetings card. She would have preferred it plain. Not dead but sleeping. Not lost but gone before. Who were they trying to kid? But he loved the old verses in doggerel, penned in all probability by the Vicar's alcoholic brother or the spinster sister with the cruel rudiments of a classical education. Bad rhymes and stretched metaphor, self-conscious reference to Arcadia, or the beloved of Athene, when what they really meant was that the body in question had devoted most of his daylight hours to shooting at things.

Charlie realised with a lurch of guilt that as he wandered around here, doing something he had forgotten he enjoyed, that he was happy. Or at least that he felt unburdened. He hadn't worried about the pub in at least six hours. He would ring Sylvia later. Or maybe tomorrow.

Chapter Fourteen.

There were unusual smells coming from the kitchen, and one in particular that was sweet and cloying. To Charlie, who had a pub child's vocabulary it was like Angostura bitters mixed with Lea and Perrin's. Contrary to the Professor's prediction he was gently pushed into a chair and given an unwieldy knife and several long spring onions. Missus Wife (for Charlie had decided that that was how he thought of her, and he would try to avoid naming her to her face) showed him how to slice one delicately and then proceeded to slice another at the speed of light. Charlie had used a knife to peel and chop for his grandmother (though the posh aunt who took holidays also had a maid for chopping things and stuff like that.) He was frustrated that this delicate task left no room for error, miscut discs staying miscut. Missus Wife just giggled, of course. The opposite end of the table was covered in flour, in the middle of which was a pile of what appeared to be dusty string. There came a sudden hiss and spitting from the range as the diminutive cook (now wearing a cotton flowered housecoat with the buttons done up the back, which on reflection made quite good sense) dropped something into a pan of hot fat. She did this several times, then lifted the things out with a long holed spoon. She placed them on a linen napkin which rested on a large plate with a little bowl in the middle. Eventually she was done and gave the heavy dish to Charlie and gestured him away.

'Professor's room.'

Charlie took it, knocked over a now empty saucer in the

corridor (the cats had gone to find a comfortable bed to wash on, no doubt), and tapped on the door of the beautiful room.

'Ah, Charlie. Do come in.'

He spotted the plate and rubbed his knuckles.

'These things are something of a treat, you see. Mrs Boldero's precious eggs, a little flour and water. Probably a splash of sake. Vegetables from the garden, although I admit mostly young carrot and cabbage. Sit down here.'

This was not conventionally possible if he was to join the Professor. He stepped onto the platform, having removed his floppy slippers. He placed them next to the larger pair, which were pointing away from the platform and turned his to face the same way.

'Jolly good.'

Said the Professor. At least it wasn't 'That's right.'

The low table was surrounded by flat, square cushions and the old man was sitting on one of these, cross-legged as before. He told Charlie to sit down and stretch his legs under the table. There he discovered a hole into which he could lower his legs in order to sit on the cushion as on a bench. Getting in and out was a bit undignified, but the idea was sound.

On the table, next to where the Professor had placed the linen-covered plate of whatever it was stood a charming blue and white bottle that might serve as a vase for a single flower. Next to it were two china thimbles for very large thumbs, the same pattern as the bottle inside and out. Whatever was in the vase was steaming.

'Your father I believe to be a publican.'

As so often with the man the statement appeared to be a

question to which Charlie must furnish some response. To this less than usually abstract example he could confidently nod. His father liked the word Publican, although he also called himself a licensee.

'Then I may assume that you have in the past taken alcohol.'

His mother and father allowed him a miniscule sweet sherry on a Sunday while he peeled things or sat in the parlour watching his grandmother knit silently. Charlie reckoned that this was not a treat to boast about. He nodded anyway.

'Splendid! then please join me in a little sake. My wife does not drink alcohol, although her intake of a variety of teas might be described as prodigious - you will no doubt have been offered her particular favourite. It is dusty brown stuff with twigs floating in it.'

He raised his eyebrow humourously. Charlie giggled and was met with approval.

'You have a ready laugh, Charlie. Now, this little ritual is one that I much enjoyed when I lived in my wife's country.'

Here he paused and looked at Charlie. He could not read the required response and so gave none. He was dying to ask, of course, but that would have opened up a whole can of worms. The Professor looked down and continued;

In this game you must not pour your own drink and must ensure that your drinking partner does not run out of sake. However, this will require you to do most of the pouring as I do not expect you to enjoy the actual liquid yourself.'

He poured a little of the clear liquid into one of the thimbles and pushed it toward Charlie, indicating with eye and eyebrow that Charlie should do the same for him. As Charlie did so the Professor lifted the little cup in his left hand where it was overwhelmed and put the fingertips of his right hand under the bottom, slightly tilting it towards the bottle. It was an elegant, if rather effeminate gesture for such huge hands. Charlie took a tiny sip from his thimble. As predicted, he did not much like the taste, but then he was not all that impressed with sweet sherry either. The difference here was that he was in the beautiful room, his legs stuck down a hole in the floor wearing a dressing gown embroidered with big blue birds and talking to an incredibly tall old man who giggled more than he did and liked throwing dirty bathwater out of an upstairs window. Better than shuffling his scrawny backside and trying to avoid dislodging the starchy antimacassars in the upstairs parlour.

The Professor now produced two bits of wood from his sleeve. At first Charlie took this to be a feeble attempt at conjuring, but the tall man proceeded to use them to pick up one of the fried things and dip it in the bowl of brown goo at the centre of the plate. On the sauce floated a couple of Missus Wife's lacy slices of onion. Charlie's would have sunk.

'You had better use your fingers, Charlie. Lessons in the use of chopsticks, which these are, can wait until we know one another better; it can be a messy learning process.'

Charlie was happy to go along with this. He had seen chopsticks before in the hair of Chinese villains' girlfriends, from where they could be transformed into lethal weapons when cornered.

Charlie picked up a lukewarm lump of chopped vegetable held together by bubbly batter and looked at it doubtfully, but being a well-mannered boy, and trusting the Professor, he dunked it in the goo and took a tiny bite. It was delicious, though apart from the vinegary tang of the sauce it was difficult to identify a specific taste. It was more to do with the texture of crisp vegetables in a slightly spongy batter.

'You seem to like the pictures on my walls.'

They had been eating in silence. Charlie realised he must have been gawking again and checked himself.

'Oh, yes. They're everso nice.'

The Professor chuckled at that, rather than giggled.

'They are indeed, everso. Do you know where they are from?'

Charlie shook his head, his mouth full of fatty little delicacy.

'They are, like my dear wife, from Japan.' He paused.

'Does that upset you?'

Charlie was at a loss. In a way yes, it did upset him. But these lovely things, including Missus Wife could not be lumped together with enemies and the stuff of war he was told or had witnessed.

'You have met Mrs Desborough. This afternoon. She does not approve of Yumiko.'

(Ah, that was the name, thought Charlie and instantly forgot it again.)

'She told me that you were most obstructive when she wished to gain access to our house.'

Charlie looked ashamed and stuttered;

'I'm sorry, I didn't know.'

'On the contrary, Charlie. I am most grateful for your protection. Unlike Mrs Boldero she is neither a kind nor a well-intentioned person. However, she is rather necessary to us, because you will have to attend the village school, and as head of the Parish Council she is in charge there.'

At the mention of school Charlie's face must have revealed his emotion, because the Professor smiled again and said

'Not yet. Cheers!'

and he drained his little cup, nodding and squinting towards the sake bottle until Charlie got the message and filled his thimble again.

He was resigned to the slow trickle of information from adults but held his tongue rather than hear anything he didn't want to. When you're twelve 'Not yet' could be an infinity.

'My wife, Charlie, despite her country of birth is a British citizen like you and I. And even Mrs Desborough. Yumiko is under my protection, for what its worth. And yours too, now. Don Charlie of the kitchen door.'

Charlie grinned with delighted incomprehension.

'She is the kindest and goodest person I know, if you will forgive the lapse in grammar, and she will look after you, as she does me, as long as you need her to.'

Charlie nodded solemnly, filled with relief that Missus Wife was a British citizen wherever she came from. He took another fried thing and celebrated with a mouthful of sake which was much better mixed with food. A pity they didn't serve this stuff at home with the sweet sherry.

'I think she's everso nice.'

The Professor, being as quick a study as Charlie recognised high praise when he heard it.

'Everso. Cheers! Oh, dear we're beginning to sound like Phyllis Calvert.'

Charlie let that fly way over his head. He would try to remember the name.

Chapter Fifteen.

Charlie was not given to introspection or even self-definition but walking back to the car through the late afternoon sunlight he was struck by the Englishness of what he was doing. Not the knee-jerk Englishness of the local Tory type, which was more to do with reading certain newspapers, be they broadsheet or tabloid, and not liking the French very much, but nevertheless comforting and probably middle-class, in the younger Charlie's parlance. Nothing wrong with being middle class. He had argued with his son (when Bridie was not around to change the subject aggressively) that the reason Marx was wrong about the revolution starting with the downtrodden of England was that the downtrodden aspired to wear the boots.

From foreign tourist to fellow publicans on courtesy visits (endurance tests for both parties) people were always telling him how very English his pub was. Eccentric, he supposed they meant, a bit old-fashioned; he hoped tolerant and with a tendency to laugh at itself. And just a little bit of tone. Charlie always told these romantic souls that it was also thoroughly endangered and remained only because he and Bridie could afford to refuse the Breweries' relentless ambition to fiddle with the formula, prettify the pub and fictionalise it out of existence. Let's face it, the brewery families who bought their titles from Lloyd George and rode on the back of Bertie's shooting parties at Sandringham modernised the aristocracy by turning it into a parody of itself and roughing up the bloodlines. Even then it can't have been the quality of their product that earned recognition, the beer was crap. Charlie was grateful, as was his bank manager, to the Campaign for Real Ale, which had recreated the much earlier diversity of English beer (and inadvertently destroyed his ability to drink the stuff) but he had no illusions about the historical authenticity of the Abbott Ale that frothed from his pumps. Unless Bridie was pulling the pint, bless her. She could flatten lager.

Since his childhood the England he aspired to, first coloured by the Aunt who took holidays and then by his brief evacuation to Norfolk, had had little to do with the towns where he habitually ended up. Nor did the vision of rural greenery and relaxed skies have much to do with the business of living and working in the countryside, which seemed fraught with difficulty. Before he had met Bridie, when he was a lowly locum pub manager for one of the breweries, he had sometimes been sent to country towns like Sudbury to cover for tenants on holiday. This was when the big companies were beginning to consolidate their grip on the nation's pubs, or more to the point on the beer that they were allowed to sell. In some ways it was a sorry time for the English pub, although the financial rewards had never been better, unless you counted the Gin shops of the eighteenth century. With fizzy, pasteurised beer on every tap (and unlike today advertised on every telly) the art of brewing 'live' beer all but disappeared. If he was honest Charlie had to admit a localised role in the process, especially when he became area manager. The formica and vinyl conversions he had overseen made once lovely little boozers indistinguishable from the local bookies. Complete with television. There were still a few of these places left in the slip-stream of 'theme pubs' if you could call untreated wooden walls and germanically titled lagers brewed along the Trent and served out of preposterous brass pumps a theme. In terms of decor the King's Shilling was such a survivor, but the food improved on authenticity. The real thing was the Albert Victor near the old pottery at home, run by a tough old widow with her hair in an angry bun, to whom Bridie had taken a bit of a shine. They had visited sometimes on a Thursday night, Bridie and the widow would play hard darts for an hour, while Charlie looked after the bar. There were no other staff. The only food was in a glass cabinet at one end of the bar; cheese and onion or corned beef and Branston. The landlady survived on what was left at closing time. There was also a box of Mars bars, and a few bags of crisps. The customers were mainly students who needed something cheap. Not doing food in this day and age should have been suicide. The margins on beer were squeezed to the limit, but you could clear 500% on food if you knew what you were doing. And if you got your contract sorted the Breweries couldn't touch it.

Charlie shook his head. He found himself in front of a hotel and looked through the door, but it was early yet, and he had half decided on another place to stay, so he got back in the car and drove to Lavenham. Here was another kind of England yet, perhaps the most insidious. It was perfect. Heritaged to within an inch of its life, an inflated Legoland populated by Charlie's betters. He 'phoned Sylvia. She was cross and told him to get on with his holiday. Everything was just ticketyboo whatever the hell that was supposed to mean. Becoming more irritable by the minute he tried the number of the pub he had picked out of Hilary's book, but there was no reply. He decided to risk it.

A few miles north of Lavenham a signpost directed him to the left down a reassuringly small road. The village and pub presented themselves simultaneously. There were no warning satellite houses straggling along the road and he arrived directly at the village green. This held a small pond surrounded by unconnected white knee-high posts, presumably to stop the thoughtless from parking on the grass. To the left and right were houses of varying size and prosperity mostly washed in pale blue or pink, or what Bridie would have called Magnolia. There were also a couple in plain brick and flint. There was greenery everywhere, including an impressive magnolia which in bloom would have given the lie to Bridie's ideal of its colour. The pub was set back from the road behind a broad lawn with a couple of rustic benches on it. It was a long, low building with a thatched roof at one end and red tiles the other, lower than the original gable. There were half a dozen dormer windows along the roof. The walls were painted what Charlie would call cream.

The carpark was signposted to the rear of the building. Charlie pulled into it gently, avoiding the muddy ruts and abysmal puddles among the gravel as best he could. At the furthest point from the building was a royal blue Bedford van, in considerably better nick than the one he had seen earlier. He reversed to face the back of the pub and noted with approval the neat stacks of colourful crates of empties behind a low fence. There was a sign above the rear door saying 'To Bars and Restaurant' but he wanted to have another look at the village green, so he went round the front. The place looked refreshingly lived in after Laveham, even a little scruffy, but there was not a soul in sight. Still, it wasn't quite six.

He tried the door marked 'Lounge' anyway, but it was bolted. In the central window was a panel of black and white glass with the word 'Chequers' scrolled in it. He thought the omission of 'The' a bit pretentious. The other door also failed to open. He had forgotten that he was out of town. Different trade: his after work custom came at five-thirty when offices closed, here it was probably a good hour later. Or perhaps people went home to eat first. He went back to the car and checked the pub book, where it said opening time was six. So he browsed pettishly through the Shell guide, which didn't even mention the village. He supposed you couldn't mention them all, however pretty. He was surprised not to have seen a church anywhere but recalled a newspaper article about village drift. More economical to walk a mile to church than build a new one, he supposed. Anyway, it was too late to go looking now, and any church worth a look would probably be locked.

At ten past six a turquoise Fiat scrunched into the carpark and spat out a young woman in a black skirt, pink blouse and sensible shoes. Staff. She opened the back door with a large key, but without a glance at the strange car in the carpark she also shut it firmly behind her. Charlie decided to give her breathing space and was rewarded a few seconds later by lights at the windows and above the door. He picked up his precious books (he left his bag in case he didn't wasn't to stay) and sauntered round to the front again. He tried the public bar door, thinking this the most likely entrance early in the evening, but the girl's face came to the window, smiling and she pointed to the Lounge. When he pushed it open, she was already behind the smart wooden bar with a cloth in her hand.

'Sorry, sir. The sod's Opera doesn't open until seven. Are you alright in here?'

Charlie was tempted to ask what constituted a Sod's Opera but didn't. He was a little hurt that she should consider him public bar fodder, but then he had tried its door first. So he said 'Fine' and ordered an unaccustomed scotch and soda to put her in the picture.

'Do you have a room free for tonight?'

Charlie had been rehearsing ways to put this question as he drove down. 'Accommodation' sounded a bit permanent, and 'Vacancies' took him back to his bloody Aunt and Blackpool. Not that she lived there, but she was always going on about having had the most fun in her life there. Poor creature.

'I'm afraid I'll have to ask Mrs Williams about that. She's not down until seven.'

'Could you ask her now. If I can't stay, I need to move on.'

She looked dubious, probably terrified of this Mrs Williams.

'I did try to call this afternoon, but there was no reply'
he didn't know why he had to justify himself.

'She'd be out in Sudbury. Or Bury.'

Charlie didn't need to know this.

'Would you just ask her, please?'

Reluctantly the poor woman picked up a small handset behind the bar and dialled two digits. There was a long pause, and then she said all in a rush

'There's a customer here who wants to know if you've got a vacancy because if not, he'll have to move on and he called this afternoon, he says.'

Charlie resented the 'he says'. After a tiny pause the receiver was banged down, and the woman turned to Charlie with less of a smile.

'There's two rooms free. She'll be down when she's ready.'

Charlie offered her a drink with his thanks, but she declined.
When he said

'Well, perhaps later.'

 She said

'Mmm'

and went off to fill the ice bucket.

Chapter Sixteen.

There was no electric light upstairs in the house, which Charlie had only realised when it began to get dark and stayed that way. Downstairs seemed dim, too, apart from the Professor's beautiful room. Nor did there appear to be any gas. At a surprisingly loud call from the diminutive cook the Professor led him out of the study and into the hall, where Charlie saw a small oil lamp set into the newel at the foot of the stairs, giving off a dim glow. The Professor, who clearly read minds along with everything ever written said:

'You will do well to exhaust yourself during the daylight hours here, Charlie. We have limited resources for your entertainment in the evenings, and limited sources of light by which to pursue such diversions as we may devise. You will also find that like most dinosaurs I prefer to retire rather early, if not quite with the sun. You are used, perhaps, to the hours of a public house.?'

'No, sir. I go to bed at half past seven.'

'That will suit us all admirably.'

He pressed the small of Charlie's back with one hand and opened the door of the dining room with the other, a feat possible only for one with extremely long limbs. Charlie was tempted to ask him how he got so tall, or rather long, but knew that it would be impertinent (his grandmother's favourite description of talkative little boys, whatever the object of their questions). The rules were clearly different here, but he didn't want to stretch his good fortune at this early stage.

Missus Wife was already in the room. It held a long conventional dining table and a dozen chairs in dark wood. There were three places laid at the end nearest the fireplace. There were woven mats with a pattern of fish in the weave, small bowls and chopsticks for the adults, but the place Charlie took to be his own, with its back to the fire, had a fork and spoon laid side by side. There was a lovely smell coming from the fireplace where his hostess was crouched over a large earthenware pot which rested on a metal plate above the coals, now mostly embers.

Charlie was gestured into place. The Professor took his bowl to his wife who filled it with a wooden ladle, and when all three had been served the adults sat down too, with Missus wife at the head and the Professor opposite Charlie.

'Once more we are being treated, I see. This stew, for want of a better word, is a speciality of my wife's home town, and contains as you will see some substantial pieces of that rare commodity meat. It should really be beef, but this is cured pork and none the worse for that. Actually, it comes courtesy of a beast that I once rather admired. What was his name?'

He looked quizzically at Charlie, who hesitated only for a moment:

'Pig?'

'Quite so. Even here in the country meat is something of a treat, and one can become distressingly attached to one's diet, as it were. I no longer have the luxury of pigs, as they tend to get commandeered, only of a single pig. You will also no doubt find some goats on your explorations, which are not regarded as meat in the same manner, and many rabbits, which under the gentle eyes of Yumiko are fecund enough to fill the pots of several of our neighbours also.'

At this point Missus Wife slurped loudly and urged Charlie to eat. He tried some of the soup with his funny porcelain spoon; it was almost clear and looked insipid, little beads of clear fat floating on the surface, but it tasted pretty good. The pork, which was really closer to bacon tasted lovely and he ate slowly because it was a very small bowl. He saved the biggest bit of bacon for last. The Professor looked concerned and asked if perhaps Charlie didn't like it, but Charlie explained that he wanted to make it last.

'My dear boy, that pot is full of it. We simply use a small bowl to ensure that it is always hot.'

And as Charlie could see that it was a big pot, he followed the example of Missus Wife in lifting his bowl to his mouth to get the last of the soup. This was great, as good (well almost) as tipping bathwater out of windows, although he was pretty sure he could never bring himself to make a noise when he ate, as seemed to be the rule here: at home that would have set off a chain reaction of tutting starting with his grandmother and guttering round the table like a dud firecracker.

Charlie was bursting to ask about school, but he was a wise child in the company of adults, knowing that asking might precipitate the event, so he kept quiet, like Missus Wife. The Professor alternately babbled away to her in very foreign, which Charlie took to be Japanese, and addressed statement questions to Charlie about diverse subjects. He had brought his ration book? It was upstairs in the cardboard suitcase stashed under the bed next to the huge potty which had made Charlie giggle. The precious book would be surrendered to Missus Wife in the morning. The availability of beer in the towns is weakened by current circumstances? This latter he reported to be 'fairly steady' according to his father's last overheard report, but he had also said Lord knows what they put in the bloody stuff these days; Charlie knew that his father watered the ale a bit and poured all the slops into the dark mild barrel where they wouldn't alter the colour. Adds a bit of flavour, his father chuckled. Charlie, who had strong opinions about right and wrong, however unformed, did not chuckle, just as he did not approve. His father called him a budding Methodist, which he assumed was not a term of endearment.

While Charlie and Missus Wife cleared up and washed the dishes, the Professor disappeared into his study for what he called an 'evening cap'. Charlie followed the lady around as she cleared things away so that he would know where to put them next time. Missus Wife clearly understood what he was trying to do, as once or twice she opened a cupboard (of which there were dozens) and pointed out important items like dinner plates, which they hadn't actually used.

'You good boy, Chiarry. Say goodnight.'

This was the longest speech he had heard her make, but it still seemed rather abrupt.

'Oh. Goodnight.'

She laughed her hilarious little laugh.

'Not me. Professor.'

and she pushed him gently towards the door which led through the cats' dining area to the hall.

He was beginning to notice all this pushing around; at home he would have resisted it from his fellows and resented it from adults. He just wasn't used, he now realised, to gentle physical contact.

'Today'

said the Professor from his dais, to which Charlie was not now invited. There was a little bottle on the table in front of him. Only one thimble.

'has been Thursday.'

Charlie nodded on cue but did not marvel at the insight.

'Which means that there is but one school day left in the week.' Again, Charlie smiled and bobbed, wishing the old man would get to the punchline.

'Do you then wish to attend the school in the village for a single day before the weekend? What a melancholy word that is when you are old, and the weather is being so kind.'

Charlie ignored the last bit as too difficult at this time of night but recognised that he was on tricky ground with the question. Clearly, he did not wish anything of the sort, so he gave what he hoped was a discouraging, melancholic shrug of resignation.

'I thought not. Splendid. Tomorrow we shall explore a little, if you don't mind.'

Still unsure of the procedure when asked for an opinion by a grown up, he didn't reply but tried to look pleased. The prospect was at very least nice, and possibly came into the 'everso' category. This appeared clear to the Professor who genially waved him away with a crisp 'Goodnight Charlie Moulton.'

'Goodnight, Professor. Thank you everso much.'

Missus Wife appeared, as she was in the habit of doing at just the right moment before indecision set in and handed him one of a pair of candles in Wee Willie Winkie holders. She pointed upstairs with hers (no pushing this time) saying something musical that probably meant 'Goodnight' in very foreign, and he carefully made his way up to the bedroom.

In the darkness the room felt much bigger; he could barely see the recessed walls on either side of the fireplace, which anyway were painted dark green. In the grate a couple of embers the size of fag ends still glowed. The window was wide open and there was a faint but not unpleasant scent of bathwater.

Charlie was relieved to see that there were no cats around. Presumably they had used the window as an exit, so he closed all but a crack too small, he hoped, even for a slinking feline. He was still a bit suspicious of them, since their truce was only a few hours old, and he checked the bed before he climbed in. He was asleep before he could even think to blow out the candle. It must have been the country air.

Chapter Seventeen.

Nursing the scotch that he didn't really want, not least because there was no ice yet, Charlie awaited the arrival of the fire-breathing Mrs Williams. He already a mental picture of her as Bridie's age and size, with the same weekly shampoo and set hairdo, the same gentle makeup; the same bossy torso, assertive hips and no-nonsense stance, one hand on the pump and the other on her waist. He was therefore unsettled by the appearance of the pretty young woman who stood over him and asked if he was the gentleman wanting a room.

'Yes.'

she smiled a little tightly:

'Perhaps you would like to see it before you decide.'

The perhaps was obviously superfluous. She walked away from him still speaking, expecting him to follow, and he had only seconds to decide what to do with his drink. He drained it quickly and took a couple of long strides to catch the door just as she was ceasing to hold it open for him.

'There is no separate staircase indoors, but I don't think customers should get behind the bars.'

It sounded like a zoo, but then that was one way of looking at a pub. Charlie agreed that customers should know their place but said nothing as he didn't want to let on that he was in the trade. It would only lead to fatuous conversation and gentle rivalry, which he didn't want to incite with this particular specimen.

She led him out of the back door through which he had watched the barmaid admit herself earlier and then straight back in through another door to the right. This led past the open kitchen, which was large and clean, now occupied by a solitary woman wearing a pink housecoat and what appeared to be a shower cap. Halting at the foot of a steep staircase his guide checked that he was with her before leading him up and along a pink-painted corridor with creaking floorboards and a low bumpy ceiling.

'There is another gentleman staying, in the room next to yours. You have a private shower.'

She pushed a door open before Charlie could say anything appreciative, and he saw a room looking exactly as he envisioned in the dreaming days between decision and departure. It had two dormer windows with rectangular leads overlooking the green through a frame of thatch. The bedspreads, curtains and carpets were pink and green too fussy for a home, but appropriate for guest rooms. The shower room was pale apricot, without a toilet.

'There are two loos on this floor, one just opposite. Mr. Yamazaki uses the bathroom at the end, but you won't be wanting a bath.'

It was not a question, but Charlie shook his head anyway, for good luck. There were two other rooms with numbers on them in the corridor, but he was clearly taking this one.

'The rate is thirty-two pounds a night including whatever you might like for breakfast. We can manage most things.'

She allowed herself a fragment of a smile which if anything detracted from her prettiness. He wondered what Mr. Yamazaki had requested for his breakfast.

'Dinner in the dining room from seven thirty, although you may eat from the bar menu if you wish.'

It was said in a manner that suggested that you might have to eat off the menu itself. She obviously didn't approve of her guests slumming it.

'It all looks very nice.'

Charlie offered feebly, but truthfully. He was rewarded with another tight little smile which he could have done without

'The doors are not locked until half past eleven, so feel free to come and go, but the children are in bed by nine, so try not to make a noise upstairs.'

Charlie was surprised at the mention of children and wondered about the husband. She didn't seem the sort, to be honest.

'I'll fetch my bag.'

She let him descend the staircase first and followed him out of the back door.

'Please order dinner in the lounge bar when you're ready.'

She disappeared back into the pub, and Charlie got his well-travelled suitcase out of the boot.

A few minutes later he set it down on a pine chest at the foot of his double bed. He was pleased to see that the bed was properly made up with sheets and blankets. He had long succumbed to the convenience of the duvet but enjoyed to the odd night in a hotel with the crisp white feeling of sliding between freshly starched sheets. He opened the battered bag and took out his washthings and regretted not bringing a towel. The one provided was small and coarse. He turned on the shower to warm up while he undressed. When he got in he found it satisfyingly powerful, massaging his shoulders as he turned under it.

Drying off he noticed a small selection of books on the chest of drawers between the windows. He remembered that apart from his precious guidebooks he hadn't brought anything with him to read, a mistake when staying in strange country pubs, where he was wary of striking up casual bar relationships. He picked up a tatty paperback of Lord Peter Wimsey stories, which should prove entertaining and went downstairs, his thinning hair just towel dried and plastered to his head (not combed over, a sad pretence that Bridie loathed.) He didn't suppose there would be anyone around to take much notice.

The Lounge was indeed empty, and the Sod's Opera was not yet open. He turned down a second scotch and took a bottle of Guinness to the window seat with Lord Peter. His request for a menu had, in spite of the landlady's words, further irked the barmaid who had crisply told him she would bring him one when the restaurant opened. He was starting to feel a perfect nuisance and did not offer her a drink.

At quarter past seven he heard three cars in close succession scrunch up the side of the pub into the carpark, but the occupants must have gone into the other bar, because Charlie's solitude was undisturbed.

At last, when it was gone seven thirty and time for another Guinness and a humble petition for the menu, the huge latch on the front door was lifted and a small oriental figure of about twenty-five (although Charlie knew them to be difficult to age) came in. Presumably Mr. Yamazaki.

He was dressed as for a protracted climb up a fair-sized fell, though for the life of him Charlie couldn't think of any point more than two hundred feet above sea level in the whole county. But it was tastefully done: heavy Timberland boots with bright yellow laces, moleskin trousers tucked into tweedy socks and a cream polo-necked shirt under a jacket that hovered between Norfolk and the Tyrol. Only the floppy hat, a sick mushroom with angling flies arranged around the band, spoiled things. He smiled and bowed slightly to Charlie, who shyly nodded back, then went to the bar and won Charlie's undying admiration by calling 'Excuse Me!' very loudly.

On seeing this eastern Wainwright as she strode into the bar, probably to berate Charlie for interrupting her when she was painting her toenails, the rather supercilious girl who had failed to connect was transformed into Miss Personality.

'I would like pint of bitter please.'

The young man beamed with pleasure at having formulated this speech.

'And package of nuts.'

'We say 'packet' love.'

'Ah, yes. Packet of nuts. Thank you.'

'Which bitter would you like? There's IPA. Abbott, Adnam's and Young's Special.'

He was a bit perplexed by this and turned to Charlie, who without being asked said

'Abbott.'

He was rewarded with a little bow and a 'thank you.'

The barmaid was clearly not ready for the cessation of hostilities;

'It's a bit strong, that one.'

and looked accusingly at Charlie. Mr. Yamazaki giggled and said;

'I am strong also.'

So she smiled again, looking as if she might chuck the poor

sod under the chin. She then tried to confuse him even further by asking him if he wanted a jug or a sleeve. He looked a bit baffled for a moment but cottoned on when she mimed holding a jug by the handle. Charlie almost applauded when the young man rather elegantly used both hands to mime a straight glass.

The bloody woman even opened his packet of nuts for him.

Chapter Eighteen.

When he woke, Charlie could hear a radio playing and thought he was at home; it was the sort of dance music his mother listened to, but it slurred slowly as it wound down and Charlie realised it must be a gramophone, a machine his father detested. Anyway, the radio didn't play that sort of thing in the early morning. He assumed this must be the time, as he now heard a cock crow, and anyone knew that they only did that first thing.

He rolled over to look out of the window, bright sunlight was streaming in through the leaves outside, and he saw a melted puddle of wax in and around the candle-holder from the night before. Guilt welled up. The Professor had said something about limited sources of light. He had a bit of money stashed in his suitcase: perhaps there was a shop nearby where he could buy some candles for them.

He was still wearing his cotton dressing gown, which was probably not a good idea. It had ridden up uncomfortably under his armpits and his left arm had gone all numb, while the thing itself was crumpled beyond redemption. He climbed out of the bed and did his best to retrieve order and dignity. Outside he saw that the big dog was trotting around the drive sniffing at things like a bored bear. A couple of cats were sitting bolt upright, eyes closed, in a patch of sunlight. Close by the Professor was walking round and round the little patch of lawn in the driveway reading a book. Charlie thought this as impressive as it was eccentric. He himself had tried to read and walk at the same time on the special days when he received a new Dan Dare or the like, but usually gave up after the second or third collision with bad-tempered adults. Still, it was rather different walking in a ten-foot circle compared with a busy street on the walk to school. If that was where he was going.

Charlie's clothes, spruce and pressed were all on the board at the foot of his bed. He dressed quickly, thinking that Missus Wife must have washed and ironed them then crept in without disturbing him. He supposed that things must dry quickly in the warm kitchen. At home all the washing was sent out, except for the endless barcloths boiling on the stove. Now all his things smelt like the country. When he put his hands in his pockets (an automatic action usually followed by exasperated instructions to remove them) he found a tiny muslin bag full of dried herbs or something. He put it on the mantlepiece, not wanting to be too fragrant. He wasn't a girl.

The front door stood wide open as he came down the stairs. Strong sunlight now fell on the two figures which he had failed to identify in the gloom of the previous night. He now saw they were some kind of suits of armour, but not at all like the tiny metallic things he had seen in the museum. He had quite liked them, but they looked too small even for him. These were made up of pieces of wood and metal joined with coloured string. They looked more flexible, though even smaller than the metal ones. And they had no legs, just big skirts and wooden stirrupy things like Dutch clogs painted red and gold. What really impressed him were the helmets, which had metal horns and horrid masks with twisted mouths and empty, angry eyes. He was quite glad that he had not identified them at night, or he might have been a little more nervous about walking through the hall.

'Hah! I don't like!'

She had made him jump, which made her grin.

'Dirty old rubbish!'

Charlie was about to protest but minded his manners just in time. She called something out of the door which included the word Papa, as he had been told to expect, and the Professor turned from his perambulation, waved and headed towards the door as his wife scurried off into the kitchen.

'I find'

said the Professor as he reached the doorstep,

'that walking as I read is better for my circulation these days, and not as you may have thought an idle eccentricity. I would not read if my purpose were to walk to a specific destination, since the pleasure there lies in what one sees along the way. And I might bump into things. Did you sleep?

'Yes, thanks. I'm afraid I finished my candle, but I can buy you another one, if there's a shop.'

'A noble sentiment, but there is no need, as we will use the remaining wax again. What might under other stewardship be mere outhouses are in the fief of my wife a veritable industrial complex in which among myriad activities she dips our own candles. She will no doubt enlist your help in some of the less arcane practises.'

Charlie indicated the suits of armour and asked shyly if they were Japanese.

'Very much so, my oriental infangthief and outfangthief. That one is called Kenji, and this fellow is Yoshio, although I don't expect you to call them by name. Unless you want to. My wife strongly objects to their presence, and in protest insists that I dust them once a week, indeed insists as firmly as she resists my participation in any other domestic duties. I am regarded as quite incapable, and I know that she dusts them again when I am not looking.'

He giggled.

'She even gives me pocket money.'

Charlie joined in the laughter and resisted asking how much with some difficulty. Co-conspirators they obediently followed the summons from the kitchen, where they were apparently to have breakfast. His hosts rightly reckoned that he would not thrive on the plain rice and cremated fish served to the Professor, nor would he relish a dish of insipid green tea. He was given a whole fresh fried egg to himself and a slice of bacon half an inch thick; he even surprised himself by liking the glass of milk, which the Professor explained had come from a goat. They lived in the lap of luxury here.

Charlie was urged not to stand on ceremony, and after he had eaten, he was invited to go outside and explore. The Professor, it appeared, worked in the mornings, although the nature of his work was unspecified, and he said they would meet again for lunch. When he asked what time he should return, running as ever to the hands of a pub clock (which was actually five minutes fast, to facilitate the chucking out process) they seemed a bit nonplussed.

'Lunchtime. I call you.'

He had to be satisfied with that as he was shooed out of the back door. He struggled with his stiff boots; he noticed that they had been cleaned and felt a little embarrassed. And irritated.

'I can clean the shoes Missus. I do it at home.'

'Alright. Tomorrow.'

'Fear not, Charlie. Unlike my feeble and decrepit self, I am sure you will be assigned tasks more various than shoe shine boy ere long.'

Charlie smiled a little nervously and walked out into the sunny cobbled courtyard.

He decided to begin with the side of the house he had not yet seen, so turned right outside the kitchen door and walked through a gate in the centre of a range of outbuildings. In front of him was a high wall with a single door painted the ubiquitous peeling institutional green. It hung three-quarters open and was, by the looks of it, stuck that way. He saved that up for later and turned right down an alley formed by the high wall and the outbuildings. They ended simultaneously and a huge garden opened out, overlooked by the tall windows of the Professor's study and a second bay of the same size, but with French windows. Steps led from the windows down to a sunken area with a rectangular pond in the centre. In the middle of the pond was a large green metal fish on a pedestal. He walked down the steps and peered into the greenish water. There were six astounding goldfish each the size of the stuffed salmon in the parlour of the pub. He squatted on his haunches and watched for a while as they milled around, bumping into each other in the confined space, and sometimes breaking the surface with their ugly round mouths or with the plop of a tail. They certainly beat the hell out of the fairground fish his friend Roy, one of the few boys allowed to keep pets, had fed for a few days in jam-jar before finding it floating belly up. His only friend.

What he thought must once have been another lawn was now a broad allotment, complete with a scarecrow. It was throwing up greenery largely unidentifiable by Charlie, but which he assumed ended up in Missus Wife's kitchen. There was also an old figure in a filthy khaki great coat, incongruously held together with what appeared to have been a sumptuous bell pull or curtain tie. He pulled himself almost upright to stare at the intruder and was muttering audibly when Charlie waved experimentally. But he didn't spit or grunt as expected, or say anything that sounded like 'Arnin', so Charlie decided to retreat.

In a small paddock beyond the crusty gardener, Charlie had spotted his old companion the donkey along with what he took to be several goats, but placing discretion firmly above valour, he went back towards the gate he had seen hanging open. Through it he found something more like the country gardens of his imagination. A criss-cross of gravel paths led up and down, back and forth through beds of flowers and small bushes: all along the wall was a greenhouse. It contained whole trees at one end and shelves of smaller plants in the part closer to the gate. In the far corner of the garden opposite the green house was a plain triangle of grass, two sides of which supported what Charlie took to be rabbit hutches in double banks. On the grass in front of them was a rickety construction in plain wood and chicken wire with no floor.

At that moment Missus Wife rattled up the garden path behind him.

'Come on, Chiarry. New job.'

She led him to the hutches clutching a wicker shopping basket of discarded kitchen greenery. She opened the first cage just enough to put her hand in and pulled out a rabbit by the scruff of its neck, most unmagicianly. It was a fat and docile beast, unlike the skittering things he had seen from the train on the way to Norfolk. He had pointed them out to the other children in his compartment, but one just scowled and the other told him to bugger off. It also differed in being black and white. Having introduced it to Charlie Missus Wife dropped the bored creature through the little hatch in the chicken wire contraption, followed by a couple of handfuls of limp greenery and shut it in. The rabbit sniffed them and began to nibble.

This process was repeated until each of the six compartments was occupied.

'Not play together. They fight. Afternoon swap rabbits. You see,'

Charlie was not at all sure about accepting this responsibility, having no fondness for fluffy animals that actually moved, especially those that had to be kept separate to avoid violence.

'I help you, you see. Bye, Chiarry'.

And off she tootled to her next task, stopping on the way to pluck something from a bush. Charlie looked despondently at the rabbits, who admittedly didn't look all that prone to outbursts of fisticuffs. He decided to explore the greenhouse next, fully expecting to find it stuffed with man-eating plants.

Chapter Nineteen.

Dinner had been a pretty dismal affair, and Charlie was beginning to lose his good humour respecting this particular place. He was alone in the dining room and would have preferred to stay in the Lounge Bar to eat, but this apparently went beyond the bounds of acceptable behaviour for an overnight guest. Foolishly he had acceded. It turned out that the restaurant menu was little different from that chalked up in his own pub advertising Larry's unspectacular achievements, and even he could manage better starters than Egg Mayonnaise and Prawn Cocktail. He had wearily ordered the former only to find half of it covered in a sauce better suited to the latter and the whole sprinkled with paprika by way of decoration. It was like Leighton Buzzard in 1971. Main courses (announced on the menu as Entrees) stretched to Surf 'n'Turf, an idea that should have expired along with the Berni Inn, and deep-fried Scampi Tails with French Fries and lemon wedge. He closed his tired eyes for a moment and thought of the King's Shilling. It was a mistake; he almost wept. When he reopened them, he was being served, if the plonking action of the Mrs Danvers of the bar could be so dignified. The fillet of plaice, well-camouflaged in breadcrumbs, was generously over-cooked, the chips limp. No doubt they hailed from the same fryer. And a lemon wedge. He would have accepted a lot of poor attitude in exchange for the pleasant dinner promised by the Shell, but no, he clearly needed another guidebook.

Having polished off most of what was put in front of him out of sheer hunger he returned to the Lounge Bar with the Shell guide and a bottle of Guinness, Lord Peter having proved too whimsical, and thought about his next move. Most likely seemed a sharp pull to the east and a visit to Aldburgh. Charlie was not a musical man, although he liked something mindless on the radio or cassette player while he was driving, but Duncan (of all people) had once given him tickets for a recital in the arts centre at which a young man with a very nice voice (Bryn something, he thought) had sung a lot of dull Germanic stuff confirming a good number of prejudices, but as an encore (unsupported by Charlie) he sang a song by Benjamin Britten, about the sea. The East Anglian North Sea figured in Charlie's memories, and he had liked the song very much. Not enough to find a recording, but it slipped into his mind as he contemplated a visit to Britten's home. Then there was the problem of Southwold. Where he and Bridie had spent their honeymoon and young Charlie had been conceived. Poor and aspiringly genteel as they had been, it was a little paradise to Bridie. She had even then said she might like to retire there. So probably no stay in Southwold.

The latch of the back door to the bar clunked heavily and Charlie automatically glanced up. It was the Japanese man he had seen earlier. He now looked even younger, having changed from Alpinist to man about Suffolk in beige slacks and an apricot sweater that would have looked fine in downtown Newmarket but did not really fit the back bar of the Chequers. He bowed slightly to Charlie who nodded back and took a seat at the bar, smiling his charming smile. Once again Charlie was able to admire his bellowed

'Excuse me!'

which was once more answered by a pink blouse and nauseating niceness. Charlie supposed he was just jealous and recalled with quiet pleasure how his girls dealt with all customers using the same brusque and indifferent politeness that served all types and relationships, even including that between Sylvia and her Ivan.

It must have been fairly busy in the other bar, but Charlie could tell she was reluctant to leave Mr. Yamazaki alone in the Lounge with that awkward bugger with the old car and the better room upstairs. Eventually duty called and she went.

Meetings between strangers from two of the world's most reticent cultures are never easy, but Charlie wanted to talk to this boy. He also wanted to bury his nose in his book and forget the idea, but he emptied his glass and went up to the bar, smiling. The young Japanese smiled back, and, not having a book to retreat into said

'The Abbott was good choice. Thank you.'

'I've always been fond of it.'

That was clearly not understood.

'You should call out or she will not come here.'

Charlie risked a male-bonding joke;

'She might bite.'

he mimed the bite with one hand. Mr. Yamazaki's hands fluttered as he laughed, eventually covering his mouth in a way that was familiar. Which was odd. He finished his own drink and called out to attract attention from the bar next door.

'What will you have?'

Charlie surprised himself, but he meant it.

'No, please. I will buy some.'

The barmaid had reappeared looking sourly on this fraternisation between favoured customer and bloody nuisance.

'No, I insist.'

'I would like to do this.'

'So would I and you can always get the next one.'

Charlie smiled inwardly at the familiar ritual. Two people deciding to socialise and sniffing around.

'I'll have a Talisker, please.'

He chose the whiskey at random but knew that Japanese men liked their scotch. The barmaid gave a smile and an apology without meaning either.

'Glenmorangie, then?'

'This is good whiskey?'

Charlie nodded and they had one each, Charlie with soda, but young Mr. Yamazaki took his straight with a separate glass of water. It transpired in the next few moments that he had attended something called a 'Scotch Seminar' at some Highland distillery;

'I couldn't remember name.'

They tried the products of several more distilleries together: not something that Charlie did as a rule, but he was on his holidays. It was as a publican that he couldn't afford to get tight, and he always drove when he and Bridie went on their little jaunts. He had learned to make a bottle of Guinness last a long time. Bridie sometimes had a gin or two too many, but she just got gooey and sentimental, which was alright by Charlie and surprised the hell out of those who had never seen her a bit the worse for wear.

The young man finally introduced himself as Kenji. Charlie was tempted to say that he had once known a suit of armour of that name but doubted that their common language skills would stretch to an explanation. Anyway, there was no need to get into all that. Kenji had an exaggerated way of pronouncing Charlie, like an American impersonating an upper-class twit in the theatre. In fact, after the third scotch his diction deteriorated alarmingly, but Charlie loosened up enough to come out with the odd word or phrase of Japanese learned long ago and polished up by Mr. Matsui.

Kenji lived in Yokohama 'There is big place of dead foreign people'. It turned out to be a cemetery on the bluff. He was on a cultural exchange in London, somehow gone awry. Though he had to stay close to London he was free to travel so East Anglia had seemed his safest bet. They hadn't gotten around to jobs yet; Charlie was still keen not to act the landlord, but it was one of those conversations with unspoken limits, destined not to go beyond closing time. Which was soon upon them. They left the bar together without saying goodnight to the barmaid and walked up the steep staircase, Kenji taking an unsteady lead. At the top he turned to Charlie with the index finger gesture of a sudden idea.

'I have small whiskey bottle if you have a time.'

Charlie hesitated, having already drunk too much. But he thought he would have a hangover anyway and didn't wish to appear churlish; he shrugged and said it was a good idea, which clearly pleased his companion.

Kenji's room proved to be half the size of Charlie's, and they would have had to sit on the bed, so they gathered up the bottle and Kenji's toothmug and went to the other room where there were a couple of chairs by the empty fireplace. They became quite giggly as they crept along the corridor, remembering the children would be in bed and tiptoeing with exaggerated quiet.

Settled with a generous last drink, Kenji volunteered that he was moving on tomorrow, having stayed here for three nights. Charlie forgot to keep his idioms to himself and had to explain why greedy people liked punishment. Kenji planned to take a cab to Bury St. Edmund's and think where to go from there, armed with a rather dodgy looking guide book he had brought from his room. It was a Japanese guide to the whole of Europe and seemed to be disproportionately given over to the shopping potential of each venue, bristling with adverts for Gucci, Louis Vuitton and Hermes. More impressively he had three volumes of Pevsner's 'Buildings of England' in the old brown bordered paperback editions, picked up in a bookshop in Colchester.

It was late, and Charlie had had far too much scotch to consider carefully before offering this unknown quantity a lift. But it removed from Charlie the onus of deciding what to do next.

Chapter Twenty.

'Originally, of course, it was a farmhouse, but most of the land had been sold off years before we came here, and I got rid of the rest myself, apart from the gardens, which while being quite enough work in themselves, have proved invaluable during this avoidable tragedy playing out around us.

Charlie assumed he meant the war, but the only sign of it here were the aeroplanes that sometimes sang in the skies above the house. It was not the first time that Charlie had had to guess at the Professor's meaning during his tour of this temporary home.

Lunch had been thick soup with bits of meat. He was told afterwards he had eaten rabbit. On reflection he didn't mind. He had been encouraged to pull pieces from the loaf by hand which was an enjoyable alternative to cutting decorous slices at home. There had also been butter, which he hadn't tasted in ages: another barter with the neighbours, apparently. When they had finished the Professor went to 'put his head down' for an hour, so Charlie had gone to his room with a copy of 'Children of the New Forest' which the old man had sort of recommended to him, by saying that it was the only book in the house likely to prove of even the vaguest interest to one such as himself, but he promised to rectify that situation on his next visit to Walsingham. He was pleased that Charlie liked to read but was not familiar with any of the few titles that Charlie could recall recently borrowing from the library. Charlie liked adventures and books about foreign places. His mother had called him Thursday's Child, although he was actually born on a Tuesday according to his grandmother, a more reliable if less affable witness. He even confessed to the Professor that he had forgotten to return the library book about the Chinese princess who looked a bit like Missus Wife (although he thought better to leave that bit out). The Professor was most sympathetic and suggested that they write a letter to his mother about it, even if he was sure that she would have realised and rectified the situation by now. Charlie doubted it. He had never actually written a proper letter, so the stratagem seemed a bold one. He had learned in school how to do it correctly, with the address in the top right-hand corner and the date in the middle. The letter itself had been gobbledegook and was addressed to 'Dear Sir or Madam' which was not how Charlie addressed people in real life. His father called one or two of the customers in the Saloon Bar 'Sir', but women hardly ever went in there except to serve, and the women in the Public Bar were all called Florrie or Madge or something like that. The floorwalker in Bassingers' in the High Street called his mother 'madam' when they went in to buy his school uniform. He had gone into long trousers last year. Charlie's pride had been exchanged for deep embarrassment when later he had to follow her round the women's department while she bought stockings and things he would only name when sniggering among other boys. Which he didn't do all that often.

The details of the ground floor he already knew except for the pretty sitting room full of pot plants. No cut flowers as the Professor said that his wife believed things should be allowed to die a natural death: Charlie didn't comment on the early demise of the rabbits. This was the room with French windows. They led to the small terrace where the strange brick thing with a grille on top sat. The Professor said it was for cooking things on, which didn't fully enlighten Charlie. His experience of outdoor dining was limited to sausages toasted on sticks by Boy Scouts on Jamboree; even this he had only read about. He suspected that the reality would actually be pretty horrible. Enforced camaraderie was not his bag. He was most impressed that the house had its own Library. It was lined with books in all sorts of languages and even some scrolls which looked really fascinating. He got the impression that while not out of bounds it was a rather private place. It was also, unlike the rest of the pristine house, a total mess, so he surmised that Missus Wife didn't get in here much either.

Two enormous bookcases with their own rolling stepladders almost filled one wall. Between them was a full-length life-sized portrait of a young man with rather long fair hair and a ginger moustache. He was dressed in a bizarre outfit consisting of a pin-stripe skirt to the floor and a kind of short dressing gown. He wore a long, gently curved sword on his right hip, one hand on the scabbard and the other grasping the hilt as if about to draw. But the look on his face was entirely benign, not at all that of one about to attack. More likely to show you around his house. Charlie peered at the label, but all he could see was a peculiar squiggle. He looked up at the Professor, who was now wearing the same benevolent smile. He nodded;

'Yes, that was me a long time ago. In Japan. The sword is over here.'

He led Charlie to a low wooden box like the ones in the hall that Kenji and Yoshio sat on. Here indeed the sword was resting on a black and gold lacquered stand. The Professor picked it up and drew it, nasty and beautiful, out of its scabbard. The blade was slim and very shiny, with small engravings up near the hilt. Charlie was impressed but did not wish to get any closer to it and was glad when the unlikely warrior put it away.

'You are wise to be wary of such things, Charlie. It has a terrible beauty, though I do not think it has ever been drawn in anger.'

Charlie nearly pointed out that you wouldn't need to be especially angry to take someone's bloody arm off with it. Just a bit careless. But as usual manners kept his opinion to himself.

Missus Wife bustled past them in the hall as they closed the Library door. She was singing a thoroughly orientalised version of 'We'll Gather Lilacs' in a high warbly voice and disappeared into the Dining Room. The Professor looked after her fondly;

'When we first met, she used to sing Japanese folk songs.'

As they walked up stairs, he pointed out some bright landscape paintings which Charlie had not noticed before.

'They are the work of my wife's older brother. Her late brother, who before the current unpleasantness was a well-thought-of artist in Japan. Before the army took everything over. He was not much respected by them at all. He took his own life in the end.'

Charlie let this sink in and was shocked, Suicide was a terrible business, he knew. One of the regulars had been discovered by a delivery boy, swinging from the rafters in his abattoir. 'Handy for hooks' his grandmother had said, although Charlie didn't understand and his mother said 'Hush, ma!' stifling a giggle and gesturing not quite discreetly enough towards Charlie. It had been the talk of the Public Bar for weeks after. They didn't think that Charlie was listening in as he bottled up the shelves or dried glasses. He was so quiet they sometimes forgot that he was there. Occasionally someone would swear, and would get a sharp dig in the ribs and a gesture towards the boy as badly disguised as his mother's. However, the Professor seemed on this occasion unwilling to elaborate, and they continued upstairs. 'Mostly boring bedrooms up here, of course, but I think you might be interested in this.'

He opened the door in front of Charlie so that he could enter alone. The room was directly above the Professor's study, the beautiful room, and was the same shape and size.

'This is called the music room, not, alas, an accurate description. We don't actually play music in it, as the Gramophone and piano are both in the sitting room downstairs.'

Charlie wasn't listening. He thought he may have died and gone to heaven. The study downstairs was lovely, to be sure, but this was everso lovely. Three of the walls were the same white and one was simply a curtainless window that flooded the space with light and apart from one folding screen at the end opposite the windows there were no pictures. All around the walls were low chests of drawers in simple red and black lacquer with delicate brass fittings. On top of each was a wooden stand with two cross bars at the top, the higher of which curved upwards slightly at the ends. Draped apparently casually over these were swaths of coloured silks. The colours were almost overwhelming. Gold and crimson and purple, embroidered with flowers and birds and trees and dragons. He knew his mouth was open, but he couldn't bring himself to shut it. The Professor said:

'And now my utmost mystery is out:
A woman's beauty is a storm-tossed banner:
Under it wisdom stands, and I alone –
Of all Arabia's lovers I alone –
Nor dazzled by the embroidery, nor lost

In the confusion of its night-dark folds,

Can hear the armed man speak.'

Then he laughed at Charlie's uncomprehending face, the mouth still gaping, and picked up one of the lengths of silk and held it up to reveal a dressing gown of the same shape as the one Charlie had worn in bed. He slipped it on over his tweed jacket and turned to face Charlie;

'Aren't they beautiful? Here, try one.'

He picked out a purple robe embroidered with water and white birds.

'But aren't they for ladies?'

'Well, technically, no.'

Charlie had no idea what the technicalities might dictate, but the 'no' was good enough for him and he slipped his arms into the proffered sleeves. He saw that it was equally densely decorated on the inside and found it surprisingly heavy. Even the Professor's gown trailed slightly behind him, so Charlie's was long enough for a wedding train. He swished it around and the two of them stood there admiring each other.

'Was that a poem you said?'

'Hmm? Oh, yes. Yeats. I met him in Dublin just after he published it. About 1930, I think. He was very pleased with it. I thought the 'dazzled by the embroidery' part appropriate, although obviously we are in Japanese and not Arabian silks here.'

'My mum likes poems.'

The Professor raised his eyebrows slightly.

'Does she, indeed. Perhaps we will read a few together. That is, if you also like them.'

Charlie thought it might be alright, although his mother never actually read them to him. She sometimes quoted bits at him which he found either soppy or irritating.

There was a small shriek of laughter as Missus Wife poked her head around the Music Room door. They both looked bashful.

Charlie removed his kimono and tried to hang it back on the frame, but Missus Wife took it gently and rearranged it so that the pattern showed properly.

'Come on, Chiarry. Change rabbits.'

She made them sound like nappies.

Chapter Twenty-One

The barmaid's duties fortunately did not include serving breakfast: it had so far been a slightly dismal stay, despite his meeting Mr. Yamazaki, and her baleful presence in the morning would not have improved his mood. Kenji had knocked on Charlie's door shortly after the landlady had called them down to eat and informed him that he couldn't face solids this morning. Presumably Charlie should inform madam because the lad couldn't face having his head bitten off. Charlie had a thick head too, but not thick enough to countermand the full English breakfast that he had ordered the night before, before the trip down whiskey lane. He was unsure why this particular combination of foods should be universally considered either full or peculiarly English. The only places where the English consumed them were holiday hotels and guilty dawn transport cafes. Certainly, he could not envisage cooking one himself so soon after waking up. The motor responses did not fully gear up for an hour. Worse with a hangover.

The first meal of the day was undertaken in the same empty room as the last, although this morning the heavy salmon-pink curtains were drawn back on a pleasant view of the village green, which at eight o'clock was surprisingly alive and bustling. A flock of straight-backed mothers in flat court shoes and navy blue or goose-crap green padded waistcoats milled about, toting or dragging various sizes of child in two similarly expensive uniforms. The majority were bundled into a white minibus announcing itself as headed for a school in Sudbury. A smaller and cleaner vehicle turned up about ten minutes later, and the remaining mothers, those with the more brittle hair relinquished their blazered offspring to a man in a peaked cap who drove a minibus identified only by a spurious coat of arms in Harrods green and gold.

The landlady was doing her best to be pleasant, but the obvious effort negated the attempt. She clearly enjoyed waiting at table as much as did her barmaid. Charlie could sympathise, but you didn't bring your opinions or problems in to work. The place had been a write off for him, but then you must take your chances.

The bill was at least reasonable. He packed his meagre luggage and trudged down the staircase to the carpark. There he found Kenji dressed in freshly pressed jeans (with a crease, yet) and a lumberjack shirt, a cashmere sweater draped across his shoulders in studied ease. His luggage consisted of a large rucksack and a small leather carry-all with a brown designer logo on it. Charlie heartily despised these artefacts. It was a bloody cheek to be expected to part with a small fortune to advertise someone else's product. Bridie liked Chanel with its little 'C's. It passed through Charlie;s mind that he would offer her old clothes to the daughter-in-law. Too good for Oxfam. Jenny would hate them, and say that nothing was too good for charity.

Charlie wondered how many costume changes you could fit in a rucksack, and felt uncharitable again. As he had expected he was regretting the offer of a lift, but would have to follow through, so determined to be as civil as the strange boy. His car having made its debut a good few years before central locking, he unlocked the passenger door first and instructed his companion to hop in. The young man looked puzzled, but apparently decided to understand. He held up his rucksack in one hand as if to say, 'What should I do with this?' smiling his charming smile and daring the question. Charlie took it from him. He needed both arms to carry it. He heaved it into the boot along with his suitcase, jamming them tightly against the spare wheel to stop them shifting around in the huge empty space. Loose items tumbling around the innards unnerved him. He always had to stop to reassure himself that it was only the luggage. He knew the various noises emitted by his lovely car as well as the varied cries of a baby, although as with babies he had never known what to do when there was something wrong. As he and his motor got older, he worried that it ought really to be looked after by a specialist, after all he didn't want to conk out in the middle of nowhere. But Larry's eldest Ian seemed to know what he was up to, and he was both cheap and glad of the cash. Best leave it at that.

Happily, Charlie's passenger was comfortable without chatter. Once they had decided on Bury Saint Edmund's as a destination he had lapsed into companionable silence, looking out of the window with apparent interest. Charlie opened the glove compartment and indicated the small selection of tapes, which Kenji rifled for a moment before pulling a Sony walkman from his Vuitton bag, extracting the tape and rewinding it in the old car machine. Charlie prayed it wouldn't be anything offensively modern or lively, which he would find difficult to drive to: he was not a young man and felt entitled to the predilections of his age. The opening strains of 'Gigi' put paid to his qualms. One of his and Bridie's old favourites, although he was alarmed and then amused as Kenji began to sing along in heavily accented but word-perfect unison. And he had a very nice voice.

Halfway through a spirited rendition of 'It's a Bore!' they arrived at the unfamiliar outskirts of Bury Saint Edmunds and Kenji switched the music off without being asked.

'Go right here.'

Charlie raised an eyebrow but did as he was bidden.

'O.K. Take next left.'

Within minutes he had guided them to Angel Hill, and they had found a place to park. This was an awkward moment: Charlie didn't really know what he intended to do next, and wasn't sure that his travelling companion, for all that he had just demonstrated a finely tuned understanding of the one-way system, knew either. Taking a very small bull by the horns Charlie suggested a cup of coffee.

'Yes, that will help my head.'

Charlie had quite forgotten that the boy had been performing Lerner and Loewe assisted only by a hangover

'Would you like a Neurofen?'

Once more Kenji looked baffled, so Charlie fished around in the glove compartment until he found a small packet of the only drug that could cure his occasional headaches.

'O, no thank you. Coffee is good.'

So they went to a large and familiar hotel, which was a bit tattier than Charlie's guide suggested, but such is life. Or age.

'You know Bury quite well?'

They were sitting in the coffee shop surrounded by modern illustrations of characters from Dickens. Little Nell looked like an elderly Mickey Rooney as Widow Twankey. Charlie was fishing, but gently.

'I was here for one night last week, a man brought me in a Taxi, so I remember the streets.'

Charlie was impressed by Kenji's memory, and said so. They were silent for a while.

'Have you seen Ickworth?'

He pronounced it Icku-worse, but however you said it Charlie had never heard of it. Kenji got out his dodgy Japanese guide book and showed a photograph which was unaccountably overprinted in red ink, but from which Charlie could make out an impressive rotunda.

'It says not finished but very old and many silver and paintings.'

A certain amount appeared lost in the translation.

'Have you been to Aldburgh yet? That's a nice place. Our famous composer Britten lived there.'

He hated the tone of a salesman that seemed to come with keeping it simple.

'With his friend Peter Pears. Yes. I like his music, but I have not visited.'

Once again Charlie was caught offside by the young man's information. He mentioned that he intended to go there that day.

'I will stay here tonight, I like this town, and I will take a taxi to Ickworth.'

He seemed to have an uncommon and expensive attachment to taxis. They fell silent apart from the odd slurp from the fairly average coffee whitened with fake cream stuff in a little plastic pot which had the consistency of gloss paint.

'Where are you staying?'

Kenji looked at him quizzically, as if at a struggling pupil.

'I will stay here tonight.'

He repeated it slowly. Charlie laughed quickly, feeling obtuse. At last he capitulated to the inevitable. He couldn't for the life of him think of a good reason not to, and he was warming to this eccentric chap, although not too eccentric.

'I could drive you down to Ickworth if you like. It sounds interesting.'

Kenji looked pleased but not overwhelmed. What Charlie had expected he was not sure.

'That's good idea. I must check in here first.'

They both went too the car to fetch his rucksack, and Charlie waited in an overstuffed chair near reception while the desk clerk accepted Kenji's booking and demanded cash in advance.

Chapter Twenty-Two.

Charlie slept very little on Sunday night: he burned three candles, not without guilt, but lessened by the knowledge that they were at least partly a redeemable resource. He read quite a lot of 'The Children of the New Forest'. It seemed to him to most awful tosh but as the Professor had given it to him, he was determined to finish it. He anticipated questions. Actually, 'tosh' was a new word learned from his host, who had used it to describe the editorial in the Parish Magazine, a single sheet of faint carbon type signed by the industrious Mrs Desborough. He had crumpled it up and tossed it into an empty fireplace, whence it was retrieved by Missus Wife, who put it in the range.

There was no escaping Monday morning here, any more than at home. Charlie dressed and went downstairs as soon as it was light. He had decided to leave the curtains open for the time being, to serve as an alarm clock; this actually meant re-opening them as Missus Wife shut them at some point before he went to bed, although he couldn't work out when she did it. The sun and clouds and big skies had suddenly become part of his extraordinary new life. They existed in towns, too, he knew. When you did pictures in school there was always a blue sky, white clouds (he liked to put in plenty of clouds so there was less sky to colour in) and a sun of unnatural yellow, which had to be drawn with rays, by some childish artistic convention. But here in the fabled country the sky was everywhere.

He had hoped to be first up but was neither surprised nor

disappointed to find Missus Wife at the kitchen sink cleaning the cats' dishes while something evil-smelling boiled on the range. This was probably, but not certainly, for the cats. She seemed pleased to see him, and he went straight to the galvanised bucket which held the stuff the rabbits ate, but she stopped him.

'Sit down, Chiarry.'

With slightly exaggerated delicacy she put a porcelain cup with a handle on a saucer in front of him, then a tiny jug of cow's milk. Next to these she put a small dish of sugar shaved from a loaf and finally she produced a real tea pot with the handle in the right place and poured him what smelled like a cup of proper tea; it was dark and hot, anyway, and with great care and reverence he put in a whole spoonful of white sugar. Never mind that the milk went in last.

'Missus Bo'do sent you. You say thank you.

'Thank you.'

 She laughed'

'To Missus Bo'do.'

Charlie laughed with her and drank his tea, which was almost as good as the stuff he made at home for his father. In fact better because of all the precious sugar. Then he went to attend to the rabbits, wondering all the while when this bartering of precious foodstuff got done. Very early in the morning he supposed.

The Professor was overly solicitous at breakfast, as if he could sense Charlie's own anxiety. But the boy knew that he could not accept the proffered lift in the battered Austin as petrol would be a rare commodity. He was even more sure that he had no intention of making another entrance on a donkey. Still, it was difficult to stay polite and smiling while grappling with the terror of a new school in a strange land.

Missus wife gave him a parcel wrapped in cloth, like Dick Whittington only square and no pole to sling over his shoulder.

'Is lunch. No sharing.'

The Professor walked him to the gate with a hand on his shoulder, and while Charlie appreciated the concern it was far from reassuring. He felt like he was going off to the front.

'Stick on this road, it's about a mile, won't take you long. School looks very like a school. You know, clock and all that. Make sure you go through the gate marked boys.'

Charlie knew it was a joke, but he gave the Professor a sharp look which he regretted as soon as the old man said

'Sorry.'

Until this moment Charlie had thought of him as mostly big, but at this moment he looked old.

"Well, see how it goes, Charlie, eh? Options open. You'll be fine, nice polite chap like you.'

Charlie set off with a smile and a wave before his new protector ran out of platitudes and started to blub. Or he did. At least there had been no nonsense about soon making lots of nice new friends.

The road ran down a slight incline. After twenty minutes walking Charlie could see the church with the school next to it. Even from this distance there seemed to be an alarming number of children milling about in the yard. The fields had come to an end and he was walking down a street lined with cottages of brick and flint. A few larger houses either wholly brick-built or with painted plaster facing were set back from the road behind small gardens with iron gates and railings. This seemed a bit unpatriotic. All the iron at home had long since been ripped out for the war effort. His father had even raided the kitchen for copper and aluminium; his mother went bonkers, throwing the ones he had left at his escaping head.

'Ello, Jap. Why haven't you got slitty eyes if you're a Jap, then?'

It was a little voice, reedy and insinuating, a girlish noise that he recalled from the constant bickering on the train that brought them to Little Walsingham. Sure enough a male sibling chimed in:

'Her, her.'

This appeared to represent mirth but was quite without amusement or warmth.

'Chin Chan Chinaman.'

'Shu'up, Ronnie.'

The girl was clearly in control of the relationship. Although she was a lot smaller than her simian brother, she was perhaps not a lot younger. It was difficult to assess. She evidently did not share his confusion over oriental nationalities:

'Vicar says you live in a Jap's house.'

'Shut up, that's not true! She's a British citizen!'

The outburst was a mistake, as was Charlie's delivery which had been refined by his mother and father. His grandmother helped with her unfailing detection of hard vowels and dropped aitches.

'Eeow, aim seeow sorry yer bleedin' lordship, aim shyooer. She's a fuckin' nip, alright, and we're at war with 'er.'

This was said with such sneering and righteous authority that Charlie could think of no reply. he put his head up and walked past them as quickly as seemed dignified. This also was a mistake because the lovely Ronnie dealt him a ringing blow to the left ear which deposited him against the unpatriotic railings of a particularly fine Georgian house. The two others walked away towards the school, he still chuckling moronically 'Her, her' she swinging her small satchel and smirking nastily.

It was a close call, but Charlie decided that he must get up and continue schoolwards; he did not want to upset the Professor any more than he had already done this morning. And he had been declared defender of Missus Wife against these cruel and stupid people who clearly did not understand that she was a British Citizen. And everso nice.

The school gates were crowded with shouting children and Charlie held back unnoticed, trying to see what was going on. There was a primitive chant of 'Townie, townie, who's got nits?' and he saw that his two tormentors were at the centre of all this, standing with their heads held down as a thin yellowish man poked around the boy's hair. He cuffed Ronnie lightly to one side and abandoned him to the boys' gate while he turned his attention to the girl. She too seemed to pass muster. The willowy man glanced up and saw Charlie.

'Ah, look, Class. Our other evacuee has finally graced us with his presence. I think we should check him too.'

Charlie's fists clenched as the schoolmaster approached him, limping slightly. The crowd of children surged around him like bees to a queen, quieter now, as if sensing a less easy kill.

'Don't!'

Charlie beat the man's bony hands away with one hand, the other clutching his lunch as the teacher tried to reach into the carefully combed hair.

'I don't have lice. Sir.'

He added this last with little conviction but knew enough about schoolmasters to allow them status.

'I'll be the judge of that.'

Again, Charlie swatted his assailant away. This time the tall thin man suddenly stood up straight and clapped his hands brusquely.

'Inside now children.'

The word 'children' seemed to sit ill in his mouth. As the crush turned away, muttering towards the segregating doors that led to the inexplicably unsegregated playground, Charlie heard a familiar voice:

'Are you running late, Mr. Rutter?'

'New arrivals, Mrs Desborough, a little unwilling to submit to head inspection.'

'As would I be, Mr. Rutter; your nails are none too clean.'

Charlie looked with astonished gratitude at this woman who had pinned him to the kitchen chair with questions and hostility, but this dissolved as he realised that she was just nasty to everyone. She pulled him roughly towards her by the shoulder and proceeded with very sharp nails to inspect his head.

'Hmm, well. They do at least say that Orientals are clean.'

'She's a Brit....'

Charlie didn't finish his protest.

'Take him with you, Mr. Rutter, you're already late.'

She bustled off and Charlie was treated to a punitive shove in the solar plexus.

Chapter Twenty-Three.

Ickworth proved to be only a few miles south-west of Bury Saint Edmunds and was a mild success with both. Charlie got to see some good English portraits in the setting he approved. An English country house, albeit a somewhat eccentric example. He could have done with a little less silver. Kenji was able to confirm the slight information in his Japanese guide book (no Gucci outlets here) and asked Charlie several difficult questions about the Pevsner entry.

For lunch, inevitably they retired to a pub, although the younger man with the larger and more persistent hangover stuck to fizzy water.

'After tomorrow I go to Norwich.'

They were finishing off the last of a lunch fit for an effete ploughperson. The bar's main decorative gimmick appeared to be its dinkiness. The chairs and tables were undersized and the bar counter unusually low. The bar stools were squat and ugly. The whole place appeared to be awaiting a coach party of Munchkins on a works outing. Charlie resisted the temptation to try this line out on his friend: explanation might prove tortuous, although he could be confident that a man who knew the lyrics to Gigi off by heart would be familiar with The Wizard of Oz.

Charlie also intended to head for Norwich soon, but first he was determined to wander east to Aldburgh and the sea. He was anyway wary of getting too entangled, even if Kenji was a pleasant and entertaining companion. A little solitude was in order.

'Perhaps we could meet up for dinner. I'll be there in a couple of days.'

It was a suitably vague arrangement, and he wrote down the name and telephone number of Kenji's hotel.

When they were once again ready for the road, Charlie drove Kenji back into Bury town centre, let him out by the Cathedral and waved goodbye through the passenger window. He was thanked with embarrassing profuseness and watched his little chum in the rear-view mirror bowing and waving until some traffic lights claimed his attention by changing unexpectedly. It was not a long drive to Aldburgh, but he wanted to take it slowly and bask in the lovely rolling, green countryside. He didn't put any music on the machine.

At Aldburgh he parked his chariot on the sea front near the Guildhall and walked back into the main shopping street where he was sure he would find a bookshop. Now that he was alone again, he wanted something absorbing for the lounge bar after dinner. He also wanted to browse a pub guide or two, since the one he had, pace Hilary, had proved unreliable so far.

Sure enough there was a nicely rambling bookshop with tables piled high. A lot of biographies, as usual, but he wasn't really all that keen on other people's lives. Their misery seemed to rise in direct proportion to their fame, and he was, all said and done, on his holidays. He was almost tempted by Thora Hird, whose television things he liked and who looked likely to be more upbeat but was also likely to be a bit too lightweight to hold his attention. The fiction was all spine out by alphabetical order of author. This hindered Charlie in his choice, he always liked to read the cover.

It was quite a highbrow joint, presumably because Aldburgh had a festival. There was a table display of hardback Booker prize-type stuff. Unpronounceable names and portentously silly titles. How could a road be famished? You might just as well have a poorly sofa. Eventually he picked an Anthony Burgess which looked weighty but unthreatening and had a snappy opening, although he would have to look up 'catamite' in the dictionary.

This was such a pleasant street that he put off the sea for a while and strolled through the shops. In one he bought a frilly potpourri pillow for Sylvia, who liked that kind of thing. Lizzie was a bit more difficult as she didn't approve of frivolous gifts. She always gave him a shirt for his birthday. He toyed briefly with the idea of a massive stick of rock, but didn't think she would see the joke, so he postponed her gift until Norwich.

The sea front was strange; with your back to the water it might almost not have been the seaside at all. The scents and gull cries gave it away, of course, but the buildings just looked comfortably urban and domestic. Turning back, the water, even on a blue-skied sunny day looked melancholy and uninviting. There were a few boats far out to sea, but the small beach was deserted. He skimmed a couple of stones for luck and went off to find the three-star hotel he had picked out of his new guide book. He knew the stars guaranteed only the facilities and not the subtleties that make a good hotel, but he thought two stars a bit close to B & B and four likely to prove expensive. He liked to strike a balance.

Because the season had not yet begun the brick and sea-blistered white woodwork of the hotel contained a pleasant air of geriatric hush, which for some reason Charlie found faintly nostalgic. In the lobby, old Axminster carpets lay over a darkly polished parquet floor with smallpox scars from fifty years of genteel high heels. At the desk he paused for a couple of minutes but sensing no sign of life he took his British reserve by the scruff of its neck and tinged apologetically on the bell which sat there, although there was no accompanying sign to suggest that it might summon anyone.

A small, elegant woman of about Charlie's age appeared from behind a green baize door next to the old-fashioned cage lift. She wore a simple black dress with a flared skirt and a silver brooch shaped like a seagull; her lead grey hair was pulled into a severe bun, like an Ealing comedy ballet mistress, and she was wearing surprisingly racy spiked heels. Poor parquet. Her discreet smile was warm enough to erase all memories of the Chequers, and she said 'Good Efternoon' in an accent that could have played Miss Jean Brodie, if a little past her prime.

Negotiations for a room were swift and successful. There was no extra charge for a room with a sea view 'should you prefer it'. However, seeing that Charlie carried no luggage she did ask him how he intended to pay. Meaning cough up before we go up.

The room was a perfectly preserved example of hotel decor from 1950. The colour of the threadbare carpet was somewhere between pink and purple, the lampshades of parchment and the fitted, lightly quilted counterpanes on the two narrow beds were splashed with roses. A discreet, plain bedside cabinet separated the beds. Not a honeymoon suite. His sea view was precisely that: from a seated position in the grandmother chair by the gas fire ('Welcome to Suffolk' on the sleeve of a box of kitchen matches in the hearth) he could see only the North Sea, stretching across to the Low Countries, whose uninviting name had never tempted Charlie (and certainly not Bridie) to visit.

'Do you have somewhere I could leave my car for the night? It's on the front just now.'

She showed him graciously to a small courtyard behind the main building, where there stood a Rover of the same model as Charlie's, although he was pleased to note that it was in considerably poorer nick.

'You can leave it here with mine. We have very little parking space now.'

She waved airily, perhaps a little dismissively at a new red-brick block reminiscent of out of town supermarkets which announced itself as a Banqueting Suite.

'But this early in the season space is hardly at a premium.'

When he returned and parked his pride and joy next to hers, he saw her smiling with raised eyebrows and hands on hips in the door to the kitchens.

'I should perhaps trouble you for the name of your mechanic.'

Charlie said it was a secret and she laughed. He went inside in search of tea and cake in the empty, charming lounge. It had stained glass panels with seagulls and sailing boats swimming in the upper lights.

Chapter Twenty-Four.

Charlie never returned to the school after that horrible day. To cap it all on the way home after an afternoon of apparently ritual humiliation at the hands of teacher and peers alike he had received a black eye from the ape lodged upon the Vicar, who had been raucously applauded by his sister. She it was who had led his new playmates in identifying him not just as a Jap-lover, which was bad enough, but in some obscure manner as of oriental origin himself.

Missus Wife was there on his return to the house with Boldero tea and a squashy lump of something not sugary but nonetheless of almost unbearable sweetness.

'Japanese sweets. You try.'

She was expecting only a tired Charlie, not a bruised and humiliated one. She said mercifully little but must have galvanised the Professor for he rose with an anger the more spectacular for its lack of warning. Even sitting in the kitchen nursing his cup of tea he could hear the Professor's side of the conversation on a hitherto unsuspected telephone as clearly as would the woman at the Post Office who operated the switchboard.

'My dear Mrs Desborough.'

The tone of his voice made it perfectly clear that she was in no manner cherished, and Charlie felt that even the honorific 'Mrs' sat uneasily on the Professor's tongue;

'I am an accredited teacher at Universities in parts of the globe of which you are no doubt unaware - do not be facetious madam -

and I will be able to impart to my charge a great deal wider and more reliable information than the lily-livered scrimshanker you have procured for the village school.'

There was a pause during which the long man tutted irritably and shifted audibly from foot to foot. He drew a deep breath.

'It is not the law at all, woman, and what is more I do not believe that the law protects those who abuse their responsibilities and indeed the very children whose education is entrusted to them. Furthermore, I can assure you that in my house at least he will be free from such infestations as it appears that you are accustomed to dealing with. Good day.'

There was a magnificent clang as the telephone receiver returned to its rest, and after a short harumph the Professor called out to Charlie to join him in the study. Charlie felt some unexplored guilt as he picked his way through catfood alley, as if he were responsible for bringing down shame upon the household by being thoroughly disliked, although as far as he could see there was only malice and no fault of his own in his downfall. It was true that at home any misdemeanour, however rarely he was actually punished, was always his fault, even when he could not identify the transgression. His mother would rattle the washing up and his father would ask rhetorical questions like 'Is this how you want to grow up?' and 'How do you think your mother feels?' To this latter there could be no useful reply. He hadn't a clue. His grandmother would click her knotting needles accusingly like Madame Lefarge and tell him to sit up straight when he was talking to her, as if he could have got a word in edgeways. Guilty nervousness accompanied all of Charlie's encounters with authority. He actually felt less guilty playing truant because then no one could be cross with him just for being there. He wasn't.

He knocked on the door of the beautiful room but having returned his voice to the accustomed gentle mode the Professor spoke from the library door.

'No, Charlie, I want you to come in here.'

Tone of voice or no this did not seem to bode well. The old man was now bent like an angle bracket, clearing books and papers from a pair of deep armchairs which faced each other across a low table. They were enormous leather-covered objects of the sort Charlie had seen on a fleeting visit to his father's club in town; the seats were longer than the backs were tall, and the tobacco-coloured leather was cracked and worn, with patches that looked and felt like cardboard. The fronts of the armrests were studded with round-headed brass tacks but there was no other buttoning. When Charlie eventually sat in one and put his back against the upright his feet stuck straight out in front of him and he felt as daft as Christopher Robin always looked.

'This, Charlie Moulton, is our new classroom, although I don't anticipate spending a great deal of time in it, as there is at this time of year, weather permitting a whole world outside, abroad in the Norfolk countryside.'

Charlie, being a nice polite boy, nodded in total incomprehension.

'I have, er, arranged with the appropriate authorities, that is Gillian Desborough, that you shall hereafter be my personal student, for the time being at least, since I feel that the school is a little too far away, and as I myself have some pretension to being a teacher of sorts. Perhaps you would not object to my taking on the duties of schoolmaster to yourself.'

Charlie could not believe that the Professor would honestly think he had not overheard the altercation on the telephone. Too far away indeed. As usual he was exasperated by the adult inattention to timescale: 'for the time being' was another of those weaselly phrases that meant 'Don't ask questions or something nasty might happen. Or recur,' which fuelled childhood neuroses.

'I rather take it'

And here the Professor permitted himself an embarrassed titter,

'That your day at school was not a success.'

The raised eyebrow and sympathetic tilt of the head seemed to demand a response, so Charlie, unable to stem the inner tide, did something more than nod.

When the tears and heaving sobs had subsided and Charlie had concluded the case for the defence of Missus Wife against the perfidious evacuees at the Vicarage (Ah, stout Don Charlie, muttered the Professor) he was a bit taken aback to find himself perched on a mantis-like knee, being patted affectionately but manfully on the back.

'We're not having a very good war, are we.'

Back to vague incomprehension, albeit somewhat snotty, Charlie sniffed and shook his head, comforted and grateful if not entirely comfortable. He slid off the bony knee and stood looking carefully into the Professor's eyes.

'I will go back to school tomorrow.'

'There is no need.'

'But it might be illegal. I heard you talking to Mrs Desborough, and when I don't go at home, they send letters.'

A long speech for Charlie. The Professor seemed to struggle for a moment, probably with the temptation to ask about his truancy and the nature, origin and recipient of the letters, but overcame it to reassure Charlie that all was above board.

'Now what would you like to learn first?'

Of all bloody questions.

Missus Wife, never one to miss her cue, skittered in hands aflutter and asked;

'You want upstairs bath, Chiarry?'

Charlie hesitated as one should at moments of catharsis and said

'Is it very hot in the bathhouse?'

'Not yet.'

The little woman's glee showed only in the sharpening of her smile. The Professor muttered something along the lines of

'Oh, well played, sir!'

And Charlie went upstairs to put on his flimsy dressing gown, regretting slightly that by this concession he was unlikely ever again to throw bathwater out of his bedroom window.

As he was undressing, he heard the clang of the front doorbell, and was thrown into panic when he heard the Professor say

'Good evening Vicar',

He feared that further confrontation might be imminent, but voices were not raised, and the Professor murmured

'Please come into my study.'

The door to the beautiful room was opened and shut. So it seemed not to be Charlie's fault after all.

He slipped downstairs accompanied by an uninterested but not too scornful cat and accepted a towel, (very small,) from Missus Wife as he shuffled through the kitchen, into the Professor's slippers and out to the bath, well on his way to becoming a junior member of this exclusive, baffling club.

Chapter Twenty-Five.

Charlie set out for Southwold very early in the morning. Unusually he had not slept well, perhaps because of a self-indulgent dinner of scallops in vermouth sauce and a glorious coulibiac of Salmon. Sitting in the guests' lounge afterwards and talking to Miss Jean Brodie about the vicissitudes of hotel ownership in an increasingly corporate age had been viscerally pleasant. She was hilariously indiscreet about the blandishments of predatory hotel chains, while he let off steam about the dread breweries to an unusually receptive audience. Much port had also been consumed, a more likely culprit for his sleeplessness than the excellent food.

He approached the little town with a strange feeling of guilt at being without Bridie. Not so strange, really, after his enjoyment of last evening's conversation: he could never have enjoyed another woman's company with her. She was too brittle with her own sex, too possessive both of Charlie and of conversation to allow such matey intimacy. And she didn't like port. Or scallops.

Even more than in Aldburgh the sea seemed absent from Southwold, especially as he walked through the town centre. The time of day barred him from the Swan, where he would have relished afternoon tea, but where the residents would now be enjoying fry-ups (otherwise labelled on the menu) and prunes. It was even too early to pop into the Adnams shop for a couple of good bottles of wine for the folks at the King's Shilling, who deserved a treat. There were a surprising number of people about, but Charlie didn't linger. Bridie would have dragged him to the beach with its ridiculous genteel huts. Crooked pinkies had no place in a saucy postcard. Give him Sutton-on-Sea any day. Southwold was precisely the mistake he had anticipated, so regretfully he walked back to the Rover and let himself in.

The car purred for him as he drove back inland with Dolly Parton singing her Tennessee heart out in an oddly harmonious response to the gentle greens and occasional violent yellows of the Suffolk countryside rolling around him. It was at last inevitable that he should head upwards into central Norfolk, and by mid-morning he was parked rather awkwardly on a steep verge outside the churchyard walls of a small, perfectly East Anglian treasure.

A finely copper-plate-scripted note, encased in a ziplock freezer bag informed him that the key was in the charge of the large house, presumably once the rectory, behind the church. There was an impressive handled bell pull, but it made no sound that he could hear. The only response to his knock was some thoroughly pretentious woofing from what must have been a large dog.

As he began to walk away, unsure whether he was disappointed or relieved, an elderly woman appeared around the corner of the house clutching a trowel as if prepared to audition for an American adaptation of Agatha Christie, and said in a manner that suggested she expected all callers to be in search of the Church key;

'Actually I don't keep it here.'

Charlie must have looked quizzical.

'It's under the square stone in the guttering on the left side of the porch.'

Charlie's failure to respond galvanised her further;

'Oh, I know it's not terribly original, but I do go out sometimes, believe it or not, and there are always village people wanting to arrange flowers or dust things, although that's a bit Herculaean if you ask me, or do I mean Augean? Anyway, the kind of yobs who rob churches are hardly likely to worry about the damn key, not that there's much left worth pinching as it's all in the bank. Shame really, I like a bit of circumstance with my wine and wafer. Wymondham's quite good for all that. Are you from around here?'

Charlie was reluctant to become tied in conversation, though she seemed a nice woman for another day. He shuffled his feet and demurred gracelessly. She didn't seem surprised or put out when he muttered his thanks and headed back down the drive. He had never seen this house where his childhood tormentors had been lodged in the war. Not as nice as the Professor's place, though it must have changed since then, been smartened up a bit.

The richly coloured stained glass in the church proved a better reason than a quick bit of dusting for using the key. Perhaps not if you lived here. The paintings of faceless saints on the truncated roodscreen still twisted their legs around each other and dragons. The colours from the windows danced like the weird light in a modern aquarium on worn floor tiles with little traces of their original slip. Despite the best efforts of the irredeemable hooligans of the reformation, and thanks to some recent restoration, there still shone the blue and red and gold of holy Norfolk and the Sainte Chappelle. Bridie had liked that, although Charlie found it a bit vulgar, to be honest (which he hadn't been at the time, of course.) It appeared that this little jewel had escaped Victorian intervention in the process of necessary decay. Bridie definitely wasn't to be found here.

He ran his hand over the shiny top of a poppy-head bench finial, never having been able to see any resemblance in these chunky organic carvings to a real poppy and sat rather suddenly in the pew where he had sat next to Missus Wife at her husband's funeral. She had looked everso nice in that last Kimono, but she had left no trace here.

Signing the visitors' book, he glanced up for inspiration in the 'comments' column and saw an ugly beaten copper vase holding some nearly fresh star-gazer lilies. It stood at the side of the main door in a niche which presumably had once had some higher Catholic significance but was now adorned with this nasty artefact and the plastic jollity of the flowers. A small pewter plaque on the vase: 'Gillian Vera Desborough 1902-1980'. Not a bad innings; only the good and all that.

He didn't know if he expected to find anything in the graveyard, so he wasn't disappointed. It was well-kept in front but very overgrown round the back, where the stones had not been tidied up. There was a plot of graves that dated from the end of the war up to the nineteen sixties, but no sign of Guntons.

Sadly the great yew hedge around the remembered house was gone, but the Ilex tree still stood proud in the middle of the lawn with its perfect noontime circle of scorched earth beneath it. It didn't seem bigger, oddly; they had both grown and grown older. He was pleased to see that beds of flowers had been dotted around the lawn, where once he had regretted seeing only green.

There were three houses now, all sharing the drive that he had first traversed on a donkey, all sharing the inoffensive neo-Georgian style that Prince Charles favoured for those who weren't born to the real thing. Thick twit. He didn't go close enough to see whether the sash windows were real or double-glazed fakes, but he could guess. The outbuildings were all gone, and the cobbled courtyard had been replaced by an uncobbled tennis court. There was no ghost here, either.

He had, unsurprisingly given his age at the last visit, never been in the pub. It was across the green from his day-long alma mater which now appeared to be a glass blowing business. The interior of The Feathers had meticulously been returned to the state he would have encountered in 1945, if a little cleaner. There were even battered old photographs of battered old men sitting around the bar to prove the authenticity. He wouldn't really have recognised Joe Boldero, husband of another protector, or his gardener father (who had seemed indistinguishable from the rags he wore) after all this time. Better that way, facial hair and string enough for the memory.

The beer was Greene King, so he had a potentially disastrous pint of Abbott and some home-made roll-mop herrings. They seemed to have been a little too long in the pickling, although they tasted good enough. At least driving through the country, he wouldn't have to worry about finding a loo.

'You on holiday? Nice motor you're driving.'

She was about his son's age; pretty but tired. Probably had school-age kids and a house to run. He said yes to the question and thanks to the observation.

'I used to live here, a long time ago.'

He didn't know what prompted him to say it. Just that there was no one here to confirm his former existence.

'Really? Changed a bit I expect.'

'Not as much as you might think. Tidier, though.'

The bar was empty, and she cleaned tables around him as they spoke.

'Your family from round here, then?'

'No,'

He paused but said it anyway.

'I was evacuated here, in the war.'

'Oh, dear, that must have been hard. Missing home and that.'

'I was with very nice people, actually.'

Careful, Charlie: your son says 'actually' is the most defensive word in the English language.

'The house isn't there anymore. I was looking for it.'

Were you, Charlie?

'Out on the Walsingham Road. There are three new houses there, now.'

The cloth she was using was getting very grubby, now; she emptied the ashtrays and wiped them with the same rag she was using on the tables.

'Oh, I know, you mean where Desboroughs built. Nice places, but they're a bit pricey. One's still empty and it's been two years now. They'll bring the price down. Have to I reckon. You looking?'

'No, no.'

He checked himself because she looked a bit put out by the vehemence of his denial;

'Way out of my range.'

She laughed, satisfied.

An old man came in and let the door slam shut behind him. The barmaid tutted mildly and shouted;

'Hello, Mr. Boldero.'

Charlie left half of his roll-mops. He didn't recognise this Mr.

Boldero, but he looked old enough to have been in the war.

***

Norwich was not all that far, but he took his time, not wanting to arrive too much before it was time to eat properly. The Abbott ale appeared not to have upset him, for a change. He cruised past church towers on the horizon, but as inviting and melancholy as they looked without him, he hadn't the heart to stop and explore; he stopped at the Glasshouse in Langham and bought a pretty wine goblet for Hilary, which was a bit extravagant, but he wanted to thank her for the ropey guide book. He wouldn't tell her the truth about Schloss Chequers. He was already thinking about going home. Maybe because Dolly Parton was going on about it so much.

At first Charlie hoped Kenji wouldn't be in his hotel when he called and was not sure that he wanted to meet up. Nevertheless, however vague their earlier arrangement, he felt responsible. Which was daft, the man could clearly look after himself. But if he were honest a little company wouldn't be unwelcome. It was Saturday night, after all. So they had arranged to meet in a pub which Kenji had already checked out, named obscurely after Edith Cavell.

There was a football match in the city that afternoon, and it was with ears and eyes open that Charlie walked through the fine-sounding Tombland to his rendezvous. There seemed to be a little trouble in the offing, but he knew that it was none of his business and not particularly clever to make it so when he saw two yellow and green scarved morons backing a much smaller figure into a corner and calling it a 'Fucking Pouf' Then he realised

'He's not a fucking pouf, he's Japanese!'

Running towards them shouting was enough to dispel their interest in Kenji. They didn't seem willing to engage an old bloke with glasses, but they had already bloodied his friend's nose, and he would have a black eye. The poor lad was staring after the retreating backs of his guffawing assailants in wonder. Charlie put his arm around Kenji's shoulder, muttering 'Young bastards!' abstractedly to himself. They were in the lobby of the Maid's Head before Charlie realised that that was where Kenji was staying anyway. The receptionist offered no comment as he took the key and sent the wounded Japanese upstairs to sort himself out. Charlie had a Guinness in the bar to calm himself.

Chapter Twenty-Six.

Charlie struggled to wake up despite the sunlight from the window and discovered that he had some new clothes. At the bottom of his bed there had miraculously appeared a pair of vastly altered corduroy trousers and a white shirt made of what looked suspiciously like bed-sheet. It did not have the fittings to attach a collar or cuffs, it was just collarless. He assumed the trousers to be ex-professorial and the shirt to have been made by the busy-fingered Missus Wife. It felt appropriate that as he was not to continue as a conventional schoolboy, he should acquire a new costume. He didn't much like all that grey flannel anyway, and his new wildly baggy trousers were a rather fetching shade of rust red.

The Professor caught sight of Charlie as he himself disappeared into his study with a handle-less cup of tea. He let out an appreciative chuckle but made no comment bar

'Eight thirty in the Library, please.'

How Charlie was supposed to know when that would be in this clockless time zone was beyond him, but he supposed that fate or Missus Wife would push him gently in the right direction at some point. She grinned hilariously when he entered the kitchen and took his place at the breakfast table:

'Very nice, Chiarry.'

She drew him to his feet and turned him round to tuck in the shirt properly at the back, something he had never truly mastered at the getting dressed stage.

'Like potato picker.'

This sounded less than complimentary to him, but he let it go. It hadn't occurred to him before this moment that potatoes needed picking at all, never mind what the pickers might dress like.

'No bacon, Chiarry. Two eggs.'

Feeling like a pasha he nodded vigorously, would indeed have agreed to anything short of the funny soup that the Professor and his wife favoured of a morning. They were both being particularly sunny this morning, which at home would have aroused vague unease, but here seemed simply how you went about mornings.

The Professor was sitting (spread-eagled might have been a better description) in one of the leather upholstered armchairs when Charlie knocked on the open door, having been prompted as expected by Missus Wife.

'Come in, come in. First day at school. Both new boys, eh? Sit here, that's the idea. Now. We're going to start with a little natural history.'

Charlie groaned inside. At home, where his parents lived, there was a museum with a natural history section. It was full of unsanitary-looking grey-furred stuffed animals in glass cases, labelled in Latin. A school trip there had consisted of a lecture about insects by a curator who looked a lot like the stuffed emu. He kept pulling out drawers full of beetles with pins through their middles, saying how rare they all were. Hardly surprising if old emu-features kept sticking pins through them. He had been rulered on both palms for that one: no wonder he had learned to keep his thoughts to himself. His grandmother was particularly disapproving of what she called "Charlie's remarks", so he had decided to be seen and not heard. It was a form of revenge simply to nod and simper when the old dragon wanted a response. His mother was caught between 'That's enough, Ma.' and 'answer your grandma, Charlie' as if between warring siblings.

'I will, of course, be working this morning as usual, so it will be for you to, as it were, set the ball rolling.'

Charlie nodded and simpered, he hoped brightly.

'I suggest you walk up the lane opposite the drive entrance and look at the pond and so on. Pick up a few interesting bits and pieces, something for us to talk about after lunch. How does that sound?'

'What, anything?'

'Well, yes. Nothing too lively of course and try not to kill any plants that look unusual, but otherwise whatever catches your eye and that you can catch.'

He gave a little snigger at his own joke, and he presented Charlie with a leather rucksack with lots of little pockets on the outside, an item the boy had never seen before. There was a piece of cheese and some bread in one pocket, and a bottle of cold milky tea in another.

'Put wet things in this side and dry things here. There's some old newspaper for anything delicate, but only empty eggshells, please, we don't want to lose any chicks.'

It all sounded a bit messy, but Charlie submitted to being shown how to wear the bag over his shoulders and the Professor pointed unnecessarily at the door.

'Off you go.'

then he turned away towards the bookshelves.

Missus Wife waved him out of the back door, so that he felt like a pioneer from one of the cheap westerns he borrowed from the library, the happier half of the building which also held the bloody natural history museum.

Sensibly he decided to start at the top of the slight hill and explore on the way back, so he set off at a scrunching pace down the drive. Striding up the gravel towards him was the statuesque figure of Mrs Boldero, who waved expansively, and when she got a little closer boomed

'Hello. love.'

He bobbed his head and thanked her profusely for his tea.

'We all need a little civilisation, don't we?'

Her broad wink convinced him just in time that it was a joke and he didn't have to leap to the defence of his new friends again, but he didn't smile, just to register whose side he was on.

'Don't worry, sunshine. She's my friend, too.'

Her stride strengthened as she set back off up the noisy stones and Charlie noticed that she was wearing trousers just like his. He would bet that she was a champion potato picker.

There were no further encounters as he walked towards the clump of trees on the hill (more of an incline: this was Norfolk, after all) that was his objective. Except for a dozen rabbits, a noisy brace of startled pheasant, some lovely red and white butterflies and lots of fragrant shit of varying hues. He was dazzled by the country; it had real animals in it without collars on. When a small grass snake slid across his path, he simply thought he must be dreaming. The smells were so different as well. Horse shit he could identify, thanks to the massive dray horses that delivered beer to the pub. It mingled with the coal smoke that was the other pervasive scent in their yard. But here there were clearer, sharper smells that he couldn't place. The flowers he was used to had a sweet and domesticated odour, like women's perfume, but in the sunny lane all was harder and less human; which he did not dislike.

For the pond he had envisioned something ornamental and tidy, like a boating lake or his aunt's fish pond, so he was a little surprised by the sight of a dark patch of water in the centre of a ring of trees surrounded by stinking black mud, dried and cracked at the edges.

Reluctant to get his boots dirty, (not least because he had volunteered to clean them) and, heaven forbid, his spiffy new trousers, he skirted the pool carefully. He was surprised at how marked it was with signs of humanity. There was a single woman's shoe and a few scraps of cloth, the valves from a radio and a bicycle frame without wheels, saddle or handlebars. He toyed with the idea of producing the radio valves for the lesson but knew the meaning of facetiousness from past experience.

In the blacker, wetter mud near the dark water he spotted a whitish oval something and edged down for a closer look. It was about the size of an egg (hen's; he didn't know any other sizes yet) but not so evenly shaped. Gingerly he bent down to pick it up; he didn't want to engage with smelly nature too fully but thought this might make for a good start with the Professor, whatever it was. It was a skull, tiny but recognisable. Perhaps a rabbit, he thought. There were other bones, too; he identified the spine and ribs, among others he could not name, too tiny and fragile to rescue. He decided against washing them in the stagnant water which was lifeless and dirty anyway, or so he thought until a newt like a tiny dragon splashed away from him as he was pulling the ribcage from the mud. He carefully wrapped the bones in newspaper and put them, after consideration, into the dry things pocket.

His fingers, even though he had used only the tips, he scrubbed on the newspaper because he felt peckish enough for cheese and cold tea, an abomination in his other life.

As he walked back towards the house, the rooftops of which he could clearly see, comforting above the yews and ilex leaves, he was surprised to hear the car start up and begin to chunter down the drive. The Professor was supposed to be working. He then watched astonished as the topless antique emerged from the gates with a stiff-armed Mrs Boldero at the wheel and Missus Wife riding shotgun, holding grimly onto her hatless head. They did not see Charlie wave, as they concentrated on the road to Walsingham.

In the kitchen there was a cold lunch spread over the big table, and the Professor soon joined him, having poured himself a large pottery mug of cider from the barrel in the pantry and a similar mug of water for Charlie. Missus Wife made the tea in this house.

'Oh, good chap. Wash your hands, yes.'

Said the Professor when Charlie had finished washing his hands. The long man's own fingers were distinctly inky, but he was already tugging chunks from a loaf of bread and digging his knife deep into the butter, unlike Charlie who pared a whorl or two from the top of the pat.

Chapter Twenty-Seven.

Perhaps he was in shock, but the young man seemed to be responding with equanimity to his earlier ordeal, didn't mention it, in fact, when he came down to the bar looking battered but spruce. Charlie put it down to a perceived oriental horror of losing face, an unfortunate expression given that he was almost unrecognisable.

Charlie guessed that finding a Japanese restaurant in the wilds of Norwich was a forlorn hope, and he was not surprised by the slightly patronising demurral from the heavily made-up woman at reception. In mild revenge he had smirked when she offered several Chinese venues as an alternative and said that it was hardly the same thing. Actually, it was a long time since he had eaten anything even remotely Japanese, and he wouldn't have known where to start if presented with a whole meal, so he was quietly relieved that Kenji seemed keen on the Chinese option ('I had too much hamburger'). Charlie felt that he had burned his bridges at reception, so they decided to look for a likely restaurant themselves.

On a broad, quiet road leading down towards the station (ever a good place to look for Chinese restaurants in Charlie's experience) they found one of those peculiarly English establishments furnished with tatty silk hangings (probably nylon) in parrot hues and with the tables divided from each other by flimsy lacquered fretwork. No doubt it would provide what they were after, and they were seated immediately in the half-empty dining room, ordering Tsingtao beer, which Charlie didn't expect to enjoy and some evil brown concoction in a small red-labelled bottle which reminded Charlie of medicines resisted in childhood. And might therefore be considered appropriate for his wounded friend.

The food, which came swift and plentiful, was apparently just what the doctor would have ordered if Kenji had agreed to see one; he wolfed it down noisily, wincing now and then from a bruised jaw. Charlie felt he couldn't be any more forceful about getting it seen to. Into their second beer Charlie found his guard dropping much against his professional custom.

'What do you do in Japan?'

A tilted head of incomprehension.

''What job do you do?'

'I am actor.'

Charlie had had no contact with the profession, so made mildly impressed noises.

'Films, is it? Or television?'

'No, I am actor of Japanese traditional Kabuki.'

The term Kabuki was not unfamiliar. He had seen some of its lavish costumes, and even worn one or two, but he wasn't about to go into all that now.

'Years of training, I expect.'

'It is my family. I am performing eight years only, but all my life studying.'

Charlie whistled appreciatively but could think of no clear avenue of conversation.

'Different from our stuff, then. Shakespeare and so on.'

Charlie had sat through Stratford performances several times with Bridie's gun in his back and his son rapt beside him, but he was not much exercised by it. Bored him to tears, in fact. The comedy wasn't funny unless you liked slapstick and the tragedy was so overblown as to be laughable. Mind you they had been watching Titus Andronicus, and even he knew that one was a bit excessive. His daughter-in-law did local amateur dramatics a bit, but the yearly whodunnit and the inevitable pantomime with her bloody accountant friend dragged up as Widow Twanky was hardly in this league. Or even in Kenji's vocabulary, most likely.

'No. Shakespeare has many same things. Traditional story, comedy and sad drama. Many love stories. Also it is for common people.'

Not any more, thought Charlie, but kept his council.

'Also his girls were boys. All Kabuki ladies played by men.'

Charlie raised his eyebrows, recognition stirring.

'I've seen pictures of them dancing. They don't look like men.'

Kenji smiled and winced again.

'Many years training. And nice kimono and many make-up.'

'You do girls parts, then?'

Charlie could not help sounding a bit disapproving, he knew.

'Not every time, but often.'

Charlie thought of Mr. Matsui's beautiful present.

'You wear kimono, then? I've got a lovely one at home. A customer sent it to me.'

'Of course I wear. Kimono is very beautiful but very expensive. Your friend is kind, I think.'

Charlie felt exposed all of a sudden; if he wasn't careful, he would have to start talking about his own life. He changed tack but merely set himself a new trap:

'What are your plans now, then?'

'Well, I don't like Norwich.'

They both laughed unreasonably loudly at this.

'I would like to go Walsingham.'

He pronounced it like dancing charcuterie, but there was no point in such subtle correction at this late stage. Anyway, it sounded rather charming. Bridie would have rearranged his every sentence for him. Nicely and for his own benefit, of course. Charlie was feeling guilty and not a little protective by now, the Lao Chu working its evil-smelling spell, no doubt.

'I used to like Walsingham. I'll take you over there in the morning, if you like. We could drive around a bit.'

He was going back on himself, although he hadn't finished with the area yet, and he knew that in the morning he wouldn't want to do it, but there was only himself to blame. And the poor bugger deserved a treat, after all. So Charlie paid for dinner as well. They called a cab because it was getting near chucking out time, and one close encounter with the football fraternity was quite enough for the night.

Charlie woke in his nasty modern hotel room with a furry tongue but no other apparent after effects. He breakfasted in the usual uncomfortable buffet fashion with warm tomato juice (an abomination) and lumpy microwaved scrambled eggs. He drove quickly into town and picked up his scrubbed but spectacularly be-shinered travelling companion. They drove equally rapidly and without regret towards the coast.

Charlie had decided on a rather circuitous route to Walsingham. It involved stops at Cromer, Blakeney and the narrow-gauge railway in Wells. Cromer was not a great success. Just a nasty cup of coffee in the once grand brick hotel above the beach. The Blakeney visit was much more pleasant. Lunch in the nice hotel restaurant on the hill was only slightly marred by the large gin and bogus yachting shoes brigade in the bar, who almost certainly only ever got their feet wet in the gents. Kenji's black eye attracted some welcome clucking from the barmaid.

'Do like me, love; I always tell 'em I bumped into a door.'

Charlie couldn't even begin on the ramifications of that one in explanation. They had a bottle of wine and calvados with lunch, for which Kenji insisted on paying (it cost considerably more than last night's dinner) and so it was with caution and a Dolly Parton song in his heart that he drove on to Wells-next-the-Sea.

It was a bit chilly on the little open train to Walsingham, but the calvados helped with that, and Charlie got quite expansive pointing out church towers along the way. He didn't really remember them from this perspective but a long time ago their shapes and names had been brought to his attention by an old man on a bicycle.

At Walsingham he was intrigued on making a small detour to the Greek Orthodox church to find a postcard of an icon of Saint Sophia that was a dead ringer for Duncan in the back bar. He was delighted to realise that this beautifully kept, onion-domed place had been carved from the station where he had first arrived in Norfolk at the end of the war. Most returning to their refuge would these days find a Traveller's Fare or some such nonsense. Or more likely no station at all. He had an Orthodox church. He felt half a bottle of wine at lunchtime proud.

Charlie found himself telling the sweetly attentive Kenji about the day he had sat here with his cardboard suitcase and his label, waiting for someone to come and confirm his existence, but he stopped short of saying that the woman who finally arrived was his compatriot. Anyway, she had been a British citizen as the Charlie of those days had been at pains to broadcast. He did, however, tell of his own first black eye at the hand of his fellow evacuee; he had barely talked to Bridie about all this, but he somehow felt released in the company of this solicitous and attentive boy who probably understood about half at best.

They walked through the town with its oddly un-English Catholic trappings. Charlie found the Shrine of Our Lady itself sinister. Kenji said it reminded him of Japan with the smell of old incense and tiny guttering candles; a Buddhist temple. Not wanting to walk much more, but not wanting to let go of the feeling of contentment and nostalgia they both felt, they repaired to the inevitable pub in the town centre. There was a signed photograph of Gary Lineker on the bar. Kenji recognised him with excitement. The fey young man standing behind the bar looked at Kenji's eye for a little too long and then glanced archly at Charlie;

'What he needs for that is a nice bit of raw meat.'

Kenji tittered with what was presumably embarrassment, and Charlie gruffly ordered two pints of Abbott. They sat down in a corner and Charlie nearly spat out his first mouthful of beer when Kenji told him that the Japanese pronunciation of Lineker's first name was 'Geri' which means diarrhea.

It was more by luck than judgement that they reached Wells before the Abbott struck Charlie's gut, and there was little question of his driving on to King's Lynn as they had tentatively planned. He spent a nasty twenty minutes in a public loo of no special qualities. They decided instead to check into a small hotel on a green above the town, another area that showed no sign of being by the sea. It was reasonable and friendly, and Charlie wasn't able to think twice about this unexpected intimacy before it was confirmed.

Chapter Twenty-Eight.

'Well, now. Hmm. This is most interesting.'

Charlie could tell from the tone of voice that the Professor did not find it interesting in quite the way he had thought it to be.

'And where do these come from?'

Charlie explained about the pond and the mud, mentioned the newt and even threw in the bit about the radio valves, although it didn't get a laugh.

'Can you tell me what they are?'

Resisting, with considerable self-restraint, the temptation to say 'Bones', since this clearly wasn't a time to be flippant, he settled for 'rabbit remains.'

'Indeed. Well, they are remains, as you so delicately put it, but actually of a puppy.'

Charlie recoiled slightly and involuntarily wiped his fingers on his russet cords. He looked down and then remembered with guilty relief that his hands were clean.

'You see, Charlie, as I have mentioned before, I think, people here in the countryside are a little less sentimental about animals than we essentially urban creatures.'

Charlie was not sure that he was a creature, but let it pass.

'The farm is not really a place for pets, as we might see animals, but for those that can serve human ends.'

'So did a dog have puppies, but they died?'

'Yes and no.'

Oh, bloody typical. Charlie waited expectantly for an

explanation of his discovery of the remains of a sweet fluffy puppy on the top of an otherwise dogless hill, but the Professor seemed a little reluctant to go on. Charlie tried to look keen to know the answer.

'You see, Mr. Boldero, who is the father of Mrs Boldero of tea fame, and not her husband as you might reasonably assume except that he is currently otherwise engaged in this unfortunate conflict, takes the unwanted litters of farm dogs to the pond up there and disposes of them in the manner he thinks best.'

Charlie could see that the Professor was not enjoying this much, but he needed to get to the bottom of the story.

'What does he do with them?'

'He drowns them.'

Charlie was shocked that anyone would so calculatingly murder puppies: the Professor said that they were unwanted, but Charlie knew the mother dog would have wanted to keep them. He picked up the newspaper which he had discarded with rather reckless messiness on the floor and wrapped the bones again. The Professor looked thoroughly miserable.

'Perhaps you might like to give them a decent burial in the garden? I'm sure a sensitive lad such as yourself will find a nice place.'

Charlie nodded. It was the least he could do.

'Do take care not to put them anywhere that Mr. Boldero might dig them up when he attends to the garden. That would be a most unfortunate irony.'

Charlie looked up sharply to see if the Professor was making fun of him, but he appeared deadly serious. In a sombre frame of mind, he excused himself stiffly and took the bones out of the room with him.

He went through the kitchen to the back door, where fortunately there was no Missus Wife to explain himself to. He assumed the puppy-slaughterer Boldero would have no cause to uproot the large Rosemary bush in the walled garden. While he was burying the bones, he heard a series of minor eruptions which signalled the return of the car and presumably of his hostess and her beneficent companion.

After fiddling with the rabbits for a few minutes Charlie felt a little less outraged on the puppies' behalf. He knew that it was hardly the Professor's fault what his knobbly old gardener got up to. He went back into the house and looked in the library, but the Professor wasn't there. He started when the familiar rich voice called to him from the stairwell above him, and he bounded up the stairs two at a time (they were low and broad enough for him to do this easily) eager to dispel any unfortunate atmosphere he may have helped to create.

'In here, Charlie.'

He was calling from the room with all the lovely kimonos: Charlie pushed the door open and was surprised to see Missus Wife, dressed in one of them. She looked suddenly very foreign, but the garment she was wearing was a bit disappointing: all the dresses that he and the Professor had looked at the previous day had been richly decorated, but this was all patched with strips of unmatched material, more like the housecoat that the cleaning lady wore in the pub in the mornings. Still, if that was what Missus Wife liked, it was alright by him.

The Professor was looming fussily over an old-fashioned phonograph, the type that played wax cylinders. His grandma had one the same: she brought it out once a year, and she only had only one cylinder that Charlie knew of. That was why she rarely played it, she said; to preserve the recording. His father, in a rare aside had said that it was more to stop him from strangling the old bat, but he'd had a few by then. The recording was mostly hiss, but there was some biddy warbling in the background, neither tune nor language recognisable to Charlie. Throughout the performance his grandmother would sniffle unpleasantly and mutter about her poor dear mama. His father once said that he had enough to put up with, with his own dear mama 'And yours, Charlie' although he had never elaborated on the latter. Charlie knew exactly what he meant about grandma.

'Please sit down, Charlie.'

He appeared to mean on a flat, square cushion on the floor. There weren't any chairs, so Charlie did as he was told as nearly as he could.

'I do regret that our little lesson got off to such an unfortunate start.'

Charlie smiled and half-shook his head to dispel any thought of his feeling aggrieved at anyone but the demon gardener.

'So I wish now to transport you to Japan with the assistance of my wife.'

Charlie couldn't help but feel that the Professor looked and sounded like a bad music hall conjuror but kept his smile to himself this time.

'Yukiko comes from a small town in the north of the main island of Honshu in a district now known as Akita.'

The words sounded scripted, and the way he held himself made Charlie suspect that this was a well-rehearsed routine. He didn't interrupt but wished that grown-ups wouldn't leave such big holes in their information. How many other islands were there, and what had this place been called before, and who changed it and why? Infuriating.

'In the winter it is very cold, with deep snow, but in the summer, it is very hot and humid, even at night. Most of the people of Akita are farmers and fisherfolk, but my wife's family are rice merchants, and live in a large house on the main street of the town.'

This was better, a bit of local colour. And anything to do with Missus Wife was fascinating to Charlie.

'When I was a younger man I lived in Japan, researching my first book.'

First? How many more were there?

'Inspired by the example of Ralph Vaughan Williams in England, I was touring the country observing, and where possible recording the local festivals, of which Japan has as many as it does settlements.'

If that meant Morris Dancers Charlie wanted none of it. They came around the pub every spring and autumn carrying their own tankards which held more than a pint, sending his father into fits. They danced around for ten minutes like a load of ninnies then got falling down drunk.

'Yukiko's home town has a very special dancing festival in August, at the time when the ghosts of ancestors return to their family home.'

Charlie shuddered at this;

'Nice ghosts, Chiarry.'

'Can you see them?'

'Only in heart.'

The Professor harrumphed slightly in order to regain the stage, and to discourage frivolous sidelines to the script. He wound up his machine and placed the needle gently on the cylinder. It gave out a familiar hiss. Charlie unconsciously prepared himself for the wobbly contralto, but instead there was a riotous and hypnotic chant, accompanied by the most thunderous drums. The Professor smiled as if he had pulled a rabbit from a hat.

'That two-minute extract is from a repeated sequence that is performed for several hours at a stretch over three nights.'

'Drumming is my older brother.'

'And singing is your father saying rude things about your uncle.'

They both laughed about this for a while until Charlie asked why the song was about her uncle. Was he famous?

'No, he drunk.'

'The song's tune and rhythm'

the Professor wrested back control of the proceedings

'Are fixed and repetitive, but if the words were fixed it would get frightfully dull to sing. So, they make up topical references about local people to spice it up a bit, as it were.'

The Professor placed a large album on the floor in front of Charlie, who thought it looked a lot like the account books in the pub. He opened it at a marked place and there was a lovely sepia photograph of a woman in a kimono similar to the one that Missus Wife had on. At least he assumed it was a woman, because her face was hidden by a most extraordinary hat. It was a bit like the Hollywood conventional Chinaman coolie hat, but it had been squashed flat from the sides so that when it was worn pushed forwards and downwards you couldn't see the face.

'This is Yukiko's mother.'

'She looks everso nice.'

The couple smiled at the awed compliment.

'This same kimono.'

Charlie looked again at the photograph and then at Missus Wife. Gingerly he touched the sleeve.

'But this bit is a different pattern.'

'These kimono are passed on for generations, and it is traditional to add patches to them as the years pass. This one is more than a hundred years old, but I doubt that the original wearer would recognise it now.'

'Gosh.'

He touched the sleeve again but could think of nothing to say. Missus Wife was rummaging around in a drawer as the Professor returned to his notional podium.

'Every night for the three nights the main street of the town is lined with burning braziers, and the townspeople gather to dance or watch the dancers.'

He turned the page of the album and there was a rather amateurish picture, taken from above, of a street lined on both sides with people dressed just like the lady in the other picture, all making the same languid gesture with their hands.

'They dance up one side of the street and down the other in a long circular procession for hours on end.'

'Get sore feet.'

Charlie and Missus Wife laughed, but the Professor didn't join in.

'This photograph was taken from the roof of my wife's family home. The upper floor has a removable window onto the street, designed specifically for the viewing of this annual ritual.'

'Are they all ladies?'

Charlie was pointing at the picture in the album.

'A most incisive question. Officially yes.'

Charlie recalled that he had said something similar about gender when they had been trying on Kimonos before.

'Boys dance, too. They do different. We show you.'

And they did. First Missus Wife arranged her feet delicately and did something fluttery with her hands, which bent back into a graceful curve. Then off she shuffled in a complex repetitive routine. The Professor joined in behind her, and though the movements seemed the same there was a subtle difference, a rougher motion. At first Charlie thought it was because the Professor was built so differently, but with repetition he could see that there were little variations built in to make the bearing less delicate. They tried to teach Charlie, but he was too shy, until the Professor started to sing the chant and bang his fists on a low table just like the recording, and this invitation to license loosened him up.

'Why do the hats cover their faces?'

Another good question he thought, but the Professor looked a little sheepish and Missus Wife laughed again.

'Well, hmm.'

Here we go again, thought Charlie.

'Have you heard of what the Europeans call 'Droit de Seigneur'?'

Charlie looked blank. He was too young to do French, which is what this sounded like. The Professor looked disappointed.

'Well, you see. A long time ago it was considered acceptable for the lord of a particular place to make free with the virtues of the local feminine population as he saw fit.'

This was going way over Charlie's head, but he knew better than to interrupt the flow. So he nodded encouragingly.

'Indeed. Well, the same applied in old Akita. In order that the local lord would not become inflamed by their beauty, local girls wore those hats to conceal their charms and the patched kimono to conceal their status.'

'Also give poor and ugly girls a chance.'

Missus Wife went into spasms of mirth, which infected the largely uncomprehending Charlie, and eventually the Professor, thus wasting several minutes. At last Missus Wife excused herself to go and start preparing dinner and Charlie asked to hear the recording once more. This obviously pleased the Professor, and Charlie's first conscious word of Japanese came from it. He was not a musical child, but the rhythm was infectious, and after the most exciting drumbeats the people on the cylinder always called out 'Tagasasa!' He would ask what, if anything, it meant, another day.

***

Charlie didn't really know what the Professor intended when he asked if he had enjoyed today's lesson. They were putting things away in the music room, the Professor shuffling around aimlessly. As Charlie opened what he thought might be the correct drawer for the kimono and raised an enquiring eyebrow, hoping that he might receive some indication as to whether he was on the right track. He was becoming used to the old man's slightly abstracted air, but that didn't make it any less frustrating.

'Yes, yes. In the bottom, there.'

Charlie opened a different drawer, tried to fit the kimono in and assumed that Missus Wife would sort it out later. The Professor seemed about to say something, but instead he led the way out of the door and downstairs. Charlie shut the door behind himself reverently.

'Was all that a lesson?'

'Indeed. I believe that you have learned a little of a different culture. Always a useful thing for an absorbent young mind. Rabbit for dinner.'

Charlie thought 'No kidding,' but didn't say it. His mother complained constantly about the language he picked up from the flicks and his beloved comics. No doubt the Professor would share her distaste.

The rabbit was very good, with a kind of mustardy sauce, which Missus Wife rather lamely claimed to be her husband's creation. It was eaten mostly in silence. The was a definite unease developing, but Charlie knew that he would have to wait for someone else to break it.

After they had finished eating Missus Wife bustled off to the kitchen and the Professor solemnly led Charlie into the beautiful room, where this time they both sat with their legs down the hole. Still the Professor did not have anything to say for himself, and Charlie tried to fill in the silence. But he was no conversationalist and was relieved when Missus Wife came in with a tray laid out with the little bottle and three thimble-cups. She sat with them and poured sake into two of the thimbles. Despite some heavy nodding and eyebrow twitching Charlie did not catch on, so the old man poured some for his wife as well. She said something twittery and took a tiny sip. He thought the Professor had said that she didn't drink but sensing that the moment had arrived when he would find out what he had done wrong he kept his peace.

'Charlie, we live in difficult and dangerous times.'

He knew that already, and he sensed that they had not got to the point of this little pow-wow yet. He also sensed that the point would not be nice.

'There is no easy way to tell you what I have to say.

Missus Wife touched his cheek with the back of her hand, and he flinched. The first thing that coursed through his head was that they were going to send him back to school. Or back to the pub. He felt a nervous lump in his throat.

'Your mother and father have become the unfortunate victims of this conflict.'

His immediate relief at not being sent away was flooded out by a vague sense of distress.

Missus Wife glanced sharply at the Professor and he winced.

'I am sorry to have to tell you that they have been killed by a bomb while your father was at home on leave. Your pub was destroyed.'

'What about grandma?'

It was a reflex; he didn't really care about his grandma. Perhaps he didn't really understand what they were telling him.

'Your grandmother is with your aunt. It was she who gave the news to the Vicar, who has passed to me the duty of telling you. I am most dreadfully sorry, Charlie.'

'You with us, Chiarry. We take care.'

'Thank you.'

He said automatically and lapsed into silence.

Chapter Twenty-Nine.

Charlie teetered around the stable yard a few times on the enormous bicycle without quite falling off. His feet were a good three inches from the ground when the thing was upright, and his legs barely stretched the full extent of the pedals. Stopping required that he slip off the broad, sprung leather saddle since the brakes didn't work anyway.

Missus Wife chirped and clapped encouragingly, and he knew that the Professor was watching with discreet concern from within the house. Charlie was not at all sure this was a good idea, especially as he was aware of the absence of a crossbar, which while necessary to his stopping technique made this a potentially embarrassing 'Ladies' Bike'. He could already hear the squeaky taunts and asinine 'Her, her' from his tormentors in the village, if they ever saw him again, which he sincerely hoped they would not.

There had been a distressing few days in which it had been decided without asking him, that the aunt would leave him in the country for the time being as long as that was alright with the Professor and his good lady. Which it apparently was, to Charlie's great relief. The alternative, which could probably not be postponed forever, was to join the aunt and his grandma, who were now his guardians. Charlie thought he was being very capably guarded already, thank you.

Grief was not something he felt or felt was missing. He was numbed by the news of his parents' death, didn't know what it meant or what he was supposed to do about it. These two lovely people had not asked him to do or say anything except yes or no since they broke the news, so he was content to carry on as if nothing bad was happening.

Another outing was now promised as one of his strange but so far fairly interesting educational activities, this time in the company of the Professor, and so he persevered with a few more wobbly circuits of the yard, until the great man himself gave his position away by calling

'Right let's be off!'

from the upstairs landing window.

He came down and wheeled his own butcher's bicycle out of the stables, and checked the tyres of Charlie's steed, although his pronouncement that the thick, squashy things were 'all in order' seemed pretty optimistic. There seemed not to be a pump about.

The Professor tossed a large moss-green hardback book into the basket of his bicycle, declaring it to be something called 'the incomparable Blomfield' in a manner that suggested that Charlie should have a clue what he was on about. He was bidden to

'Follow me.'

At the gates of the drive they turned away from the village, to Charlie's quiet relief, and headed at a stately pace northeast towards the coast. It was a bright morning with high clouds and loud with the non-noise of the countryside to which Charlie was becoming accustomed. Although he was puffing less than his small sidekick, the Professor didn't have much to say, apart from pointing out a lark and a wheeling hawk. The lark made a nice noise, but the bigger bird came under Charlie's disapproval. He knew it was hovering only in order to plummet and dispatch horribly some small furry animal. He was exhorted by the wind-blown Professor to marvel at the mastery of the thing, but Charlie remained sceptical even when the point was amplified by some more babble which he took to be poetry.

Every so often they would stop beside the road for a swig of tea from screw-top jars of the type which in the pantry held pickles. His was sweet and milky, the Professor's green and cloudy, smelling of dirty grass. He was offered a swig, but declined sniffily and was told, equally sniffily to suit himself, as he would apparently live longer, which was a surprise because that was something his mother said to his father sometimes. When tea was finished and they had cycled another wobbly half hour, Charlie was told that they were nearly there. He took to worrying that they would get thirsty on the way back: he was beginning to get hungry and his legs were tired, but he kept quiet and they soon browed a hill which showed that they really were at their destination.

At the bottom of the hill, which they had coasted brakelessly, they arrived among a group of houses set around a green of sorts. On the left side there was a crumbling ivy-clad flint and brick wall, behind which was a slightly squat church. Its lack of a tower made it a chapel rather than a church in Charlie's ecclesiastical vocabulary. The two central windows in the west end, or rather the two main lights of a larger window, had been unceremoniously bricked up but a round, flower-shaped light at the top, glazed and criss-crossed with rust, completed the infill of a plain pointed arch. On either side of this main wall were matching empty pointed windows with no building behind them, doorless arches beneath. Charlie wondered aloud that the bombs had got all the way out here. Must have been a foggy night.

The Professor chuckled at that in an annoyingly grown-up way and told him that this was the work of a different sort of greedy iconoclasm, as if that cleared things up.

They laid their bicycles on the grass verge by the wall. There were a few pointedly incurious looks from people wandering purposefully past, but the Professor just waved at them with his usual dignified distractedness and led Charlie through the gate.

'Close that, Charlie.'

The bloody thing had been open when he walked through it, and he struggled to move it. It dragged noisily through the sparse gravel as if preferring not to be interfered with, and Charlie gave up without operating the rusty closing bracket.

The Professor was looking up at the bricked in arches and beaming.

'Perfectly proportioned Early English arcaded screen,'
he announced,
'the earliest example of bar tracery in England.'

Charlie nodded.

'It compares with Rheims, you know.'

Charlie clearly didn't. It was old, ruined and bricked up.

The Professor flipped through Blomfield and read for a couple of minutes, then proceeded towards the big black double doors in the centre of the west end.

'Don't know the vicar, but I think I can tell you all you need to know.'

And the rest, thought Charlie, bracing himself for an avalanche of unwanted and barely apprehended information. The Professor was pushing open the door, not seeking approbation.

Charlie expected the interior to be gloomy, and his eyes had to adjust, but when he got inside and had smelled the musty mouse-droppings and old hymnbook smell, he looked up and saw the sun. It was floating in the dust through three tiers of rounded arched windows and the oddly domestic square one at the far end. He breathed

'It's very nice.'

The Professor beamed at him as if he had said exactly the right thing.

'Yes, Charlie. Isn't it?'

Wrought iron brackets sprang from the walls dangling upturned metal baskets which in turn sprouted light bulbs. In front of him on two stone platforms too high to use as steps was a font carved with little headless figures. There were plain washed-out looking pews with carved bench ends.

'Poppy heads.'

Said the Professor, but they looked to Charlie nothing like poppies, more like the fleur-de-lys on the shields of King Arthur's knights in one of his library books.

'Hmm. Interesting thought.'

Charlie wished that when he said something the tall old man disagreed with, he would just say so.

He looked closely at the writing on the back of one of the pews. It was black and looked very like real writing, but he couldn't read it. From under it peered faces and patches of gold. He wanted to ask why someone had written on the nice paintings, but feared appearing silly, or worse still getting too comprehensive an answer.

The Professor sat in one of the pews and read his Blomfield while Charlie sat on the lower of the font steps and looked up into the plain soaring roof. The three tiers of rounded arches (pronounced Norman by his teacher) rose around him in yellow stone. He could see the masonry lines where they were joined and was fascinated by how snugly they fit together. But mostly, rather than noticing things he just looked at the light and breathed in the dusty, empty smell. There were flowers and candles to show that someone must use the place, but somehow he could blot out the people. It felt good and warm, its obvious age comforting.

Eventually the Professor had had enough of the big green book and they went back outside where he showed Charlie humps in the Churchyard and pronounced them to be kitchens and dormitories and parlours, but they all looked like lumps in the grass to Charlie. His mind was still in the lovely church which felt not like a church, but just like a big room full of nothing. No colours but brown and cream and sunlight. It made him feel full up even though he still felt hungry.

They walked through one of the empty doors under the glassless windows back towards the grassy space in front of the church and he saw a donkey clipping a bush outside the churchyard. Then Missus Wife waved at him from a tan-coloured tartan rug spread out under the wall. There was a basket in front of her.

'We come on fields. Not so far.'

Charlie wondered if she was not allowed into the church, despite being a British Citizen. And incidentally why couldn't they all have walked across the fields if it was not so bloody far.

Chapter Thirty.

Kenji had decided to take the train and his Pevsner back to Walsingham. He was keener than Charlie on the details, and wanted to see the church in Great Walsingham, which they had missed out. Charlie was content just to wander around these places and decided to give Wells this random treatment this morning before heading down to the sea.

The church was a step inland from the hotel, which was already strangely alienated from the sea. It was a pleasant enough Victorian rebuilding with a stormy history according to the potted version on a board outside. And it was locked. He walked a couple of empty residential streets. They did not seem to be exclusively for summer rent; some showed tatty evidence of continuous occupation. He dropped into yet another pottery in yet another converted (it would have been unfair to say disused) station building. He contemplated a rustic mug as a tankard for Sylvia's Ivan's beer, but did not like to ask the bearded young man about the accuracy of its declared pint measurement. This would have exercised Bridie more than himself; still he had enough bother with the precious personal tankards of the old buggers in the back bar as it was, and pottery would be a liability in the glass-washing machines. Talked himself out of that one with no bother.

Once back over the brow of the slight hill he could smell the sea behind the banks of its wall and hear the weird slap of rigging on the aluminium masts of the small boats that lay at rakish angles in the ugly, pungent mud. The sea was still a long way from here. On the quay an industrial building with a gallows winch three stories up had been converted into flats. Probably very nice, but a grumpy souvenir of the place's past. A small market was under way in a modern pub car park. It was little different from any other, the usual tat and cheap jeans, distinguished only by a stall selling fishing tackle and particularly monstrous bait. The weather had turned cold and windy, promising rain, but Charlie set out along the straight road to the sea. A welcoming restaurant on the corner by a deserted amusement arcade caught his eye and he went to take a look at the menu. It was yesterday's. Still, a daily menu was a good sign, and he would look again on the way back. Kenji was due to return in the late afternoon; perhaps they could have dinner together.

Hands shoved into his unsuitable car-coat pockets he walked briskly along a path on top of the sea wall, a muddy inlet to his right. Antique wooden piles and possibly not forgotten hulks of boat stuck out at random. The air was sharp with scents associated with advancing silt. On his left a semi-permanent caravan site was doing sluggish business, or perhaps these people lived here all the time. They scuttled about in the chilly wind, not dressed for the holidays to be sure.

Through a deep gap driven between dunes he came upon the beach. Pine woods on his left stretched away towards Holkham. They seemed somehow wrong for the seaside, though he couldn't think of a clear reason why pine trees should be out of place here. Must have been planted for protection. The sea proper was far away across ribbed expanses of sand, water rippled in a visual echo by the gusty breeze; whorls of worm cast dotted about like miniature cartoon dog-mess. His shoes were far too good to go down in the wet, but he had the upper beach pretty much to himself as he walked away from the town towards Holkham, past brightly painted, tightly shuttered beach huts.

Melancholy thing, a deserted beach with rain waiting off shore to slap him at any moment. He had been aware of the sea's existence when he had lived here briefly as a child, but it had not figured in the programme of discovery set out for him by the old man: perhaps it would have eventually. The little village where he had stayed was an entirely land-locked farming community, not only physically, but socially. There was quite a bit of fish eaten in the big house. Mostly for breakfast and therefore not by Charlie; at the time he had put its regular appearance down to the dietary peculiarities of the Japanese, rather than the proximity of its source.

Bridie liked her seaside hot, preferably with a jug of Sangria and a straw hat. Fair enough. It was strange to mix memories of her with the little Japanese woman. Bridie had just begun her life as a memory. He struggled to mourn either of them. Years ago he had shunted from his mother to Missus Wife, lost one to circumstance and the other to a bomb. His aunt had filled a gap, inadequately, until Bridie came along and took him in hand. He didn't know how or what to feel, but he knew that nothing wouldn't do.

The rain started without asking, blowing at him from the north and drenching his right side, cold and appropriate. He turned up and over the dunes in order to walk among the displaced pine trees, although he expected to get a good soaking on the exposed road along the sea wall. He could always find a nice pub to warm up in. It would be about opening time when he got back.

***

When Charlie asked for his key at the hotel, the nice lady with the grand embonpoint and gold bifocals on a fancy chain handed him a message. Kenji was staying in Walsingham for the night. Oh, well. It's a free country. He couldn't help feeling something akin to betrayal, even knowing that it was he himself who had been reluctant to get into a travelling partnership. Where was the boy staying all of a sudden? But they had both set out on solitary trips around the country: why that should now seem less alluring escaped him.

The pub had been one of those out-of -season seaside places that were a bit soulless at any time and completely lost without grockles aplenty eating greasy food. But they had a nice bottle of warm Guinness and a Calorgas fire to dry him out. He asked the lad behind the bar about the restaurant on the quay, having forgotten to check the menu as he scurried for this haven, and was told that if he waited a few minutes he could ask the owner, himself as he usually popped in about now.

As Charlie reached the bottom of his glass a round fellow with a beard and steel-framed square spectacles appeared. He sported a fisherman's smock which looked as though it might have seen action with a real fisherman cleared his throat and declared:

'Brian Preston. From the Maltings.'

Charlie started and the man apologised.

'You were asking about the restaurant?'

He indicated the barman with a jerk of his head. The lad smiled and inclined his head at a job accomplished. He wiped the pint glass he had been drying for a while more vigorously.

Charlie hesitated. Did he want to eat in a restaurant alone?

Then he felt silly; he hadn't counted on Kenji when he began this escapade. It was no different from eating alone in his hotel. But of course, it was: there was a world of difference between a solitary guest in the place he was staying and a middle-aged man dining alone in a good restaurant.

'Do you have a table for dinner?'

'Just you, sir?'

Brian Preston did not seem to find the idea unusual, so Charlie said yes, as early as possible.

'Rightho. See you at seven, then. You'll be staying at the Bell?'

Charlie didn't argue with that, though through what seaside telegraph this information had arrived he couldn't imagine.

'The name's Moulton. Charlie Moulton. Would you like a drink?'

Charlie realised that he must be lonely.

***

At six o'clock he went down to the hotel bar for a drink with his book. Burgess was alright, it seemed. The hero of this book was a rum bugger (and Charlie used the term in its purest form, not being given to words like pouf or fairy, and not really minding the nice distinction) but it was a good modern historical romp. Clearly written. He was just settling down when, dressed in a Burberry raincoat (where the hell had that come from?) Kenji appeared looking distinctly sheepish.

'I made mistake.'

Charlie raised an eyebrow.

'You alright?'

Charlie automatically checked out his shiner, but it was now a less ugly shade, and appeared not to have been augmented.

'Yes, but I didn't like the place to stay in Warsingham.'

Each syllable of the name still carefully pronounced but now with a shakier L sound.

'Sit down and have a drink. I'm eating in town if you would like to join me.'

'Thank you, yes. I change.'

While Kenji went upstairs to rifle through his apparently bottomless luggage, Charlie telephoned the restaurant, having secured the number from the nice lady with the impressive frontage.

A few minutes later they walked across the strangely unsituated green surrounded by its nineteenth century middle-class suburban houses, then down a hill lined with proper shops (not a Boots or a Smiths in sight) to the cheerful restaurant. Charlie was surprised to find the dining room almost full at seven o'clock; Brian Preston greeted him by his mister, complimented Kenji on his shiner, then brought them a home-made kir aperitif at the table. It was not something that Charlie would have chosen for himself but was actually rather nice. Not too sweet. He read the hand-written menu, which avoided most of the usual pretensions. Everything sounded imaginative and local, although perhaps the venison was from farther afield. He decided to start with monkfish gravlax cured in brandy and move on to mushrooms stuffed with venison and juniper berries, after he had been assured that both mushrooms would be the size of a side plate. Disappointingly, but given the language situation understandably Kenji decided to follow his lead. He would probably enjoy the fish, anyway.

As they shared a bottle of wine the poor lad told Charlie parts of a story about his day in Walsingham: being charmed by the landlord of the pub with a photograph of Gary Lineker on the bar into staying Bed and Breakfast for the night. But he found the room had a small single bed and no washbasin and was right next door to the landlord's. Charlie kept his suspicions to himself and merely said that he was lucky that the Bell still had his room free.

'O, I tell them to keep it and I pay.'

'How did you get back from Walsingham?'

Charlie could guess.

'I take a taxi.'

The boy clearly had more money than was good for him.

Mr Preston and his wife, who did most of the cooking, apparently, came and spoke to them while they had coffee. Very nice people. She was round and American and they reminded him a little of the folks at the King's Shilling. Charlie wondered what they made of this odd pair of diners, especially the one who whom turned up at the last minute with the remains of a black eye and rudimentary English. They seemed unfazed. The trade does that to you.

Back at the hotel by half past nine, they retired to the visitor's sitting room with a couple of whiskeys, not intending to repeat the excesses of the night they met. There was a fire burning in the grate and no one else about.

'What's your job, Charlie?'

It was the first time Kenji had said his name since the Chequers and he pronounced it very carefully. Charlie quite liked the fact that a limited grasp of the language allowed for such directness. He had been expecting the question at some stage, of course, but he hadn't decided on an answer. The truth, he supposed, since he could think of no reason to hide it now; it was only with others

in the trade that he did not wish to get trapped in shop talk.
Kabuki could hardly be further from the pub.

'I'm a publican.'

This clearly did not register as one of the professions covered in
Kenji's Cambridge English Course, so he had another stab at it.

'I'm the landlord of a pub.'

'Ah, you have tenant.'

Oh, dear.

'No, I own the pub, but they call me the landlord.'

'Yes, but who pays rent?'

'Well, nobody does. I am the landlord and I run the place as
well.'

Not a perfect explanation but it would have to do for now.

'Is good business?'

Kenji decided to leave the semantics of landlordship for the time
being and try another equally direct tack.

'Yes. Yes it is.'

It was what Charlie knew, so it was good. He had never wanted
anything else. Apart from his wife.

'You are married.'

It was a statement, Charlie was wearing his wedding ring.

'Yes,'

Charlie felt guilty. He didn't know why he couldn't just tell the
man. He would have liked to try out the words for the first time.
She's dead. Perhaps it was unfair to match blunt with blunt. But
then he probably wouldn't have understood any of the stupid
euphemistic alternatives. Passed away, passed on, passed over.
Past, anyway. Like the moment.

'Look, I'm ready for my bed. What would you like to do

tomorrow?'

He sounded like a guilty parent clearing up the tears. It seemed that they both assumed that they would be doing something together, at least for one more day.

'How about your Queen's house?'

Charlie thought for a moment.

'Oh, you mean Sandringham?'

'So. Shall we go?'

That might be amusing for a foreigner, Charlie thought, but said 'Why not?'

Chapter Thirty-One.

The leather rucksack felt uncomfortable with a heavy green-covered book in it, but Charlie was under instructions from the Professor to take it with him and read the marked passages when he got to the church. His protestation that he could read it first and remember all the stuff when he got there was rebuffed with the words 'context' and 'atmosphere'.

More half-grasped explanation, but he was grateful to the understanding old man for recommending him to turn off the road before the village, skirt around the back of the church and hop over the stile 'to avoid any unwanted encounters with 'our dear Vicar's houseguests.'

He struggled with the huge iron ring of the latch, but the door opened easily enough, then he stopped, remembering to look up at the roof of the porch as he had been told and saw a carved cream stone boss with a little figure in the middle. He (it was probably a he, although the person was wearing a sort of dress with a hood, so he couldn't be certain) had a bag over his hunched shoulder, like Charlie, and a rather stupid grin on his face. He hoped the Professor didn't expect him to identify with it.

Closing the door behind him he breathed in the nice old churchy smell. The church at home wasn't as old as this, he knew, because it had the date 1864 on the board outside with the Vicar's name and the times of 'Divine Worship'. Not that he ever went, unless the grandma collared him before he had been assigned sufficient Sunday morning tasks to present an excuse.

201

Also that one smelled different: still empty and dusty, but sharper, with an edge of floor-polish on the red and yellow tiles. This place had a stone floor and although clean and tidy had a deeper scent of seasoned wood and mice. He liked the odour; he thought it smelled smaller than the other church they had visited, then checked himself because smells didn't have sizes.

The next thing to draw his eye was the stained glass. Most of it was dark and greenish, but two of the windows had the most lovely colours. A figure knelt beside a tree in the first. The other was a jumble of coats of arms with bits of funny writing like on the bench back in the other place where they had a picnic. Deep blue and red dominated, glowing in the sun which could only struggle through the other windows.

He sat down in a pew with a bogus poppy head on the end and wrestled the heavy book out of his bag. The page was marked with a postcard of Brighton. He tried to decipher that first but gave up on the spidery handwriting and turned to the printed page. It was just a load of words to Charlie, some half of which he recognised. There were a lot of dates and a few names, but as for context or atmosphere he was stumped. So he left the book on the seat and got up to look around hoping to find something to report to the Professor. The part with pews in it, where he had been sitting, had plain plaster walls with a few marble monuments projecting from them. There were also a couple of relatively new brass plates commemorating people who had died in the Great War. There were pointy windows with varied shapes, but the middle arch, which spanned the building and must hold up the tower, was semi-circular. It had a regular zig-zag pattern around the inner edge and he could see a bell-rope hanging down on the other side under the tower. He walked under the arch in the direction of the high altar. There were some pretty wooden seats you could lift up to see carvings of plants and animals. The ceiling was a criss-cross of arches with stone bosses as in the porch but carved only with leaves; some traces of brownish pigment remained in the recesses of the worked stone. Charlie thought they would look nicer for a lick of paint.

A small pointed arch too low for a grown-up led to another room on the left of the altar, and Charlie went in. This was much more interesting. There were two knights in chain mail lying on low tables of stone. Both had dogs at their feet and one had his legs crossed at the knee, so Charlie knew from school (he paid attention to a good story) that he had been a crusader, which was pretty exciting, really. The walls were covered with painted shields and coats of arms with helmets above them. Most impressive of all, one had a real rusty helmet with a visor, resting on two iron spikes driven into the wall, snail trails of red staining the walls under them.

'Ah. Charles Moulton.'

It was a stern but thin and adenoidal voice, and he turned around to see the short, thick-set Vicar in dog-collar and shiny black jacket. Charlie nodded and said

'Yes, sir?'

The vicar hesitated and tried a snaggle-toothed smile, which seemed to cost him some effort. Or perhaps he just smiled like that.

'I was most sorry to hear about your parents.'

Charlie shuddered. He didn't want to hear about his parents, was trying very hard not to think about his parents.

'If I can be of any comfort to you in your, er, bereavement, you may call on me at any time, you know. There is great solace in the church.'

Not bloody likely, with those two monsters running around. Anyway, he didn't think this odd little man could comfort him much. And solace was another funny word.

'Thanks. I'm alright. Thank you.'

'You're admiring our helmet.'

The Vicar was obviously pleased to be able to move onto something less nebulous than solace.

'It is fourteenth century, you know.'

'No, I didn't.'

The ugly smile faltered as he checked for signs of cheek, but Charlie was too subtle for him.

'I like the paintings.'

The Vicar, it seemed, wished to talk about the helmet.

'Sir Gervase de Court, who was the great, great etcetera grandson of this chap'

He tapped the crusader on the knee

'Wore it in jousts, we believe.'

Charlie nodded and wondered if he should mention Blomfield, but that would be dangerous showing off, because he didn't understand a word of it.

'Well, I must be getting on. If you would like to talk to me....'

'Thank you. Sir.'

The Vicar made a kind of benediction and went back into the main church, leaving Charlie to try, unsuccessfully, to read the funny writing on the walls.

'Is this yours?'

The vicar was back with the big green book in his hands. Charlie snatched it rather rudely and looked sorry.

'No. It's the Professor's.'

'Hmm. I should like to read it.'

'You'd best ask him then.'

He automatically put the book behind his back.

'Indeed.'

The man looked as if he might scold Charlie for his manners but thought better of it.

'Well, goodbye Charles.'

Charlie opened the book when he was alone again and looked for the name Gervase de Court. He must try to make some sense of it before he went back.

***

'I don't lend books.'

Charlie told the Professor about his encounter with the Vicar at lunch.

'Did Blomfield have much to tell you about the church?'

'Not really.'

'No, well, he's not much of a story teller.'

To Charlie's relief the old man seemed not to mind that all he had had to say about the church was that the glass was nice and there was a very nice old helmet. He had forgotten the name of its owner as soon as he left. In fact the Professor seemed quite pleased.

'Now'

Apparently the church was old news in the fast-paced education of Charlie.

'This afternoon I shall be working in the Library.'

Missus Wife grimaced at Charlie over a baton of raw carrot and mimed sleep.

'I would like you to look very carefully at the Japanese objects in my study and in the room above it and choose one that you particularly like for us to talk about before supper.

'You help me in garden first.'

Charlie smiled cheerfully at both of them, not caring which he did. Both seemed potentially educational but helping in the garden would probably be more practically entertaining.

In fact, he was just instructed in how to clip the Yew hedges, which was all very well up to a certain height, but even with a step ladder he and Missus Wife only reached half way.

'Go and find nice thing, Chiarry.'

She said after an hour of clipping and giggling about her poor balance on the steps. So Charlie trotted off into the house. He looked first at all the paintings in the study, and at the vase of peacock feathers in the grate. He was tempted to choose this, but he reckoned that they were not what was required, so he went upstairs and stood in front of the picture that he knew he liked the most before he had even started.

Having chosen but knowing that he was probably expected to take rather longer than a few minutes Charlie went to his bedroom, sat on the edge of his bed and looked out of the window. A cat purred in the deep dent it made in his bedding but didn't deign to look at him. He could see Missus Wife down below putting their hedge-clippings into a wheelbarrow its green and collapsing wooden axle looking beyond the task being set. Mr Boldero wandered through the yew arch, spoke to his uncomprehending employer who bobbed her head cheerfully, and then shambled away again. The dog jigged around, sniffing things at random. There was no real noise, just the vague sounds of birds rustling and clearing their throats. Charlie lay down on his back and looked at the ceiling.

It was clear that he would never see his mother and father again, but he was so far from what he decided to call their context and atmosphere that he couldn't come to grips with the idea. As far as he really knew they still washed dishes in the kitchen sink or poured the slops into the dark mild barrel. What did dead mean? Did they really go to heaven? Because that would probably be quite a good thing. But what would he do now? When he came to Norfolk it had been without any sense of a future; just the next moment's trials. At home he was given things to do from one hour to the next to keep him out of mischief. Was it really any different here? There didn't seem to need to be a purpose.

There was a gentle knock at the door.

'Are you ready for me, Charlie?'

The Professor pushed the door open a little, as if it wasn't his house.

'Perhaps we could talk now.'

Charlie jumped from the big bed and said

'I like the big picture in the music room.'

'Show me, then.'

They walked around the bannisters and into the bright room. Charlie pointed at the colourful screen. The Professor looked a little surprised.

'A most mature choice, Charlie. Most mature.'

Charlie took this in his stride as the Professor lifted the hinged picture from its brackets on the wall with some difficulty and folded it in two.

'Let's take it down to the Library.'

He started off downstairs.

'Naturally this is a nineteenth century copy, otherwise I should not be manhandling it quite so willingly.

Naturally, thought Charlie.

The Professor opened the screen out to about one hundred and sixty degrees and balanced it on top of some large books on a side table.

'This is a very sophisticated selection. May I ask what attracts you to it?'

'I like the shape of the wooden thing next to the wavy cloth.'

'Hmm.'

The painting was of kimono folded over wooden stands whose cross-pieces turned up at the end. The fabric was folded so that the sleeves were draped downwards, showing a pattern of flowers and water. The background was plain gold leaf, showing the bold outlines of cloth and stands.

'This is a folding screen called in Japanese 'Byobu'.'

Charlie tried to say the strange foreign word, but it sounded a bit daft when he said it.

'Byobu. Quite.'

The Professor smiled at Charlie's repeated effort.

'The subject is one of deep resonance in Japanese art. We call it 'tagasode'. Try that, 'tagasode.'

Charlie obeyed and it sounded better than the other word.

'Just so. It means, literally, 'whose sleeves'.'

Whose sleeves was almost as much of a tongue twister as the Japanese words. Charlie didn't try it out, for fear of causing irritation.

'Iro yorimo

ka koso aware to omokyure

tagasode fureshi

yado no ume zono.'

The Professor's voice seemed to soften and deepen as he said this, and although there was obviously no meaning that Charlie could discern it sounded less foreign than when the old man babbled with his wife. Like some kind of magical incantation.

'Is that Japanese?'

'It is very old Japanese, written in the year 905, before the church you visited this morning was even thought of.'

'Gosh.'

The Professor chuckled, pleasantly.

'Japan is a very old and sophisticated culture, Charlie. Ours is old too, of course, but Japanese culture was more refined than ours until quite recently.'

'Do you like it better, then?'

The Professor seemed to consider his reply carefully.

'I have studied it more closely than I have our own.'

Charlie didn't think this much of an answer.

'What does it mean?'

'The poem? My own translation has it

Deeper than the flowers' shade

Their fragrance haunts my sense

Whose sleeves so scented brushed against

Plum blossom by my door?'

He cocked an eye at Charlie who smiled encouragingly.

'It is an expression of longing for someone who is missing,

whose only presence is in the colour and scent of the sleeves of her kimono, who is missed like the beauty of the plum blossom of early spring or late winter, which is itself a symbol of transient beauty and refinement in nature.'

'It's like the poem you said before.'

The Professor looked puzzled for a moment and then clicked his tongue appreciatively.

'You have a sharp mind, Charlie Moulton.

   - Nor dazzled by the embroidery, nor lost

In the confusion of its night-dark folds -'

'That's right. I like that.'

'Mr. Yeats. He never could satisfactorily explain that particular piece when I asked him about it. Not that it truly matters, of course. Poetry doesn't have to mean anything if it's lovely enough.'

Charlie was not convinced by this.

'But if it's just a load of words, what's it for?'

'The pleasure of saying, perhaps? Like the pleasure of looking at this delightful byobu.'

Charlie smirked at the silly word but recovered his composure at once.

'Like humming a tune if you don't know the words.'

'You are a remarkable boy.'

He was beginning to feel like the urchin with the turkey at the end of 'A Christmas Carol', as if the Professor were a little too ready with such compliments. He didn't really thrive on praise, especially such nebulous praise as this.

'Will you say the Japanese one again?'

So he did, and Charlie thought the vowel-heavy sound was

lovely.

'Whose sleeves?'

It wasn't so difficult to say after all. He thought of the beautiful kimono upstairs, and how they had swished and smelled when he and the Professor had tried them on. Dusty but perfumed like the lavender in his mother's napping pillow, only heavier, thicker.

Chapter Thirty-Two.

Rhododendrons had always struck Charlie as a preposterous sort of flower. Too big, too bright and too thoroughly un-British to be beautiful. They had parked the car at the bottom of the hill in Dersingham, having decided to take a good walk around. As they entered the broad drive with its deep grass verges, Kenji was delighted, saying that some places in Japan were famous for this flower too. He produced a pocket dictionary and looked up what he thought they were he pronounced them 'Ajiaria', so Charlie had to spend a couple of minutes teaching his slightly crestfallen friend to say Rhodedendron. They spent more time on Charlie pronouncing 'Tsutsuji' which wasn't the same flower anyway. At least they missed listening to the people around them ooh-ing and aah-ing about the loveliness of all the shocking pink and purple. Kenji said something about Zandra Rhodes and Rhododendrons which Charlie didn't quite catch and giggled.

Charlie supposed out loud that it shouldn't surprise him that the women of the royal family displayed such peculiar taste in clothes if this road was decorated in their preferred colours. Except Diana, of course, who was pretty stylish. Kenji wondered if they might catch a glimpse, but Charlie said that it was highly unlikely. He didn't have her down as much of a country girl.

Charlie liked carrstone, the deep rusty-coloured local building blocks. It was mostly oddly shaped and held together with clunch, but in the better finished (and financed) buildings, like the pub they had passed in the village (The Feathers; Charlie assumed it was an estate property) it was trimmed into tidy blocks with fine lines of mortar in the walls. A warm and comfortable material. Sandringham house was another matter, neither warm nor comfortable. Pevsner described it as 'frenetic Jacobean', which Charlie enjoyed but couldn't explain. While Kenji was impressed by the sheer bulk of the rambling and jumbled pile, Charlie thought it looked like an overblown Victorian home-counties golf clubhouse, or one of those hotels that offered 'hydro' facilities. He that took to mean drying-out or cleaning up for the young and monied, whose self-control was no match for the free market. Only now were they beginning to show the effects of all that stuff they took fifteen or twenty years ago, and their successors hadn't learned from them. Still junkies, poor lads. And lasses he supposed. Look at Liz and Liza: in and out of the Betty Ford Clinic like the revolving door at Harrods. Stick to the pub and you'll go wrong more slowly.

The gardens, Rhododendrons notwithstanding, were very pleasant. Charlie liked a good lawn, which Kenji said was difficult to reproduce in Japan; they always looked brown and dry, even in the rainy season. Probably the wrong kind of turf. There was something of the Edwardian municipal about the whole place, a bit like the gardens around the Albert Memorial in London. Fit for bustles.

Inside, the house was a huge disappointment, with a fusty air of jaded guest house, a sort of stage set for country-house entertaining. Side-tables held hardback copies of Dick Francis novels and adventure travel by Ranulph Fiennes, a man with a tortured way of justifying his existence. Unread, by the look of them. Kenji took a small leather case from his pocket and produced a business card which, after a furtive glance around he slipped into a copy of Maeve Binchy's latest.

'Maybe they call me.'

Charlie laughed loud enough to gather a few harsh looks from the blue-rinse brigade on the other side of the room who were dressed in full rig for their visit. Perhaps the local ladies LVA.

'I doubt if they can read Japanese.'

'O, no. I got English one printed.'

He took another from the little wallet and proffered it to Charlie with both hands and a bow. An extravagant gesture for such a tiny thing, but Charlie took it and bowed a little himself. They were standing in this neutrally decorated sitting room milling with trippers, already hostile to this apparently irreverent pair, but he read it with respect

Kenji Yamazaki, Kabuki Actor.

'This only for English, Japanese is different.'

'You're not a full-time actor, then?'

'Oh, yes, surely. But in Japan I use Kabuki family name. Everyone know it.'

Surrounded by so much evidence of the bland philistinism of the shooting fraternity, Charlie led the way out.

As they walked round the impressive red stone walls to get back to the garishly inflorated drive Kenji shouted something Japanese and Charlie swung in the direction of his pointed finger. He just caught sight of a familiar grim face at the wheel of a Range Rover beneath the tell-tale silk scarf knotted under the chin. Lucky Philip didn't have to wear one; no chin.

'It's her?'

'I think so, yes.'

'I never seen Tenno- samma.'

Charlie looked puzzled.

'Emperor.'

Kenji was extraordinarily excited, Charlie unimpressed.

'Let's go and get some lunch.'

***

They returned to the car with Kenji bemoaning the fact that he didn't have a camera. Charlie had commented on this before, believing the notion that all Japanese took photographs all the time, but Kenji explained that he really wasn't much good at it (although he had an impressive Nikon in his luggage) and preferred to collect postcards. One large pocket in his smart rucksack was indeed stuffed with them, from kitsch Dianas to some lovely old sepia things he had picked up in the same place as his antique Pevsners. It seemed unlikely that he had visited the more arcane of these locations. Like the shell museum in Dorset (not on his itinerary) which Charlie was fairly certain would no longer exist.

They had been recommended a coastal pub just a little way back along the road from Hunstanton, so Charlie drove straight up from Dersingham. They stopped at the Lavender centre in Heacham long enough for Kenji to stock up on frilly nonsense for the folks back home. Charlie didn't think any of this stuff would do for Lizzie. Too girly. And there was definitely nothing for Sylvia's Ivan, who was unlikely to have a feminine side to appeal to.

Back on the road, Kenji was much taken with the sign for the LeStrange Arms, but it came with blandishments for golf, which Charlie could not abide in any of its manifestations although Bridie showed a marked facility at clock golf in her youth. Anyway, they had a definite pub in mind, not browsing this time.

Following the admirably detailed directions of the ample lady in the Bell, he turned off the road in a small village and headed to the sea, then turned left again and came to a long low white building with a red-tiled roof and stepped gable ends. A grassy carpark was across the road from the pub, and as it was empty, Charlie parked near the gate. The sea had been here once upon a time, but even straining their eyes they could not make out anything marine where the sky met the land. Another long walk if they wanted it, which Charlie hoped they wouldn't.

The bar was little more than a hatch. It opened onto a low room divided by the grey oak skeleton of walls and furnished with pleasant mismatched armchairs and settles. There were old rugs on the stone-flagged floor, which must be a bugger to clean. Behind the bar the cellar was clearly visible. There were different sized barrels of a variety of beers at odd stages of drinkability - some spiled and tapped, some waiting. It was heartening to see the bones of the operation. It gave you faith in the correct running of the place, like open kitchens in restaurants; not something Charlie would encourage if the establishment were his own, of course. Some things were a mystery for a reason. Archie's cellars and Larry's lasagne were two such.

Charlie took his Guinness and led Kenji with his pint of Abbott (brave at lunchtime, but he's on his holidays) through a small passage to another whitewashed room. A few logs smouldered in the fireplace, even at this time of year. They had passed the entrance to a high-ceiling dining room, but they intended to have bar food, and this was more cosy.

Charlie read the menu, Kenji flicked through his Japanese guide book around a fuzzy red photograph of Sandringham.

'Shiyakunagi'.

Charlie looked up from the steaks, puzzled.

'Rhodedendron. In Japanese.'

he pronounced it very slowly and precisely.

'Ah. Do you like whitebait?'

They decided after a brief description that it sounded quite to the Japanese taste, as did herring roes on toast, Fish Pie to follow. Charlie returned to the bar to order; it was not quite twelve, and as expected the girl said they would have to wait, but she took his order and his money with reasonable grace.

When he returned to their table, he was surprised to see that Kenji had been joined in his absence by another man, a situation in which he seemed not to be comfortable. About Charlie's age, but considerably better preserved, and wearing jeans (which Bridie declared daft in anyone over forty) and a natty Arran sweater. A yachting cap sat on the table in front of him. He faced Kenji and leant in rather close. The boy showed palpable relief at Charlie's return.

'This man from Walsingham.'

he said quickly. The man from Walsingham stood up and gave Charlie a rather louche, appraising look.

"How do you do?'

'Charlie Moulton.'

He didn't offer his hand and felt unreasonably suspicious of this stranger: why on earth he should, or why he felt so protective towards Kenji he couldn't fathom; this effete yachtie was hardly the stuff of the bruisers who had attacked in Norwich. He bristled, nonetheless.

'Kenji -'

(Mr. Yamazaki to you, thought Charlie)

'Almost stayed at my pub the other night.'

The 'almost' was stressed for regret: Kenji looked panic-stricken.

'After he saw the room, he remembered another appointment.'

The man from Walsingham (Charlie realised he hadn't offered a name and Kenji either didn't know it or couldn't bring himself to say it) laughed self-deprecatingly, but not charmingly.

'We went for dinner in Wells.'

Charlie didn't know why he felt defensive, but he wanted this conversation to stop now.

'And now lunch. How nice.'

Charlie didn't like his tone, not at all.

'Yes, well. Excuse us, then.'

Mr. Walsingham seemed in no hurry to move on.

'Would you like another drink?'

This to Kenji who put his hand over his nearly finished pint.

'No, thank you.'

He didn't ask Charlie who sat himself down with his back to the standing stranger, opposite Kenji.

'Well. Nice to see you again.'

Kenji nodded and smiled. Charlie had learnt from his mother a long time ago that if you ignore nuisances, like wasps, they will eventually go away.

Kenji riffled through his book again and Charlie re-read the menu until lunch arrived. It was very good indeed. They shared their starters, which particularly impressed Kenji. And while a little fazed by the mashed potato crust and the rich cream sauce, he enjoyed his fish pie as well.

Over a forkful of mashed potato Kenji said he was moving on to London. Charlie wished he wouldn't talk with his mouth full, which was particularly disgusting in one with such otherwise delicate manners.

Charlie had come to the end of his week's holiday and had planned one last night at the Bell; an evening that he had somehow come to expect Kenji to spend with him. He had thoroughly enjoyed having this unusual companion, and didn't want him to go just yet, but wouldn't have said so. Anyway, his last visit tomorrow was best made alone.

'You going home?'

Kenji's question threw him for a moment, and he realised that it seemed a bleak prospect. For the first time in decades he had almost put the pub out of mind. He hadn't called Sylvia, worried about the ordering or thought about the old reprobates in the back bar for at least a day.

'Tomorrow. I'll stay another night in Wells. Your luggage is still there.'

'I take a taxi to King's Lynn.'

'Don't be daft. I'll drive you over. When's your train?'

'Tomorrow. I have hotel room booked.'

'I'll take you this afternoon. No other appointments.'

Kenji didn't notice the phrase.

'Lynn's a nice place.'

'You could stay too.'

'I have a visit to make tomorrow. Near Wells.'

They finished lunch in companionable near silence. Mr. Walsingham was glimpsed through the window with his cap on.

He didn't look in at them.

Chapter Thirty-Three.

Charlie couldn't sleep. His body was still rattled from the car journey and his mind was confused by the jumble of emotions that had crowded his day. He had been in the library looking through a book of old hand-coloured photographs of Japan. It looked like a grubby place; the people dark-skinned, not yellow as they were supposed to be. The telephone rang, a jarring noise in this quiet old house. He heard the Professor say "Good Lord" and 'yes, of course, I'll go immediately, don't mention it' in a childishly excited sort of way. Then a babble of Japanese and Charlie peered out of the glass in the front door to watch the old man cycle down the drive with surprising swiftness.

He was infected by an unusual sense of hurry in the house. Missus Wife told him to put on his town outfit. He struggled in his rush; the clothes seemed tight now that he was used to dressing as a potato picker. The Professor returned with Mrs Boldero on another bicycle, who called up the stairs to him to get a move on. When he dashed out of the kitchen door hopping on one foot to put on his boots she was sitting in the car while the Professor cranked it up.

'Hop in, Charlie boy!'

she called, with extra flush in her already rosy cheeks. She was wearing a big floral scarf around her head, and a dress which Charlie thought looked distinctly odd. Missus Wife pushed him towards the car as the Professor got the engine going.

'Mrs Boldero doesn't like to drive alone, and she's going to pick up another passenger, so you'll have to go with her.'

This was only a fraction of an explanation, but it had to do. He climbed into the passenger seat hoping that he wouldn't have to crank the old grid up again later and they trundled off down the drive. The Professor and Missus Wife waved them off as if they were the London to Brighton run in the Pathe News.

'It's my husband.'

As they rattled and coughed through the deep hedgerows Mrs Boldero explained that he had telephoned the Professor from the station in Walsingham. He had a twenty-four-hour pass and had come to see her but there were only a few hours to spare before his return journey.

'Silly bugger's a farmer; a reserved occupation but he still wanted to go off and do his bit. Could have stayed here and done his bit with me, but no, that wouldn't do. Been stuck in a camp peeling ruddy potatoes ever since. Never so much as washed a bally pea at home. Silly sod.'

Charlie said that he didn't want to be in the way.

'You can sit in the garden while we have a drink or something. I only like driving the tractor, and that's no use with a war on. Use the horses mostly. You keep me company, that's a good lad. Here.'

She passed him a tattered old Eagle annual.

'That's my Eddie's. You'll like reading and that?'

Charlie was delighted, even though he had read his own copy at home a dozen times, it was a blissfully far cry from the soppy children of the New Forest.

At Walsingham station he sat in the car while Mrs Boldero danced off to find her square-bashing husband. She hadn't done much dancing in her corduroys, but he could see that she might be allowed a bit of license in the circumstances. They appeared a few moments later holding hands.

'Thanks for watching the old girl, young man.'

Charlie assumed he meant his wife and not the car. He was huge, with hands that could have held Charlie's head in their palms.

'Mind the car for us will you?'

That sorted that one out. He offered Charlie a cigarette and Mrs Boldero slapped his hand.

'Get him a bottle of lemonade you daft ha'p'orth.'

She was crying, which seemed totally out of character for this blowsy countrywoman. She suddenly seemed like an oversized doll in the wrong clothes. They walked off hand in hand and left him with the car, the Eagle and a bottle of warm lemonade, which suited him fine.

When they returned, not much later, they looked a bit subdued and she was crying again. Charlie assumed that she had stopped for at least part of the time or it would have been a very distressing meeting. They ignored him as they walked past the car and towards the station, but then Mr Boldero appeared to remember him and walked back.

'Here you are, son.'

Charlie didn't much like being called 'son' by anyone who wasn't his father. This didn't leave much of an opening, he suddenly thought, but anyway he wasn't supposed to accept things from strangers. Even big men in uniform who made their wives cry and offered him half a crown.

'No thank you, sir.'

'Good lad.'

The man cuffed him on the side of his head, quite nicely but it was still a cuff. He put the coin on the driver's seat.

He walked back to his wife and kissed her in a most embarrassing way as the train pulled into the station.

She had cried all the way back in the car (which he had cranked up with remarkable ease) but pulled up and wiped her eyes and straightened her scarf before they drove back up the gravel into the yard.

'They're good people, the Guntons. Don't you forget it.'

Charlie could easily promise that as she thrust the half-crown into his trouser pocket, and he jumped away from her. She laughed.

Now sitting in bed with the Eagle she had told him to keep, but which even he couldn't face reading yet again he felt upset. It was about seeing these two nice people meeting up for a short time and being sad and happy all in the same breath. And he wouldn't see his mother like that now. Or his father.

The house was completely silent as it had been for however many hours it was since he had come to bed. He opened the window and smelled the clear air. Then he closed it again because it was quite chilly. He had one more candle. He lit it from the little pool of wax with the twig of wick floating in it and stuck the end firmly in the brass holder.

Very quietly, a stage drunk hearing more noise than he was really making, he opened his bedroom door and stepped into the hall. His candle made little guttering impression on the gloom as he made his way around the bannisters. The door to the music room opened without a creak and very sensibly he did not close it behind him. Who knew what strange locks might click shut and trap him forever? Although he didn't actually have any other engagements that night.

He looked around for somewhere secure to put his candle and decided on a lacquer side-table. It stood in front of a polished metal disc on a plate stand, about the size of a gramophone record, it had some kind of picture engraved on it. The metal was too tarnished to see what the picture was; still it served slightly to magnify the flickering light. There must be a draught from the door, but he couldn't feel it through his long underwear. He had given up on the tangly dressing gown thing which woke him up with dreams of being trapped.

Charlie moved from one draped frame to the next, touching the soft silks of each kimono, rubbing them against his cheek. The colours were less striking in the candle-light, but where there was gold or silver thread (which was in most of them) it glittered warmly, like Christmas.

Boldened by the silence of the house around him, he slid open a drawer and pressed down the tissue paper. It made a satisfying rustle as it sprang back into shape. In the biggest, blackest cabinet near the windows looking onto the garden, there were some black kimono patterned with bronze, gold and cream that were not wrapped in tissue paper. Putting both hands under one he lifted it out gently, not wanting to unfold it because he was sure he wouldn't be able to put it back together again properly. To his irritation it unfolded itself anyway, and the sleeves hung down in a most appealing way.

He let it fall open completely and held it by the shoulders facing him so that he could see the beautiful cream silk lining.

Then he slipped it on.

'Whose sleeves?'

He whispered.

'Tagasasa.'

The drumming from the wax cylinder recording filled his head and he started a vague pantomime of the steps they had tried to teach him, but he knew it was nothing like the real thing. He pulled the body of the kimono around him and did a kind of twirl; the material swished in a most satisfying way. it was surprisingly heavy.

'Tagasasa.'

He let the sleeves and lapels hang loose as he twirled around and caught the candle a cracking blow with his hand. It flew out of the holder and everything went dark. He could feel hot wax on his hand and with horror he felt it on the silk as he groped about in the blackness.

Pain of guilt and panic gripped his ribcage and as quietly as he could he stumbled around the bannisters towards his room where the matches were. Fumbling on his bedside table he found them and struck one. It was worse than he had feared. A great splash of wax ran across the black silk sleeve and down the front. He was too agonised to cry. What could he tell Missus Wife. The Professor would be so disappointed.

He had to go back for the candle so that he could see to try and get the wax off and fold the kimono and put it back where it came from. Perhaps they never used it and wouldn't notice until he was gone. More panic: he would have to leave. Anyway, this one hadn't been wrapped in tissue paper, so they probably used it more often. What would you wear it for here, apart from dressing up with Charlie?

He stumbled back into the hallway, then realising he would be a lot better off if unencumbered by an outsize kimono, he wrenched it off and put it over the bannister.

There was a light in the beautiful room. Oh, no. They were up. He ran to the door and saw a small flame flicker up a lime green sleeve. Leaping across the room he pulled it from the stand, which toppled onto him with a loud bang. It wasn't heavy and he pushed it off, but there was suddenly a burst of flame and smoke. He hit at it with his arms and fists and it seemed to be subsiding a little but then another tongue of flame leapt from a different swath of silk. The beautiful cloth had decided to turn on him and he began to cough and lose his breath, still beating with his little arms, unable to see.

He was lifted into the air, and the stupid idea that it wasn't bathtime flitted through his mind. He was dumped at the top of the stairs and would have fallen had not Missus Wife tugged him back and started to lead him down instead. He looked for the Professor who must have dropped him, but he could see no sign as he was pulled through the cats dining hall and into the kitchen then out of the back door choking.

Missus Wife disappeared and Charlie thought he had better stay put, at least for now. Then he heard breaking glass and followed the sound to the front of the house where a flaming bundle of cloth flew through the air throwing off sparks like fireworks and landed in a smouldering heap on the lawn.

"Water Chiarry!'

He rushed back and started running the tap.

'OK. No big fire.'

They filled the huge kettle and Missus Wife heaved it upstairs while Charlie filled the biggest pan he could manage and followed her to the music room where the Professor was stamping on a few smoky bits of cloth and coughing horribly. Only now did Charlie register that all this had happened in the dark.

They poured water on the remaining fire, or rather charred cloth. It was very gloomy, and smoke swirled around them, but Charlie could tell that the damage was awful.

'I'm sorry, I'm sorry.'

'Sss, Chiarry, it OK.'.

The Professor stumbled past them and vomited noisily on the hallway parquet. Missus Wife pushed Charlie towards his room.

'Wash your face, Chiarry.'

He was about to ask what with, what a silly thing to say, but the Professor was on hands and knees retching and Missus Wife was rubbing his back and crooning at him though he clearly couldn't stop. Charlie went to his room and splashed water on his face from the glass beside his bed. An early light was drifting through his window.

'You come please, Emergency. Professor Gunton.'

The telephone was getting more use this week than it could ever have known.

'He can't breathe.'

Charlie sat on his bed with his hands between his knees.

'Smoking fire. No, accident, it out now.'

Charlie thought the end of the world had come.

'Thank you doctor.'

Chapter Thirty-Four.

Driving back along the coast road Charlie asked Kenji if he had any Japanese music in his collection of tapes. They had listened for a few minutes to something called the Southern Allstars, but Kenji nodded sagely when Charlie said that it sounded a bit American, stopped the machine and slid an unmarked tape into the deck. This was more what Charlie had in mind, but it didn't make for very comfortable listening: strange pinging drum sounds, bursts of tuneless flute and shouted wailing voices filled the car, not quite what Charlie was used to as driving music. It wasn't unpleasant, exactly, but utterly alien. Kenji explained that it was the accompaniment to Kabuki dance music.

'You dance to this?'

'Sometimes.'

'It doesn't sound like dance music.'

'It tells what I think.'

Charlie left it there, and Kenji swapped it back. The Southern Allstars seemed to be singing about a Pontiac which they rhymed with 'maniac' and 'insomniac', which was impressive in a foreign language, though it all seemed a bit strained. As throughout their brief friendship there was little in the way of discussion, since Kenji was so determined to get his English right and Charlie's capacity for (or patience with) explanation was limited. Actually, that was probably the secret of their success; lack of necessity for communication beyond a basic exchange of opinion or impression. Kenji was as comfortable with silence as Charlie, who had always let others do the talking when possible.

The Kabuki music made an impression, however, and Charlie asked what the title was as soon as it was banished to Kenji's little Vuitton bag of tricks.

'Fuji musume.'

'Like Mount Fuji?'

'No. Fuji is a flower, Wisteria in English.'

He knew that one without looking it up, anyway. But Charlie didn't want to get back into the flower game, so he merely nodded.

'Musume is young girl. Maybe you say 'Wisteria Maiden'.

'Sounds prettier than the tune.'

Kenji grinned.

'You have to see dancer. Very beautiful girl.'

'But a bloke, right?'

'Bloke?'

'Man. Like you.'

'Oh, yes. I do this dance sometimes.'

Charlie could not imagine it and didn't try.

The plan had been for Charlie to just drop Kenji off at his hotel in the centre of Lynn, as he had booked himself in for dinner at his own place, but there was easy parking in the Market Place and by the time they arrived the bar was open. It was a rather pleasant wood panelled room with dark green furnishings. The prints on the walls were more interesting than usual. He ordered a bottle of Guinness and waited for Kenji to check in. A few obviously very regulars were perched on high stools at the bar offering some fairly pitiful banter to the disengaged girl. She looked to Charlie's expert eye like a receptionist waiting for the real barstaff.

When Kenji came back and bought himself a pint of IPA Charlie explained reluctantly that it stood for Imperial Pale Ale, but didn't go into detail, as Kenji appeared to know what 'Imperial' meant. The boy had brought a Filofax with him, a wretched artefact for salesmen that seemed to be everywhere these days, even infecting the old boys in the back. What on earth they had to fill one with he couldn't imagine. He obligingly wrote his address and telephone number in it. They went through a rather sad and desultory routine; yes, he was going home tomorrow night, and yes of course Kenji should come and visit anytime. No, he wouldn't stay for dinner. He was booked in alone at the Bell.

He was suddenly impatient to be away from the boy and was worried that it might show. Perhaps as a result he made solicitous noises about being careful in London. Where he went, who he talked to, that kind of thing. Kenji assumed an air of worldliness that sat ill with the remains of his black eye, and at half past six Charlie said goodbye, leaving Kenji in the bar to cope with its inhabitants or not, as he chose.

Rather than retrace his way along the coast road Charlie consulted his map and decided to take a long route across country through North West Norfolk. It was a lovely evening and he put the windows down (a manual operation which required a certain resolve, since in order to put the passenger side window up again he would have to stop the car and get out) and clunked Dolly into the cassette machine. He half wished he had asked to borrow the kabuki tape but would probably have been maddened by it in the end; Dolly seemed to like Norfolk, although she confused it rather with Tennessee and saw mountains where there were only the gentlest of rolling hills.

The Fakenham road was not particularly inspiring, but he turned north around Harpley and sailed on gently, passing Houghton Hall (his son would have muttered about Whigs at this point, so he tooted his horn, gently so as not to disturb anyone) and enjoying the well-kept estate roads until he browed a hill and caught a glimpse of what might be sea. It was good to be alone again as long as he was in the car, but when he parked on the green outside the Bell and wound up the windows (Dolly shut up as soon as he switched off the engine) got out and locked the door he wasn't so sure anymore.

There was time to wash his face and hands and put on a tie and jacket before going down to the bar to order something to eat. There was a pleasant young man behind the counter, who said he would fetch Mrs Worby, who Charlie supposed (rightly as it turned out) to be the charming lady with the impressive balcon upon which now rolled and balanced some large pinkish faux-pearls.

Yes, he would eat in the bar if there were no other diners, grateful for the option, and chicken fricassee rather than lamb curry. Rice and vegetables. And another Guinness rather than wine.

The bar accepted a few drinkers, all clearly local, as the evening progressed, but none showed much interest in Charlie, who went upstairs for his book and then retreated to the sitting room with a whiskey. Burgess was an amusing enough companion until bedtime.

At ten-thirty he rang the pub. Sylvia's Ivan answered, as usual, but Sylvia was on hand. It sounded quiet and he had a pang of nerves, but the 'phone was in the back bar, so he knew it was impossible to gauge anything from that. All was well, she said;

what he had expected he couldn't say, but perhaps a little disaster might have piqued his interest. She was looking forward to seeing him. Yes, he'd had a nice time. No, she needn't shop for him. No, he didn't want to come home: he didn't say that bit, but it seemed an awkward truth. What was he going back to?

Stupid, really, it was his life Bridie or no Bridie. No Bridie.

Charlie went to bed.

****

The morning was high-skied and windy, so he was eager to get into the car and get going. Wind always made him mildly ill-tempered. It took no time at all to chuck his meagre luggage into the boot and begone; settled behind the wheel of his faithful car. He touched the dash for luck as he increased by a fiver the amount he still owed Archie's eldest Ian. A final visit to make, he had told Kenji, which made it sound a lot more concrete a plan than it really was; half-remembered places with names that he recalled better than their appearance. Impressions of a couple of nice people he had known for a few days, a fortnight at most. He honestly couldn't remember, and he had had no one to help with his memory for forty-odd years. His aunt had blanked out the whole experience, probably to try and make him do the same. Bits stuck out, obviously; especially at the end, but he couldn't picture faces. A tall old man with white hair and long pinkish fingers. A tiny lady with amazingly black hair and a tendency to push him about. He had liked them very much, he knew that. And he still had the photograph of Missus Wife, but it could have been of any Japanese lady, a studio portrait like the many that he had seen in second hand bookshops since. And he couldn't remember Mrs Boldero's face, only her corduroy trousers and her husband's half crown.

He drove the few miles without looking at the countryside until he came to the village sign and slowed to a crawl. Not one of Norfolk's more floridly rustic names. Pickenhams and Massinghams and Cressinghams were more corn fed than this, which sounded more like a seaside whistlestop. Still, the church was a place that he very specifically remembered, and he was drawn towards disappointment.

He dove past it onto the village green. The Fairstead, they had called it, reading from a big green book while they ate a picnic in the churchyard: where did these random little memories come trickling back from? There was a market cross, or the stump of one. The Professor had said that they used to have a fair every year, but the war put paid to it. Although the gentle man never said 'War'. Of course, Charlie spotted the pub, which looked in good nick. Not open yet. In fact the whole place looked deserted. Brick and flint, some whitewashed rendering, pretty enough but hardly distinguished. A small bookshop which he would check later.

He walked back up to the church, which was now apparently in the care of the Department of the Environment, and was a Priory, no less. They looked after it well; the churchyard was very trim to the right, with a couple of large upright gravestones and some more laid flat into the well-cut turf. The left side had been allowed to grow wild with lots of grasses and wild flowers. Charlie approved in his best Bridie-trained manner. The bricked in window was still bricked in, a sad rather ugly scar on the beautiful Early English west front, but he noticed that the rose window at the top had been recently cleaned up. He remembered it as rusty. Why? He had forgotten the pretty bell-cote above it. Inside first, then.

To his surprise it wasn't smaller than his memory. The three tiers of Norman arches on the south side still rose with that impossible combination of mass and elegance, the same light- fittings still sprang from the walls, and sunlight filled it from that side and from the plain square window in the east end. He now appreciated how truncated the space had become in comparison to the church it once must have been, but somehow that made it more intimate; tailored to requirements without sentimentality.

A rather nasty tapestry hung behind the pretty plain Jacobean altar-table, but church art seemed like that these days; some of the building wasn't bad, especially the Catholic stuff (they had the cash, he supposed) but the decorative modern couldn't seem to rise to the religious occasion. Perhaps we've just forgotten how. Too long Protestant. Charlie sat on the font pedestal and looked up into the sunny dust; cleaner and brighter than he remembered it, perhaps, but still calm. There was no one here.

On a table at the back were some guidebooks and postcards and a greetings card of a John Piper painting of the West Front, all dark blues and black lines. Not the vision he had of the place, but he bought one anyway. He didn't linger, but it was a good place; he was glad to have had it to himself for a little while.

Outside on the south side a whole range of monastery buildings had been unearthed and re-pointed. Bare flint foundations, mostly. Daft exercise, really; he had liked the lumps of grass that the Professor had pointed out. Couldn't recall if his identifications of kitchen, refectory and what have you matched the tidy green metal sign plates cemented in here. He smiled at the supposed memory of the old man and a half-listening little boy. How old had he been? Eleven; twelve?

Charlie walked around the new east end (well, post-reformation, anyway) where the massive piers for the long-gone tower still stood. Must have been quite some church in its day. There were newer graves round here, and clumps of margarets were dotted prettily about. There was one plain brick tomb with an ivied slab on top, the inscription weathered beyond reading. Under a yew tree was a group of smaller, newer graves and he went to have a look. Always interesting. They were only a foot or so square, and were set flush with the grass, a few plastic flowers scattered about. One of the newest read:

'Yukiko Gunton. 1903-1984.'

He had to brace himself against the yew tree. He felt quite sick. Only three years ago. He almost ran back to the car.

Chapter Thirty-Five.

Charlie sat on his bed for a long time feeling terribly small and lonely, listening to what little was going on. Shuffling, foreign muttering and a lot of coughing. He heard the doctor arrive in a car much healthier than the Professor's old crate, then come upstairs and go into the bedroom down the hall. The door was closed behind him and Missus Wife's slippered feet flip-slapped down the stairs and into the kitchen. She must have made tea, because he could hear clinking china when eventually she came back up again.

Then the doctor came to see him; he seemed distracted and didn't ask, as Charlie felt sure that he must, what had happened. Just tapped his chest, looked up his nose, made him cough and said 'Nothing to worry about.' Charlie nearly told him he must be off his rocker but held his tongue. Not crying, anyway.

It was quite light now, and he drew the curtains back on the bright morning, not daring to leave his room. There was an ugly pile of burnt silk on the lawn, dotted with broken glass. The big dog sniffed it once then sprayed it with desultory piss. Mrs Boldero appeared with a small basket of eggs and gave the pile a curious nudge with her foot. Charlie considered shouting down about the dog's contribution, but it was too late and anyway he didn't want to break his isolation just yet. She looked up at the broken window, her mouth suddenly a little 'o' and hurried out of sight round to the back door.

'Missus Wife! You alright?'

He heard the little woman hurry back downstairs and a murmur of conversation drifted up from the kitchen, but he couldn't make out what was being said. Didn't much care. The coughing had stopped, and he heard footsteps, presumably the doctor walk towards his door, but they turned away and went downstairs instead.

At last Mrs Boldero threw open the door to his room.

'Oh, Charlie, love. You alright?'

Humanity conquered him and he pushed his face into her midriff, but still couldn't cry.

'You're to come home with me, love. The Professor's a bit poorly'.

'Where's Missus Wife?'

Mrs Boldero looked over his shoulder for some reason, and hesitated.

'She's seeing to her husband just now. Have you got a bag?'

Charlie reached down and pulled his little suitcase from under the bed.

'Pack your stuff, then, and come down to the kitchen. I'll make some tea.'

Charlie grimly did as he was told. It took very little time indeed. He slipped the dressing gown and the Children of the New Forest into his case, then guiltily peeked at the photograph of Missus Wife he had pinched from the album in the library. He hid it in the folds of his school shirt. Was this it then? He supposed he must have broken the dream. Missus Wife didn't want to see him. She must think he was about the nastiest little boy in the world, and he couldn't blame her. He was tempted to look into the music room, just to see the awful truth of what he had done, but he didn't dare.

She knocked lightly before putting her head around the door.

'OK Chiarry?'

He stayed still on the other side of the bed, open suitcase between them like something in a soppy movie. He nodded feebly.

'You stay with Missus Bo'd'o tonight. I look after Ben'dic''.

She had never said his name before, but then he had said that he didn't much care for it. Her hair was all over the place (as his mother would have said) and her face and hands were blemished by sooty smudges. Charlie felt particularly disgusted with himself, responsible for this unaccustomed disarray.

'I'm sorry. Very very sorry.'

'Alright Chiarry.'

She sounded tired.

'Missus Bo'd'o making tea.'

She reached across the bed and gently brushed his hand with the back of hers. Then she left him.

He toted his suitcase downstairs and into the kitchen, knocking over a saucer; they were all empty and he wondered whether he should suggest to Mrs Boldero that they feed the cats, but she silenced him with a cup of sweet brown tea and instructions to drink it while it was hot.

'He'll be alright in a day or two. You can sleep in Eddie's bed for now. He'll not mind.'

Charlie hoped that Eddie would not be in it too, but he was too numb to question the arrangements. He had become so used to his big bed (empty but for the occasional cat) that it felt as if he had always known this luxury.

'Come on, then, Charlie boy.'

It was a forced jollity, but he appreciated the effort. She tried to take his suitcase for him, but he gripped it tightly.

'No, thank you.'

They set off down the drive in silence, followed as far as the gate by the big dog. Charlie wondered what had become of the donkey.

***

The doctor came by next morning with a message from Charlie's aunt. How it had eventually filtered through he had no desire to find out. She would come and fetch him as soon as transport allowed, whatever that meant; as long as the people here in the suddenly-beloved country would allow him to tag along, he was content. The doctor took Mrs Boldero out of the kitchen where she and Charlie had been unwrapping, sorting and rewrapping wrinkled apples to talk in private. She came back looking grim, which was much as Charlie had expected.

'They took him to Norwich, to the hospital.'

Charlie knew who she meant, but only just stopped himself from asking anyway.

The Bolderos had different, much less educational ways of keeping him occupied. Most of them involved some degree of odorous muck, which Charlie took upon himself as a kind of penance. He could tell that he was the little townie orphan being treated with kid gloves, and the food here was at least more familiar, but he ached to see the Professor and Missus Wife. Eddie kicked him in his sleep.

Not wanting to risk a decision he kept quiet about school, but he didn't doubt that the subject would come up again eventually. One comforting thought was that Gillian Desborough was likely to think twice about trying her bully girl tactics with Mrs Boldero judging by past encounters, and the farmer wouldn't give up her new hand without a fight.

And then one evening a little figure appeared at the back door, looking stooped and a bit older. Charlie was getting ready for bed by the kitchen range as was his new habit.

'Sit down, Chiarry.'

Mrs Boldero came into the kitchen just then to see if he was safely into his borrowed pyjamas. She had worked out his shyness quickly and he suspected she tolerated it more lightly than she would have in her Eddie. Missus Wife smiled at her gently. The bigger woman looked worried and sat next to Charlie on the settle. Missus Wife appeared smaller and more fragile than ever.

'He died.'

She said it simply, like breathing.

'Oh, love.'

Mrs Boldero stood up and would obviously have gone to her, to comfort her or hug her, but the doll like creature across the room was so still that she hesitated, and the moment was lost. The tall woman sat down slowly, and Missus Wife came over to Charlie.

'He liked you very much, Chiarry. You come with me tomorrow.'

Charlie didn't understand. Was he going back to the big house?

'I meet you here. We walk to church.'

Still Charlie didn't twig. Mrs Boldero looked a bit concerned and raised an eyebrow at Missus Wife.

'The funeral already?'

Missus Wife nodded mildly.

'He died three days.'

'I'll have him ready love.'

She glanced nervously at Charlie who was sitting quite still, looking helplessly at Missus Wife.

'Alright, Charlie. He old man.'

She touched his cheek and went away.

***

Proper travel arrangements had been made, so there would be no walking to church. Charlie polished his boots as never before and was sitting in the sun outside the back door of the Bolderos' tidy house long before the car was expected. The Bolderos had gone before. When eventually the doctor drew up in his black Austin, Charlie could just see the top of a head in the back seat.

'Hop in young man.'

That was a better greeting than most he got. The doctor opened the front passenger door from inside and Charlie climbed in. Missus Wife was still barely visible, but she said

'Hallo Chiarry.'

Very softly, and he turned to face the front not knowing what else to say or do. The idea of a funeral was terrifying, and the fact that he had missed out on his own parents' send-off (an expression he had picked up from his father, who went to a lot) was not lost on him here. Death, of which he had scant understanding, did not seem to enter the picture so far.

It took only a couple of minutes to drive to the Church, and Mrs Boldero was waiting for them by the lych-gate, her Eddie looking sheepish, his hair obviously recently given the spit treatment.

Charlie got out of the car and, following hand signals from the doctor he walked around the front to the driver's side rear door and opened it for Missus Wife. His mouth fell involuntarily open.

'You look everso nice.'

She had her hair piled up in meticulous folds held in place with tortoiseshell combs which stuck out in several places. Her face was powdered white and her tiny mouth was bright red, although it did not seem artificially made up. And she was wearing a black kimono with swirling gold, bronze and cream patterns. Charlie checked out of the side of his eyes for wax stains but could see none. She held out her hand. It took him a while to cotton on that she also needed his, then she shifted both legs round together across the seat towards him. The kimono seemed very rigid and tight, but once she was upright and about shoulder to shoulder with Charlie, she pigeon stepped daintily forwards. She kept tight hold of Charlie's hand as they joined Mrs Boldero at the gate. Eddie looked dumbstruck.

'Smashing Yukiko!'

Charlie was surprised that Mrs Boldero had known her real name all along. Yukiko sounded rather good in a Norfolk accent.

The hand clutching Charlie's tightened painfully. He winced then looked up to see Gillian Desborough bearing down like a black yacht in full sail, Missus Wife turned away from her and he was sure that Mrs Boldero muttered

'Fucking hypocrite'

as she walked past them into the churchyard. Then the hearse was upon them and the big box was pulled out of the back by six ill-assorted youths and old men. Wartime as usual.

The church was almost empty. At least the Desborough woman sat out of the way at the back. Charlie didn't take much in beyond the irritating adenoidal drone of the vicar and the constant strong pressure from Missus Wife's hand. He noted the sunlight through the stained glass, though.

After the service, apparently under orders, Eddie Boldero frog-marched Charlie away from the grown-ups and they went back to the house 'to break out the booze' so he didn't see what happened to the coffin. Or to Missus Wife.

Chapter Thirty-Six.

Charlie drove home as quickly as he could, not taking in the scenery around him or the perfect weather. He had had enough escape; by lunchtime he was already close enough to home to make stopping pointless. It would have been somewhere familiar anyway and he might as well get back. Dolly stayed in the glove compartment.

He arrived as the pub was just winding down from its Friday lunchtime buzz. A lot of office people came in at the end of the week, extending the weekend a bit, he supposed, and who could blame them. He had never worked in an office, thank God. Couldn't really imagine what it would be like. The old place had all its routines and the regulars, but every day was different. New faces and the unchallenging change represented by gossip. He didn't expect to be able to slip in quietly, given that the door to the flat was behind the bar, so wasn't surprised to find Sylvia ready for her brief debriefing. She seemed pleased to see him but not so pleased that he would suspect anything had gone awry. After a while he pleaded tiredness and went upstairs.

Sylvia and her Ivan had packed their stuff into the unreasonably large suitcase lying in the dim hall. The old girl didn't travel light even to come to work every day. Still, there was an air of invasion about his little nest. His bed, where he dropped his bag, was fussily made up. When he went through to the kitchen, he found the kettle plugged into the socket behind the fridge and a new jar of the wrong sort of coffee next to the kettle. Bridie hadn't bothered with real coffee. He took a teaspoon from the drawer (at least that was in the right compartment) and carefully ran the tip of the handle around the edge of the seal. Bridie had stabbed it in the middle. But he didn't want a cup of coffee.

'Welcome back, mate. Everything alright?'

Sylvia's Ivan poked his head around the door. He was tempted to mention the coffee, in order to punish the man for calling him 'mate', which he loathed. 'He's not your mate' Bridie used to say, 'You don't rut, do you?' she could be quite coarse sometimes. But he just said

'Fine.'

Ivan held out an opened bottle of Guinness with the stemmed glass he knew Charlie preferred, upended over the neck.

'Welcome back, then.'

He didn't stay to talk, bless him.

Charlie ran a bath.

***

Saturday morning was welcome, Charlie had spent a lonely and unfocused evening with the telly on. He had been unable to get back into the Burgess book now that he was surrounded by all his own distracting bits and pieces. He had gone downstairs only after the bell rang for time. He had a little drink with the staff before they all went home and made sure as discreetly as he could that there was nothing much for the cleaner to do in the morning. He hadn't slept much, trying to put the holiday with all its uncharacteristic touches behind him.

The sad thought kept coming back to him that he could have found the Japanese woman if he had tried; she had just disappeared from his life when his aunt came to collect him after the funeral. The Aunt had been furious with Mrs Boldero for letting Charlie go to the service and would have confiscated the photograph he had pinched if he hadn't hidden it in his suitcase along with the Children of the New Forest and the funny little dressing gown. What had happened to them? He still had the picture, of course: maybe Bridie would have liked to confiscate that, too.

Downstairs Archie's eldest Ian was sitting in the far corner of the back bar with the Mirror, although it was pretty dingy without the lights on, and he might as well have been holding it upside down for all the reading he was doing.

'Just waiting on me Dad, Mr. Moulton.'

With a pang of guilt Charlie peeled thirty pounds from the wad he always kept in his pocket, 'Landlord's roll' Sylvia called it.

'You only owe me twenty.'

Ian looked delighted.

'Ran like a dream, son. I'll want you to have a look at it this week; had quite an outing.'

The boy smiled and left. Not waiting for his Dad, then.

Lizzie arrived to bottle up and clean the shelves, which she did better than anyone else. Charlie realised that he had never got her a present in the end. Too much of a hurry to get back. He would put an extra tenner in her wages for being a good girl while he was away, which was more the sort of gesture she would appreciate anyway. She asked about his trip, but didn't seem much interested, which was a relief, really. He didn't think he could explain.

At ten thirty he let Duncan in, and the old fool slid into his place, elderly and feline. Pint of the cheapest, which was still Morland's, and no mention of Charlie's absence. Pretty much the pattern for the old codgers. They didn't exactly resent his going away, but never referred to it when he came back, as if it had been an embarrassing dereliction of duty on his part. Perhaps it was.

Larry tottered up from the kitchen and asked for half a bottle of red plonk for his meat sauce; he made it in such industrial quantities that Charlie doubted if half a bottle of Hirondelle would make much impact on it: probably drank the stuff, but what the hell.

He went into the office and opened the safe; he had left instructions for Sylvia's Ivan to collect change from the bank on Thursday as usual, and he seemed to have managed alright. They could always buy some from Jim at the Talbot if he went short. Always had plenty, that man. Then there was nothing much to do. The 'phone rang. He picked it up at the same time as Lizzie in the bar, which always confused the caller,

'Alright, love, I've got it. Two Brewers, Moulton speaking.'

There was a long pause.

'This is Kenji.'

Charlie wasn't best pleased.

When he had put the 'phone down he sagged in his chair for a moment and then went through to the bar for a bottle of Guinness. Hilary was sitting, perching, rather, on one of the higher stools at the bar.

'Hello, Charlie. I heard you were back.'

She stood on the cross bar of the stool and leaned over the bar towards him. Charlie looked nonplussed, then realised that she wanted to kiss him, so he presented an embarrassed cheek. Duncan sniggered in the corner.

Charlie gave her his edited highlights of the trip. They were very few, but he did mention that he had made friends with a young Japanese man, because he thought she would be interested. She looked quizzical, but he wasn't sure why and ignored it. He added that the man in question was on his way from the station right now.

'You don't sound terribly enthusiastic.'

'I've just got back from all that.'

Ruefully.

'Where's he staying?'

This perfectly reasonable question set Charlie on the defensive: he hadn't asked and now felt a slight panic, that swamping feeling he got when it seemed that he was not in control. It had always happened when Bridie went away on her own for a night with one of her relatives. As opposed to going away for good.

Then Kenji arrived.

He had acquired a hat from somewhere, which he tipped as he put his bag down, a curiously archaic set of moves; courtly in an American manner, an oriental Jimmy Stewart, perhaps. Or perhaps an old-fashioned travelling salesman with his foot poised to block the door, except that he was dressed in the latest chic and had a rucksack on his back.

Charlie felt a surge of something like affection get the better of his irritations. He accepted Kenji's hand limply outstretched hand across the bar and introduced him to Hilary.

'Sorry for surprise. I didn't enjoy London so much.'

He picked up a glossy paper carrier bag with cord handles and passed it to Charlie over the counter.

'This is small present for you.'

Embarrassed now, Charlie peeked into the bag. In it was a battered looking picture book about the size of a posh menu.

'I went to Charing Cross Road.'

Charlie pulled the book out of its bag. The thing was falling apart, and the title was in Japanese, but he could see that it was a book of colour prints with each one glued to a blank page.

'Famous Kabuki characters,'

said Kenji,

'By Ukiyo-e artists.'

'How very thoughtful. Thank you.'

He was going to say that he shouldn't have, but that was such a daft expression, and far too late. Hilary took it from his and flicked through it less gently than he might have wished.

'Have a drink then, Kenji. Pint is it?'

He realised that he was in Landlord mode, speaking to the boy in the detached friendly manner that he adopted for those he wished to keep at a distance. Not what he really intended, but old habits die hard.

'Thank you. You have Abbott.'

He pointed to the oval porcelain plaque on a pump handle; he seemed not to have noticed the tone of voice.

Kenji settled a little precariously on the stool next to Hilary while Charlie pulled his pint and refilled her glass of wine (not Hirondelle). Lizzie had gone off to collect glasses, so he busied himself with customers as the two stool-perchers went through his new book, Kenji explaining haltingly who they were. When Lizzie came back Charlie fetched them some quiche from the salad bar. It came from a local pie company and was therefore untouched by the hand of Larry. They sat at a tiny table in the snug across from Duncan who airily made it clear he wasn't interested in these newcomers to his domain. Charlie broached the subject as casually as he could without giving out any signals;

'What had you thought of for accommodation?'

'O, I find a hotel, it's best.'

Hilary decided to stick her oar in;

'There's nothing much in town, really.'

'You could stay here, but there's not a great deal of room.'

This much was true, and he was fairly sure that Kenji wouldn't want it anyway.

'I've got loads of space. Stay with me.'

Charlie was surprised but not about to argue. Nice girl, Hilary. Kenji was even more taken aback.

'You are very kind, but I am stranger.'

'Any friend of Charlie's.'

Kenji looked puzzled, at Charlie, who shrugged and nodded at the same time.

'I mean that Charlie's friends are my friends, so if you would like to you can stay in my house. It's quite close by.'

Despite his surprise at this declaration of intimacy, Charlie was grateful for the solution. The thought flitted across his mind that they made quite a nice couple.

'I'll take you both out for dinner. If you're free, that is.'

Hilary laughed;

'I expect there's a window in my schedule.'

Charlie offered to drive them to Hilary's house when they were ready, since they would have difficulty getting a cab at this time on a Saturday. Everyone seemed to use them since the town centre became no parking, and there never seemed to be enough buses. He left them to finish their lunch and returned to the bar for the last half hour or so, feeling that the whole thing had worked out very nicely indeed.

As Charlie brought the car round to the side door, Kenji was looking up something in his small dictionary. He had said something which Hilary asked him to explain. 'Nostalgic' he came up with eventually. Charlie assumed he meant the model of the car, but Kenji explained he had good memories of riding in it through East Anglia. It turned out that Hilary lived in Wicken Street, which was a very nice address indeed. He had forgotten that she was a solicitor.

It was a little timber-framed house sitting directly on the street, and Charlie agreed with Kenji when he said that it was like a dream English cottage. Hilary looked pleased and modest as they arranged to meet in the Talbot at half past six. Charlie went back to the pub to 'phone Sylvia and ask if her Ivan was free to stand in that evening. As she was working, he would usually have been a customer anyway.

Chapter Thirty-Seven.

Eddie was untypically friendly and communicative as they walked back to the Boldero house. Charlie could easily have done without the talk, although it was mostly about chickens and a particularly malicious sow, a 'rum 'un' apparently, and he couldn't have made much contribution if he had been so inclined. He was thinking about the coffin and the impossibility of it containing the Professor. The mumblings and squeaks which were intended to represent changes in emotional pitch during the Vicar's officiation had been all but meaningless.

Missus Wife's hand had neither relaxed nor tightened its grip on his throughout the service and now he missed it. Eddie, he supposed, would not be the hand-holding type. At least his monologue on the vicissitudes of livestock management did not stray into mentioning either of the Guntons.

At the farmhouse they went into the parlour, which was every bit as fusty and fussy as those of his own family. Eddie opened the lower cupboard in a heavy sideboard covered in mis-matched blue and white china. He took out a bottle of sherry and one of whiskey both of which looked to have aged years in becoming half-consumed, like the more obscure bottles lurking on the upper shelves of the saloon bar at home. He placed them with some grubby glasses on an embroidered cotton mat on the side-table. There they entered into sullen competition with a sightless stuffed bird under a glass dome and a pair of white china dogs with a single yellow glass eye between them.

Then the boys waited in the kitchen.

Charlie was hungry, so Eddie found him a wrinkled apple which he bit into once and then passed from hand to hand as they sat at the scrubbed table. Jim had run out of surly pig stories.

Mrs Boldero arrived first looking less cheerful than she was determined to sound, followed by the doctor in whose car they had arrived. A couple of ladies from the church came in and passed straight through the kitchen, headed for the sherry. Charlie didn't think that ladies drank whiskey. That was it until the vicar arrived and solemnly patted Charlie on the head, much to his irritation. Eddie, still sitting at the kitchen table, spluttered with laughter at the face Charlie pulled under the Vicar's nose.

Mrs Boldero came back into the kitchen and gave Charlie a tiny glass with a coating of sherry.

'What about me?'

'Pull yourself some cider, boy.'

She went away before Charlie could ask her and Eddie wouldn't know. Missus Wife wasn't coming. He couldn't understand why they were having this admittedly tiny gathering here and not in the Professor's house, although thinking about it he remembered the Desborough woman saying

'Have you got anything to sit on yet?'

and supposed that the beautiful room was ill-suited to a wake. You needed a parlour for this kind of thing.

The sherry was very sweet. He wished they had some sake. There was still nothing to eat. Eddie didn't return from fetching his cider.

Charlie kicked his legs under the seat of his Windsor chair, but he wasn't particularly bored; he was quite used to sitting around on his own.

'Where's Missus Wife?'

Mrs Boldero had come back into the kitchen and was cutting up a fruit cake with some exhausted marzipan clinging to the top: it seemed very dry and crumbled distressingly.

'She's not coming, my love. Here.'

She passed him a delicate blue plate with a pile of large cake crumbs in the middle, fortunately without marzipan,

'Cut yourself some bread, the jam's in the pantry.'

'Why not? Where is she?'

'The doctor took her straight home after… She's a bit tired.'

'I could go and see her.'

Charlie was trying not to sound shrill, but he knew he wasn't being very successful. Mrs Boldero looked suddenly a bit fierce, but her face relaxed again, quickly.

'Best leave her for now, Charlie.'

And she disappeared with a pile of cake fragments on a limp doily.

Charlie could see that the point had come at which he would no longer be in the grown-ups vision of things, so he cut a rough chunk from the loaf on the dresser and slapped some apple jam on it in the pantry (disgusting stuff that you left on the side of your plate after roast pork) and slunk, munching out of the kitchen door.

He could hear Eddie tearing a strip off a pig somewhere. Charlie stood on the running board of the doctor's car and peered into the back seat. There was no sign that she had ever been there, not that he knew what he had expected. Maybe a forgotten tortoiseshell comb, or a dent in the leather of the seat or a smell of – what? He had no names for the scent of her.

Anyway, the car door was locked, so he could not have retrieved any souvenir, not even her perfume.

Abandoning thinking he walked out of the slightly shitty little farmyard and set off down the lane towards the village. He was half way to the church before his internal alarm bell sounded and he clambered through a gap in the hedge to keep out of sight of any possible assailants. Don Charlie was himself now a protector short. Mrs Boldero and her Eddie were very nice, but he didn't think they saw any need to shield him from rough and tumble. In fact, he had strong suspicions they thrived on it themselves.

He checked both ways then ran down the bank and up the other side to the back gate of the churchyard. There were no new plots around that he could see; perhaps important people got planted around the front. But the graves on the village side were all well-established, some to the extent that the tombstones were sinking graciously down to be nearer their owner.

The church door was locked.

He knew he shouldn't, but Charlie couldn't keep his feet from the road towards the house. His house. The shady lane was deserted and all around him were signals of burgeoning growth and greenery which he could barely read. Birds sang and rabbits skittered, pheasants flapped about without reason (they really were stupid birds; no wonder people shot so many) and dead things lay around seeping and stinking in their nasty countrified manner.

He didn't usually mind being on his own but felt terribly abandoned now. His solitude had always been self-willed among people who ignored him. Or latterly who were happy to give him things to do. Or even who seemed quite interested in what he had to say, which was a novelty. He didn't believe that they actually took much notice, any more than a school teacher really thought a cloudless blue crayon sky was worth a gold star, but it was nice of them to try, to recognise the effort involved in not putting in so many clouds.

All that was left was Mrs Boldero. Who was almost certainly a potato-picker and who cried a lot when she saw her husband. Who was quite a nice man, really, of the half-a-crown sort.

He didn't quite dare go to the house, but instead turned left into the lane opposite the drive and walked up the little hill, where he knew he would be able to see it; near the top before you got to the puppy-drowner's pond was a sturdy-looking tree with low branches. He could easily scramble up it with the aid of the well-hedged brush beneath it.

It was a perfect perch; he could see the ilex tree and the front door and although only part of the yard was in view, he could see the top half of the kitchen door and the window behind the kitchen sink. Actually from here he had to think of it being in front of the kitchen sink.

He was perfectly content to wait. She must be there. He stared and stared at the two doors in turn, willing her to show herself to him; naturally he spent more time concentrating on the kitchen door, because the front door was only for visitors. No sign. Once or twice he nearly climbed down and went to knock at the door, but he knew that Mrs Boldero's advice was to be heeded.

First the sky turned and then it began to get dark. He was increasingly stiff and uncomfortable, and he knew that they would be wondering where he had got to, but somehow the vigil had come to justify itself by its very pointlessness. There would be no discernible lights in the house to show her presence anyway. Wee Willie Winkie candlelight got lost in there even when you were inside with it, never mind looking down from a tree quarter of a mile away.

Just before it was completely dark, he saw Eddie cycle up the drive and pull the front doorbell, slicking down his hair and wiping his hands on the seat of his pants. There was no reply. That was all Charlie had really been waiting for and he jumped down from his perch and ran down to the village road shouting Eddie's name.

'You little bugger.'

Was all he said, then he made Charlie sit on the saddle of his bike and pedalled back towards the farmhouse standing up.

'Your auntie's here.'

Chapter Thirty-Eight.

When he let himself in by the back door the pub was very quiet. One of the lads manning the front bar popped his head through the doorway to find out who was there (good boy) and reported that it was very slow, as usual in the afternoons. Charlie tried not to interfere in the front bar anyway and wasn't much interested in the afternoon trade foisted on him by the new licensing laws. Just an irritation really; the old hours had been the clock of his life for as long as he could remember. If Bridie hadn't insisted, he wouldn't have opened up all day at all, but all the other pubs were doing it, under orders from the breweries, so there didn't seem much option. Maybe he would start shutting again now. During the week, anyway. Change for change's sake didn't come naturally. As he slipped behind the bar he glanced through and saw that the lads had moved a stool from in front so they could sit while they read the newspaper. Didn't mind them reading but sitting wasn't really on. He couldn't get Bridie to give them what for now. He let it go and went upstairs.

The coffee that Sylvia had bought to replace his Gold Blend wasn't up to much - powder instead of granules - but he made half a cup and heated some milk in the microwave and took it into the sitting room to look at his new book. The cardboard spine was missing. The webbed binding was brittle and split, so he put it on the dining table, drew out a chair to sit on and turned the pages carefully. To be honest he found the faces a bit clownish and malformed, and the way that they were cut off in odd places reminded him more of slick advertising images than proper art, but the colours and shapes were fascinating. Halfway through he stopped at a woman with a bright red hat perched on her elaborate hairdo, which was stuck with ornaments of wisteria flowers. She wore a lilac kimono with the same flower splashed over it. Very like the one that Mr. Matsui had sent him. He went to the cupboard and took out the cardboard package in order to unwrap the silk and compare it with the picture. It was actually quite different, but when he looked at the caption properly it said 'Fuji Maiden' in English then something in Japanese that he took to be the name of the artist. He was sure that that had been the title of the weird music that Kenji had played to him, however briefly, in the car on the road to King's Lynn. He would ask him about it later.

He finished his disappointing cup of coffee and looked up the number of Lampedusa in the flip up directory by the 'phone in the hall, called and made a reservation for seven thirty with no difficulty. It was a bit pricey, but he hadn't been for a while. The food had been, and he hoped still was good old-fashioned Italian. Meaning unpretentious and plentiful. Kenji said he liked Italian and Hilary said she would eat anything if he was paying. He turned on the television and was rewarded with 'Mrs Miniver'. Exactly the kind of tired old movie he could nap in front of.

When he opened up the back bar at half past five the front was already full of noisy students, probably after a game of some sort; they were loud but spent well and usually went elsewhere to get really rowdy, so the boys were being kept pleasantly busy. The stool was gone, he noted with satisfaction, but there was already wet cardboard on the floor. That wouldn't do at this hour, so he took over serving from one of them and made him strip it off, mop the floor and dry around their feet with old bar towels. He then emptied the drip trays into a bucket and took it down to the cellar. He was careful but still managed to spill some on his freshly laundered trousers. He was a bit sharp with them about spillage, even if he could see that they were busy. Business is business. They could moan about him as much as they liked when he was out.

Sylvia came on at six – Oh, don't you look smart and then a damp sponge to his trousers. Her Ivan, trouper that he was, said he would go on the front for an hour until the late staff arrived at seven, and Charlie set off on foot for the Talbot.

'Looking good, Charlie. New girlfriend?'

Jim towered above his bar, filling up so much space that the poor lass trying to serve had to keep shifting him out of the way to get to the pumps. She looked new and nervous, so Charlie gave her a friendly smile.

'Big lump. isn't he?'

She grinned at him in a slightly scared way and started like a wet cat when the cider pump spat at her.

'New barrel, love. Let it run a bit. What'll it be?'

Charlie could see Jim tending towards the Guinness on the shelf.

'Glass of red, I think. I'll be drinking it with dinner.'

Jim smirked and muttered something about a lucky lady which Charlie chose to ignore. Hilary came up beside him trailing an oddly shy-looking Kenji. She opted for fizzy water, but Kenji had his customary pint, Fuller's ESB which Charlie didn't bother to point out was the strongest thing in the pumps. They went to sit in the window seat where Charlie and his then new friend Hillary had sat after Ernie's funeral, although he didn't bother to point that out either. There was an awkward silence until Kenji blurted out

'I'm sorry about Mrs Moulton.'

So that was the problem. Hilary smiled awkwardly;

'I thought he knew. Sorry.'

Charlie just shrugged and said 'Thanks' to Kenji.

'We're not due at the restaurant until seven thirty. I thought perhaps a quick one in the Thistle?'

A change of venue might lighten things up.

The Thistle, a goodish hotel on the High Street, was a victim of changes in group ownership. They seemed epidemic to the hotel trade lately, happening with such regularity that Charlie couldn't remember what they were all called these days, Trust House, Grand Met. Must cost a fortune in new stationery every time. Hilary opted for water again and admitted to feeling under the weather. Women's things, she called it when Kenji wasn't listening; Charlie was apparently supposed to understand. But she insisted that she was looking forward to her dinner.

'Always wanted to try it but never had the occasion.'

She and Kenji appeared to be getting on famously; giggling a bit, but Charlie could live with that. Dinner was just what Charlie had hoped, huge antipasti, gnocchi with gorgonzola sauce and veal saltimbocca; traditional English Italian. Kenji eventually went to what he called the Bathroom, and Charlie took the opportunity to chaff Hilary, who he now reflected had eaten very little, about how well they were getting on. She gave him a very funny look;

'Um, I'm not exactly his type, Charlie.'

'Nonsense, you make a very dashing couple.'

She let it drop, so he did too.

Then espresso and Sambuca flamed with coffee beans. (Hilary wanted neither. She did look rather pale) Charlie talked about his kimono and the picture in the book, asking if it was the same as the one for the dance music he had heard in the car. Hilary was interested to hear about Kenji's dancing as a woman and Kenji struck a couple of poses that quite transformed his appearance, although Charlie couldn't have explained how.

'That's amazing. You're more woman than I am.'

This seemed a little far-fetched for a few gestures, but Charlie was enjoying himself. He said he couldn't remember the name of the print.

'If she wearing a red hat it's Fuji Musume.'

'Is that like Mount Fuji?'

Charlie smugly explained that Fuji meant wisteria. He must have had too much wine because he found himself asking them back to his place to see his kimono.

'That's a new line.'

Charlie laughed and payed the bill in cash. When they hit the fresh air, Hilary said she felt a bit sick. Why didn't they go on without her? She wouldn't hear of postponing it to another day. Kenji was very keen to see the kimono.

'I just need to get to bed. Kenji's got a key.'

They walked her to the taxi rank, where it was still early enough for her to get a cab straight away. She waved out of the back window, Kenji sweetly waving back until the cab turned a corner.

'She's a very kind lady.'

Charlie agreed, a little unsteadily. Suddenly it didn't seem such a great plan, but there was no diplomatic way out, as Kenji's host for the night had just disappeared, so they set off for the Two Brewers.

The place was heaving, and it was hard for Charlie to force a path through the crush saying hello to regulars, Kenji in his wake. It was so busy the staff barely acknowledged them when they finally got behind the bar. Perhaps unwisely Charlie poured two very large Armagnacs from the bottle behind the back bar and gave them to Kenji to hold as he unlocked the door to the flat and led the way upstairs switching on lights as he went.

'Nice room.'

Charlie assumed he meant the whole flat rather than the tiny hall in which they were standing and looking at it now in his slightly tipsy state he supposed it was.

'Have a seat and I'll fetch the book. The kimono's over there.'

When he returned Kenji had the thing out of its box and the tissue paper was all over the floor. Charlie held in a tut and said

'What do you think?'

'This is theatre kimono, very high sense.'

'Is it the same as this one?'

He held open the book at the page with Wisteria girl on it. Sounded like a fey superhero. Another thought to keep to himself.

'O, yes. This is famous dancer of Fuji Musume. His name is Onoe Kikugoro six.'

Charlie couldn't help wondering what happened to the other five and regretted it.

'They died.'

'How does it go, then?'

Charlie had a sudden clear image of being taught a Japanese

dance a long time ago.

'That lady taught me a dance when I was very young.'

He pointed to the photograph of Missus Wife; she looked peculiarly grim tonight.

'You went to Japan?'

Kenji sounded miffed, as if this was another thing he should have known about before. Charlie couldn't blame him. Perhaps he should have told the boy all about it, as he should have said something about Bridie. Charlie felt stupid; he hadn't told the man a bloody thing, really. In all the time they had spent together, not a bloody thing. 'No, no. She was married to an Englishman. I only knew her for a short while. When I was very little.'

It sounded pretty lame.

''What was this dance?'

'Oh, I really can't remember. It was forty-odd years ago.'

Kenji decided to return to the matter of the moment.

'Fuji Musume is long piece, about twenty minutes.'

'Blimey. can you remember all that?'

'It's very famous dance, very sad.'

The question obviously didn't warrant a serious answer, but Charlie was interested now. He made a 'go on' face and Kenji took his cue by slipping into the kimono.

'You see this picture. I should have red hat like this and stick of wisteria blossom, so.'

He pointed to the picture and then posed in the exact manner of the lady in the print. The transformation was astonishing. Kenji's face became at first blank and then full of sorrow; one hand came out in front in a gesture of tiny elegance and the other held and imaginary branch over his, no her, shoulder.

'Close your eyes.'

Feeling uncertain Charlie did as he was told. There was a loud crack as Kenji clapped his hands and Charlie opened them again, as was clearly expected.

'That is kyoshigi - sound of dance beginning.'

He began to move slowly and with great sad dignity as he told the story. He had become the lady in the picture.

'This woman sends many love letters to a man, but no reply.'

He swished his sleeves and from his pocket pulled a bright white handkerchief, which he bit at one end, pulling the other end with his free hand. His back seemed to form an S shape under the loose kimono, as his feet and body pointed away from each other.

'Light is fading. Night is soon, but she still waiting for lover to come.'

A sleeve swished close to Charlie's face and the scent was of incense smoke and lavender. He saw the tall old man and the tiny lady laughing and clapping their hands.

'Tagasasa.'

He muttered, but Kenji seemed not to hear him and kept moving gently. The scent of the sleeves now reminded him of this mother, smoke and perfumed pillows, then the smoke from a pile of burning silk on a lawn.

'The bell of the temple sounds the night, but the woman waits.'

Charlie began silently to weep. He laid his head in his hands as silk swished past his head. He thought of Bridie, but she wasn't interested in Japan.

'Then curtain closes on sad waiting lady.'

Kenji gently brushed Charlie's shoulder.

'It's alright Chiarry.'

Charlie started at the touch and the sound of a familiar voice. He wiped his eyes briskly on a rough jacket sleeve. Kenji's hand stayed where he had laid it, and Charlie looked up at him. There was more than concern in his eyes as he leant down towards Charlie's face.

'Don't cry.'

Charlie twisted his shoulder harshly from under the boy's hand and stood up.

'You'd better go now.'

Kenji smiled sadly and took off the kimono laying it on the sofa. He picked up the two glasses of Brandy, handed one to Charlie and drained the other.

'Goodnight Charlie.'

He enunciated it perfectly this time.

Charlie sat back down and took a sip of brandy, hearing the brief roar from the bar as Kenji slid out of the flat and closed the door quietly behind him.